THE TAXI

THE TAXI

JENNY JOHNSON

OAKTARA

Waterford, Virginia

The Taxi

Published in the U.S. by:
OakTara Publishers, P.O. Box 8, Waterford, VA 20197
www.oaktara.com

Cover design by Yvonne Parks at www.pearcreative.ca
Cover images © thinkstockphotos.ca: taxi in rank/Adam Dodd, 92490467;
French fries/iStockphoto collection, 94113230; scattered clouds/56359159
Author photo © 2012, Martha Evans

ISBN: 978-1-60290-272-5

The Taxi is a work of fiction. References to real people, events, establishments,
organizations, or locales are intended only to provide a sense of authenticity
and are used fictitiously. All other characters, incidents, and dialogue are
drawn from the author's imagination.

Printed in the U.S.A.

⌘⌘⌘

FOR DR. JAMES T. JOHNSON,
who showed me the path to eternal life.

Acknowledgments

I am grateful to my husband and daughters for their patience and sense of humor as I sat at my laptop to "clickety-clack" while life flowed on around me.

I give heartfelt appreciation to Ramona Tucker and Jeff Nesbit of OakTara Publishers for giving many new writers an opportunity, including yours truly.

1

Strange Taxi

The presence of a taxi waiting outside of a fast-food restaurant struck me as strange. It appeared out of place in this day and time, like something more common to the 1950s. What made me notice it at all? I guess I thought of personal cars like I thought of cell phones and laptops. *Surely everybody has one by now.*

That's not true after all.

The taxi had pulled up, not at the drive-thru as one would have expected, but opposite the entrance to the famous arched icon of short-order cooking on this particular Saturday morning about eight o'clock. The novelty of seeing someone arrive to buy fast food in a clean but slightly battered white cab coaxed my attention away from my own well-established breakfast routine. When I looked more closely at the taxi's occupants, my curiosity was piqued. The driver was a black man, maybe about thirty, wearing the traditional taxi driver cap with a bill. A young white girl about seven or eight years old sat alone in the back. I watched from my booth seat beside the window and wondered what drama might be about to unfold involving the inhabitants of the puzzling cab.

Nothing at all happened for about five minutes. I returned to my newspaper and coffee, convinced the cab was simply waiting to pick up the child's mother, who likely worked in the restaurant. Movement near the restaurant exit refocused my interest. One of the servers had moved from behind the service counter and was carrying a small white bag toward the door. Sure enough, she pushed open the outside door and moved toward the taxi. She gave the bag to the driver, who handed her money, nodded and immediately turned to pass the bag over his shoulder to the little girl.

I couldn't see or sense any significant exchange of words among any of the players. It appeared to be some sort of practiced transaction, as if all the parties understood the routine without having to speak. The little girl sat back straight and solemn against the seat, the taxi moved away, and the fast-food worker returned to her post.

I turned back to my morning paper and cool coffee with the distinct awareness that there was a Story behind what occurred…that there was much more to the event than what I saw. Who was the child? Why was she alone except for the taxi driver? Why was she visiting McDonald's in a cab? What set of circumstances would lead up to the scene I just witnessed?

I liked to think of myself as a writer. My résumé confirmed that I indeed had served in the capacity of staff writer for several modest newspapers in a handful of small towns throughout the South. It also stated that I freelanced for numerous publications from large, prestigious upscale monthlies to more than I want to remember of shoestring publications. In my twenty-eight years I had worked for everything from a hunters' weekly publication to one for economy-conscious schoolmarms. I was never comfortable in one place for very long and would take on most any reputable writing job that paid the rent for another month. So I was a writer, a pretty good one.

What I really wanted was to be an author. There was a big difference, in my thinking. The grass is always greener. I was always looking for the unique idea for a novel that would move me from the status of writer to published author. Not just any idea would suffice. I wanted a Story. My notebook was filled with ideas. I could see ideas everywhere, but good stories that will keep a plot going for a whole novel are harder to find. I will admit that, at the time, I was somewhat obsessed with becoming a world-class and obscenely rich author of adventure-filled and highly romantic novels. In my daydreams, my novels were so good that they were immediately optioned to become major motion pictures, for which I would also write the screenplays and thus reap twice the monetary rewards. Those were the motives that led me to be so interested in affairs outside the McDonald's that Saturday morning.

By now my coffee was undrinkable. The paper in front of me was *The Daily Summit*, which was also the newspaper for which I currently worked in the western North Carolina mountain city of Boone's Summit. *The Summit* was filled with names of the recently dead, whom I never knew had lived, and the recently wed, who wore blissful looks that I knew would likely turn sour within the first year. I folded the newspaper and left it for the next customer. I was going to be late for work.

My morning routine hardly ever varied. Slightly obsessive folks are sometimes like that. I would wake early in my private apartment in Mrs. Callister's Tourist Home, spend a respectable amount of time on my morning devotions, and then work out on the exercise bike or take an early run around my quiet city neighborhood. After a quick shower, I would spend as little time as possible drying my long dark hair, twisting it into a tie, dashing on some subtle face colors, and slipping into my work wardrobe, which also varied little. Ready.

From the time of my arrival in Boone's Summit, I had been eating what was considered to be a healthy breakfast at home—maybe oatmeal, bran cereal, or an occasional boiled egg and toast. More recently I had begun to include McDonald's as a most favored treat in my morning routine. After late nights of honing my writing skills on the hopeful drafts of novels, I needed a little help with wake-up. The famous yellow arches served up coffee that always promised to get my day underway, with or without my consent. I was addicted.

It took me three weeks of increasingly curious scrutiny from my window seat in McDonald's before I realized that there was a pattern to the regularity of the white taxi's visits during my fast-food breakfasts. Thursdays and Saturdays were the days. The times might vary from twenty to thirty minutes but always around 8:00 a.m. and always on Thursdays and Saturdays. The arrangement during the visits didn't seem to alter at all. The taxi pulled up, waited five minutes, counter lady walked out the door, nodded, driver turned with the bag, the child leaned back clutching it, and the taxi drove off. By now I was sure these visits were not occasional.

On the fourth Saturday, my unassuming old silver LeBaron was running and ready to ease out of place as the taxi pulled off. This would be easy…just the usual follow-that-car routine. I had to know more of the Story.

Unfortunately I had not factored in the difference in driving abilities between the taxi driver and me or the breathtaking surprises of the steep and winding city streets he navigated at faster than safe speeds. It was two more Saturdays before what I had come to call The Game ended with me as a winner. I had convinced myself that the elusive taxi's destination would be an upscale neighborhood in a newer part of the city. The child would live in a 300,000-dollar-plus home as the overindulged daughter of advantaged parents who compensated for their busy schedules by pampering her with a fast-food diet every Thursday and Saturday morning to which she was delivered by taxi, perhaps while they slept in.

I was mistaken. The taxi was parked in front of one end of a considerably shabby row of large connected brownstone apartments that had been young and elegant in the early part of the twentieth century. The apartments had not had the benefit of a face-lift since then. While they didn't look disreputable, they did appear sad and old, not unlike the rice-paper-thin face that peered down at me from the window of the second- story apartment on the end of the building.

The appearance of the face was a surprise. She was not young but yet looked ageless, aristocratic, and slightly arrogant. I tried to look away quickly. I wanted to appear as if my glance were casual, as if I were on her street for a legitimate reason. I failed, mesmerized by the silent but disapproving watcher, and after staring back at me for a good long time, she pulled a lace curtain slowly across my view of her face.

Now what? I was by this time standing on the sidewalk facing the ancient façade of the end apartment and feeling foolish. I looked up again; the window was lace-covered, and there was no face. Had there been a face? To cover the confusion and indecision about my next move, I strode with more purpose than I felt down the sidewalk and stepped with feigned confidence up the steps to the first-floor apartment, the one beneath where I had seen the watcher. What on earth was I doing there?

I rapped with indecision on the ornate but aged door, all the while chanting to myself, *Oh please, oh please, do not let anyone from this apartment come to the door*. My actions had been juvenile and superficial, with little thought of what I would actually do if the door opened by any of the people I had been following. As desperately as I wanted to know about the taxi drama, my courage was beginning to waver.

No sound came from within. My charade was safe, but my bravery now failed. As I turned to make an escape, the huge old door on which I had been knocking was pulled open with a jerk, and a child threw herself out of the opening and down the steps. I was blocking her path, and her little body slammed into my side as I turned, knocking me back against the rusted iron railing and causing her to begin a wild spin down the stone steps.

My hand flung out automatically to reach for the falling child and made contact with her flimsy sweater. I held on, clutching with the free hand for her dress. My hold broke her plunge but threw me off balance also, and we both landed sitting hard on the steps, the child in my lap. She reminded me of a feral kitten as she froze in my arms for an instant. Then she whirled and scrambled to her feet on the step below me. I realized I was staring up into the eyes of the little girl from the taxi.

She looked to be about six or seven years old, and before I had time to do more than note her wild fair mane and too-short, long-outgrown dress, she brought tiny hands to each side of my face and addressed me in an urgent whisper. "Lady, Lady, can you help me? Lady, I need your help so much!"

I grabbed the rail behind me for assistance, pulled myself up, checked quickly to make sure I had not broken a shoe heel or maybe a leg, and reached for my fallen keys. By then, she had taken one of my hands in both of her small, cold ones and was dragging me toward the open door she had just flown out of.

"Honey, what's wrong? What's the matter?" My voice sounded ragged and uneven to me as an eerie awareness of the improbability of this occurrence competed for my attention with her more urgent pulls on my hand.

"Who are you? Where are we going?" This time I spoke more firmly to get her attention.

Her eyes on mine were now large, dark orbs of begging. She dropped one hand, placed her index finger on her lips, and whispered again to me. "Shhhh! If he hears you, he will go away with no help. He's bleeding, and I don't know what to do. Don't talk, Lady. Just come on and help him!"

With that warning and final plea, she let go with her other hand, pushed the heavy old door open further and stepped back for me to go first. With a final glance at her pale, delicate face, the face so translucent that the blue veins around her eyes seemed stark by contrast, I marched through the open doorway. Once inside, she quietly shut the door, scooted around me, took my hand again, and led me through the most elegant room I had ever seen.

It was a large parlor, of sorts, with incredibly beautiful and delicately carved woodwork. The light was dim, but I could see enough to make out sheets askew over what appeared to be fine old furniture. I could see the legs of a grand piano and fine porcelain figurines uncovered on the mantle above a fireplace. These scenes flashed like subliminal photographs before my eyes to leave but indistinct impressions when remembered later. I had no time to stop and soak up the strange, masked beauty of the obviously unused room. One last look revealed a large and ornately framed painting above the mantle—maybe of a young blond woman, perhaps in a wedding dress.

By now I was beginning to doubt the wisdom of advancing further into the dark apartment. Indeed, if it were not for the child's cold hand in mine and her constant tug forward, I would have believed the circumstances to be a dream instead of real. She opened the door to a room off of the hall, at the back of the apartment judging by how far we had come past closed doors to the right and left. Natural light coming from somewhere outside now made movement easier and, as I turned to take in the scope of the room, I saw the blood smears on the door.

I stopped abruptly, my hand involuntarily pulling free of the child's and going to cover my mouth, which was as dry as powder. "Oh, dear God..." I began to pray out loud.

"Lady, shhhh," the child murmured again. "He's still here. Please try to help him."

My eyes followed two large blood spots across a linoleum floor toward a daybed under a long bank of windows. No lights were on, but the windows allowed me to see all too clearly. On the daybed lay a tall man wrapped from the waist up in a sheet spotted with blood. There was so much blood that my initial thoughts convinced me I was looking at a body rather than at a breathing person who needed immediate attention.

I remember saying out loud, "God, I ask..." before I realized that I was the answer to my own prayer. I walked quickly to the daybed where the man lay and lifted the edge of the sheet. His face was stained with the now-drying blood. His hands held what looked like an old towel to his head, and his eyes were closed. He began to shake.

AIDS, what if he has AIDS? I was talking to myself again as I stood looking down at the bloody sight before me.

"Lady, don't be afraid," a little voice beside me spoke, as if she had heard my unvoiced question. Maybe I had actually said it aloud.

"Lady, please do something."

It dawned on me that the room must be a huge kitchen. I moved toward some large white cabinets with drawers and started jerking those nearest a sink open. I found what I was looking for in the second one down. Rubber gloves, old and yellow, maybe brittle, but I grabbed them and pulled them on before turning back to the daybed and the task at hand.

The child had moved the sheet back further, and I could see that the man was dressed in formal evening wear, complete with a once-white pleated shirt and black striped tuxedo pants. I had also grabbed a handful of kitchen towels, and I placed one over the man's hands as he held the old towel to his head. Moving carefully so that my strange form of surgical gloves would not tear and so that my movements would not alarm the shaking man, I gently displaced his hands so that I could see what they were covering. The hands were large, but the fingers were long and beautifully formed. It struck me then what a peculiar impression those hands made on my memory.

The fingers were a sticky mass with his blood and so cold that I could feel it through the gloves. He moved his shaking hands back to his head.

"Sir," I said, "how badly are you hurt? Sir...?"

"No, Marta." It was not a voice but a rasp. "Please, take her away." His accent was strange and foreign to me, and his voice was so strained that I could barely make out the words. "Marta...you know we cannot!"

"She will help you, Papa! I know she can help." The child was near tears, and her voice was desperate.

His answer was a groan.

What had I uncovered here? Both the man's condition and my safety worried me more by the minute. He might be in shock already. I looked around the vast, cold room. There was a long counter down one side with an old black rotary phone sitting on top, beacon-like and signaling to me. I had already dialed 9-1-1 before I realized the phone cord was not connected to anything. My cell phone was in the car outside.

Another groan from the daybed made me turn toward the man who was now struggling to stand. His efforts brought a flow of fresh blood down his face and a small, terrified outcry from the child.

"Oh, Papa, please...!"

I began to talk fast as I moved to the bedside. "Just don't move. I have to see how badly you're hurt. You may do more damage. You have to stay quiet, please. I need to find a telephone to call for help. Is there another one in this apartment, or do I need to run for the one in my car?"

I was chattering. It happened whenever I felt otherwise helpless.

The man was sitting now with his arm propped against the back of the daybed for support. "Just my head." He spoke softly and with more control in his voice. "Not so bad as it looks."

I saw that he was holding one of the fresh towels padded over a spot above his left eye.

"A head always bleeds savagely." He tried again to stand.

"Sir, please." I moved closer to him. "Stay down."

I placed my hand on his shoulder with gentle pressure. The child, Marta, now began to sob loudly. She was kneeling by the daybed, resting her head on her hands. Some decisive action was immediately required, for her sake, if not for his. I bent beside her, placing my arms on top of hers around her frail body.

"Marta, please look," I commanded softly. "Look at your papa now. See...his head is no longer bleeding very much. I think he's getting better." I prayed I was right.

Still shaking with sobs, she raised her little head and looked first at me and then at her father's face. Indeed, the outside of the towel was clean with no fresh blood seeping through. Although his face was quite pale, he was no longer shaking and appeared calm.

"Do you see, darling? He's better, isn't he?" My answer was a nod as she placed her hand on her father's knee. "Now I need some help from you," I said, addressing the child. "Can you do what I ask? Is there anyone in this apartment building you know and trust? Not a stranger but someone safe—a friend. Someone who has something to drink? Coke, juice, anything to make your papa feel stronger?"

The child nodded. "GranJuel. She's my great-grandmother."

"Can you get what I asked from her?"

"She has juice, I think." She ran from the room through the door we had entered.

The stranger in formal wear with the bloody head and I stared at each other for a long minute. His eyes were the gray-blue color of an ocean just before twilight. I don't think I had ever seen such eyes before, and only one time since.

"What happened to you?" I finally said.

His response shocked and surprised me. He laughed. In spite of the drama that had just surrounded our meeting, he gave a brief, quiet laugh. His unexpected reply brought my hands to my hips.

"I am sorry"—he seemed to be suppressing a smile while holding the cloth to his head—"but you look...your hands..."

I looked down at what he saw and realized that I still had on the ungainly yellow rubber kitchen gloves. I flushed, as I often do when I'm embarrassed.

"I was afraid...I didn't know if..." We were communicating only in pieces of sentences.

"I know what you feared, but I assure you your fear is unfounded. Except for this," he indicated his head, "I am perfectly well."

I wasn't sure I believed him. "Then tell me what happened," I said again.

"Miss, I am not sure how you came to be here. I thank you for your assistance to my daughter and me. What I would like for you to do now is leave us and forget that you were here. Please speak to no one of this or of us. Our lives and yours may depend upon it."

That sounded melodramatic, but I knew he meant it. I also felt as if I had been somewhat rudely and summarily dismissed. His polite demeanor did not hide the authority in his voice. My first impulse was to do exactly what he asked and quickly. My second thought was to show him that no one told me what to do.

Under the circumstances, it appeared that he was at the disadvantage, and my curiosity urged me to find out more about what was going on here. Why was he in formal evening clothes? How had he been injured? And...oddly it occurred to me at this time... why did his daughter travel in a taxi two days a week to get her breakfast at McDonald's?

I obeyed my second thought. The only way I knew to stall for time was to offer to get the first-aid kit and cell phone from my car to call an ambulance. I thanked him for his concern for my well-being and proposed to assist him further with his wound. Before he could refuse, I turned and hurried from the kitchen, back the way I had come, and out the front door toward my car parked in front of the apartment. It took me less than three minutes to secure the first-aid kit from the trunk and my cell phone from the front seat.

I literally ran back up the steps, into the apartment, and back toward the room where I had left the stranger. I slowed my steps as I entered the kitchen, preparing to appear the picture of efficiency as I readied to offer what first aid I could.

The room was empty.

The daybed cover had been smoothed over, and there was no hint of the bloody sheet. There was no appearance that the room had been occupied recently. Even the blood smears on the door and floor had been wiped out. I began to doubt my own experience as I turned around, searching for any sign that I had not made up the last hour of my life. Nothing.

At this point, my head started to pound, and I was beginning to hyperventilate. Though not usually given to hysterics, the stranger's last words alarmed me. Why didn't he want me to tell anyone about him, and why would telling put us all at risk?

I turned to go. Suddenly my one consuming goal became leaving this strange experience behind. It took all of the dignity I could own not to bolt as I walked outside and down the apartment steps once more. As I started my car and pulled away from the curb, it almost collided with a passing vehicle because I turned to look once more at the front of the apartment building. I distinctly saw the curtain move in the second-story window. My exit had been observed.

I drove faster than was safe for about two blocks and turned into an empty church parking lot where I stopped the car and turned off the ignition. After making sure my doors were locked, I rested my head against the seat back and closed my eyes. A migraine was beginning to tap insistently above my left eye. It took at least five minutes for me to breathe normally again. I opened my eyes and looked into the rear-view mirror. My face looked frightened and exhausted but not crazy. The encounter was real. What should I do? Did I have any responsibility to the stranger and his child?

Up to this point, I had made a studied effort not to mind the business of others or to allow them to mind mine. I was a believer, a Christian, and didn't consider myself to be selfish. It's just that I had grown up in a home where everything was everybody's business, and there were few secrets. Opinions were freely and copiously shared, whether invited or not. It was an atmosphere of loving chaos, and I had been happy. But I knew I was different by nature and promised myself early to live a life of quiet, tranquil privacy if I ever grew up. I did, and now I made it my firm and resolute policy not to meddle or interfere in the affairs of those around me. Some of my acquaintances felt I followed this to a fault.

Then why was I worried about the injured stranger and his little daughter? He obviously didn't want my help, since he had disappeared. Still, the tiny child's anguish at her father's condition bothered me. Was action on my part breaking my *no involvement* rule or merely acting responsibly in an emergency? What could I realistically do?

I could call a rescue squad. They would arrive and take over where I had not been allowed to help... if the man were seriously hurt...if they could find him in an empty apartment. Maybe the police instead. Surely law-enforcement officers needed to know about the father and child whose lives were threatened. Just what would I report to them?

I could hear myself saying, "You see, Officer, there was a stranger dressed in a tuxedo who was bleeding profusely and saying that we were all in danger, but then he disappeared..."

Perhaps not.

My practiced non-interference policy won out. I started my car and drove home unsteadily, grateful not to be mistaken for a drunken driver.

2

Unsettling Encounter

The next two weeks were an exercise in forgetting my ill-fated encounter with the little girl from the taxi. I ate my breakfast and drank my morning coffee at a neighborhood Mom and Pop café near my apartment. I didn't even drive by the McDonald's where I had first noticed the taxi drama any more than absolutely necessary, and then I looked the other way. Relieved and proud that I had conquered my obsession with the Story, I enmeshed myself in the tasks of Section Editor of Society and Community Affairs at the newspaper office where I worked.

It was early spring, which brought new buds to the trees and a softer angle for the morning sun. I began to feel comfortable, almost good about my decision not to pursue information about the strange encounter further. In truth, it had almost ceased to be real.

My natural standoffishness discouraged most colleagues at the newspaper from becoming close friends. There were only two whom I had allowed to penetrate my polite wall of reserve. One was Jake Bean, the Managing Editor, who was the father of one of my few friends from college. The other was Albert Lanier, who served as Cultural Arts and Entertainment Editor. Al had been both a friend and an occasional date during my tenure in the city.

One of Al's duties as a critic dictated that he attend theatre production openings, art exhibits, and other similar cultural events. It was not unusual for me to tag along, either at his request or mine. We were not yet considered a romantic item on the office water fountain network, therefore allowing ours to remain a safe and comfortable relationship. I liked being safe, and neither of us liked recreational dating. Our loose arrangement also served to protect us both from the noisome pestilence of the dating predators always prowling around for new conquests.

"There's a benefit concert this Friday evening at The Metro featuring a consortium of musicians from southern African countries. I think you'll find them appealing. The artist line-up is first class, according to my sources. And the music should be outstanding—a mix of Nouvelle African sounds mixed with traditional classical favorites and a fresh, multi-ethnic twist. Interested?" he asked as he passed my desk Thursday morning.

"Hmmm." I was distracted by a particularly interesting submission for my section of the paper. "Listen to a wedding report that came in this afternoon. A local funeral home owner (who was also a minister) married the bride and groom at Riverside Cemetery so that the groom's deceased mother could be in attendance. The happy couple was whisked away in the hearse for their honeymoon."

"Love the enthusiasm for my invitation, Jannia. So I'll take that story as a yes. I'll pick you up at 7:30."

"Wait, I'll meet you at The Metro, bottom steps, 7:45. That'll make it easier on you," I responded as I looked up from the paper. That was my intense need to be independent speaking. "What kind of concert did you say?"

I forgot the commitment as soon as he left, and only remembered it as I dressed for work on Friday morning. The memory required me to re-dress into one of those ubiquitous day-into-evening ensembles featured so often in the women's magazines in grocery store checkout lanes. My usual wardrobe consisted primarily of plain black pants or longish black skirts with which I paired a multitude of highly colored and slightly offbeat tops or jackets, depending upon the occasion. This particular outfit featured black slacks and a sparkly silver top covered by a long black sweater that wasn't very original but versatile.

I used the need to stay downtown as a reason to work until almost 8:00 when I rushed to meet Al on the steps of the old, renovated twenties-era theatre, reconstituted as a state-of-the-art performing arts center called The Metro.

It would be easy to love Al because of his always casual, always positive outlook. He never hurried but was never late. This was a steady man who could make a woman feel special. We shared a Christian faith and countless other interests. We could have made it work and been more than reasonably happy. There was just the absence of a certain tension necessary to make a relationship that...well...sparkled, like the shirt I was wearing.

We eased into our special press section seats at the front of the theatre only minutes before concert time. Our view of the stage was unhindered.

"Sparkly becomes you, my dear." Al smiled as he handed me a program he had collected for us.

"As always, thank you, sir, for noticing." Sometimes I was slightly tempted to settle for comfortable-with-no-tension as a relationship criterion. But then I yawned, and that made me remember how comfortable I already was on my own. I yawned again and hoped Al didn't notice. It had been a long day.

I idly opened the program Al had handed to me. It announced that this event was a benefit concert with the catchy title of N.U.N. International Southern African Concert Tour, standing for *Ndapota Uxolo* (*Please*) and *Ndatenda* (*Thank you*) in a mixture of African dialects. The *Please and Thank You* name was in anticipation of charitable donations that could be made to benefit children and mothers in distress in a trio of African countries known to have out of control AIDS, widespread poverty, and political unrest.

Oh dear, more inducements to get involved. I knew the needs were real, but all I wanted to do on this Friday evening was just be able to sit quietly, close my eyes during the music, and not think.

The lights dimmed, and after a dramatic pause the auditorium was filled with such a beautiful and haunting melody that I knew not thinking would have to wait. The opening music was played by a chamber orchestra evoking scenes of foreign, dark, and lonely places where most of us would likely never go. This composition set the mood for the evening and was followed by a brief, but equally moving, plea for help to the land of plenty on behalf of a small group of third-world nations a hemisphere removed. Mothers were starving; fathers were dying in civil unrest; disease, distress, and war were rampant; and the children were the hapless victims of it all. If a few helped a lot or a lot helped a little...the request was simple, straightforward, and very compelling.

The evening continued as classical pieces were interspersed with indigenous music by highly accomplished artists from each of the sponsoring nations. I had attended my share of concerts for both work and pleasure, but I had never become such a part of the melodies and harmonies coming from the participating musicians as on this night.

Al and I sat, completely engaged, as instrumentalists, soloists, small orchestras, choirs, and a modern dance troupe reminded us that third world is more of a fiscal label than a cultural one. The colors of the musicians and dancers blended as the old classics of Brahms and Chopin meshed seamlessly into the unfamiliar sounds and rhythms from another world. Both were beautiful and disturbing. I followed the music rather than the program.

Just before the Intermission, there was a noticeable change in the audience. A pause in the program brought a distinct air of anticipation and expectancy as a tall, well-built, and formally dressed Caucasian musician walked alone into the spotlight. He stood completely still for several moments, looking into the audience, unsmiling, dignified. He then turned and seated himself at a large, black grand piano. Pausing again, unhurried, taking the time he needed to acclimate himself to the moment, he slowly began to play. The notes were not familiar; the composition and its execution were, at least to my untrained ear, flawless. But it was not the music that left me breathless. It was the man in the black tuxedo.

I didn't realize I was clutching at Al's arm until he put his other hand over mine and looked at me with raised eyebrows.

"It's so beautiful," I whispered, hoping that would suffice as an explanation for my unconscious actions and feeling relieved when he smiled and nodded. What I really wanted to do was stand up, point, and cry out that I knew this man; he was real after all and not a figment of my imagination. Instead I sat quietly until the end of his performance, squeezing my hands together, practicing deep, slow breathing, and wondering why his presence disturbed me so much.

As soon as the man finished playing, there was dead silence while he continued to sit quietly, looking off beyond the piano with a slight smile on his remarkable face. As he finally rose to bow, the audience reaction was unexpected. Often a standing ovation begins with one person standing, followed by three or four more, then others join in until most of the audience is on its feet either for just cause or from peer pressure.

Not so for this performer. The listeners rose silently as one body and stood still and silent until they finally overflowed with spontaneous and authentic respect and affirmation of his performance. The thunderous applause followed him as he turned and left the stage.

"Well," said Al and turned to me.

"Yes, quite so," I answered.

"So, would you like a juice?"

I didn't, but I did need to be alone for a few moments, so I tried to look enthusiastic as I responded. "Yes, please."

My hands were shaking as I fumbled with the program, turning to the correct place, desperate to find the name of the engaging pianist, the man I knew as my wounded stranger. Intermission, back one performance, there...Sir James Martin Neville. James Martin. I immediately thought of the child he had called Marta.

I don't believe in chance or fate, only in Divine Intervention. In my opinion, coincidences are oftentimes God's appointments for our favor. Encountering this mysterious man again was no coincidence, I was sure. But for what purpose? Surely not just to satisfy my curiosity.

I forced myself to sit quietly and play the scene through. The pianist had recognized me, I was sure. I had seen it in his eyes that widened slightly when his unsmiling gaze flickered over us during his leisurely bow. We were sitting that close to the stage.

Al rejoined me, and I stood to drink the small cup of juice he offered.

"Enchanting" was his evaluation of the performances so far. Albert's standards are quite high when it comes to judging the arts. A vote of *enchanting* constituted lofty praise on the part of this professional critic.

"I believe this performance is near the end for the American leg of the N.U.N. concert tour. I understand this group has had a rather long and grueling events schedule beginning in Europe and concluding here in the U.S.," he continued. "The performers are slated to return to Africa at the end of the month. The last performance is in Atlanta at the Boisfeuillet Jones Center. That's a formidable venue, and there are high hopes that this last fundraiser will be the biggest and most productive of the tour. The Atlanta charity machine is promoting the N.U.N. in a major way. Apparently conditions are grim and getting more so in the home countries of these musicians, both economically and politically. This group certainly has a dignified and high-end method of asking for assistance."

I tried to respond appropriately to this discourse and made what I hoped were timely nodding movements, but I honestly had trouble forming any sentences in response. To my rescue, the dimming lights made replies unnecessary as we prepared to profit from the remainder of the concert. The succeeding performances were as moving and technically excellent as the first had been. Clearly this was a highly professional and well-rehearsed group of musicians, third world or not. They also exhibited an amazing degree of versatility as they interchanged the familiar classics with original compositions representing their own cultural origins.

I began to see a pattern of appearances as each individual or group performed at least twice. I waited patiently, I like to imagine, for the second chance to hear Sir Neville (as the program introduced him) play his big black piano.

Just as he anchored the conclusion of the first half of the program, Sir Neville did so for the second. His final appearance was as a soloist on the piano accompanied by a large choir from a local black church. The music was all African and magnificent. He and the choir were perfect points and counterpoints. The instant and enthusiastic applause indicated the opinions of the members of the audience. Again, they rose as one to their feet in tribute to the man, the choir, and their majestic music. In a response quite unlike me, tears flowed down my cheeks as the musicians took their final bows.

Al again put his hand over mine, which was clutching the program on my lap, at the conclusion of the concert.

"You all right?" He had never seen me cry and rarely had seen me show emotion to any significant degree. Though somewhat uncharacteristic for a true woman of the South, I didn't do that very often.

"Oh yes, it was just so well done," I covered, reticent as always to be found out. I stood to signal I was ready to go.

"Why don't you come backstage with me?" he asked as I was gathering my belongings. "I need to interview the promoter and some of the performers for my review."

"Why, Al, I...it's getting late and I have to...I don't mind..." and I looked to the back of the emptying theatre as if help would come from that direction at any minute. I had forgotten that he, of course, would need to go backstage. I had no excuse not to go with him other than not knowing what on earth I would say to the wounded stranger if Al ended up interviewing him. Should I pretend not to recognize Sir Neville and wait for his lead? Should I take the offense and ask him to explain the incident at the apartment? By now, Al was looking at me strangely, clearly eager to get to work backstage.

"Sure, why not?" I stuck out my chin. "It's not that late, and tomorrow's the weekend. Lead on." I sounded more enthusiastic than I felt. Al again eyed me askance but led the way.

Backstage was a whirlwind of post-performance emotions. The performers were awash in smiles and tears, champagne, and roses. Townsfolk of the highest social echelons could be seen vying for the musicians' time along with a fiercely dedicated group of traditional African music followers. The excitement was tangible.

Al, being used to the hullabaloo from years of attending such events, pushed his way through the crowd with me in tow until he spotted the international music promoter and the socialite sponsor of the benefit who had made all of this night possible. He didn't hesitate before shaking the hand of the promoter and greeting the latter, a slim and beautiful society lady, with a kiss on the cheek.

"Loretta, you look lovely, as usual. Mr. Arbusson? Bravo! Now, may I ask you both some questions?"

As I stood by, listening to Al's smooth and estimable interviewing skills at work, I watched the backstage stir between the performers and their admirers. The excitement and mutual affection seemed genuine, and I remember hoping that the night had been a profitable one for the N.U.N. African artists and their cause.

Al's conversation took longer than I expected, and the crowd began to thin a bit before he concluded. Waiting on the sidelines, I began to sense that I was being observed. The sensation seemed odd, as there were in fact still a number of people around us, but all were obviously involved in their own conversations or activities. Yet I continued to feel...somehow...watched.

And then I heard a soft voice at my side.

"Excuse me, Miss. I have a message for you." It was a young man who might have been a theatre usher.

"Yes?"

"The gentleman, Sir Neville, asked to speak with you at your convenience," and he indicated toward a narrow hallway to my right.

As I turned in that direction, I saw the source of my vibrations. Directly down the hall were doors to what appeared to be dressing rooms, and standing in an open doorway midway down the hall signing autographs for a group of well-wishers was Sir James Martin Neville, the gifted pianist and my wounded stranger. I moved closer to Al and his interviewees and pretended not to notice the man.

"Excuse me, Miss, did you understand the message? Sir Neville wanted me to be sure that you..."

"Yes, thank you very much. I do understand. Please tell the gentleman I will be with him in a moment."

With a swift look at Al, who was deeply engrossed in his conversation, I smiled reassuringly at the eager young man and followed him down the hallway toward the performer. As we approached I heard Sir Neville excuse himself courteously from his admirers who turned reluctantly away as he disappeared inside his dressing room.

My young escort moved with confidence past the curious lingerers and tapped on the still-open doorway. We were greeted by Sir Neville, who thanked the young man, handed him a tip, and motioned for me to enter.

As I walked past him into the room, he turned his back to the open door and addressed me quietly. "Please forgive me for being so forward. I did not mean to frighten you, but I recognized you from our former meeting. Allow me to introduce myself. I am James Martin Neville." He paused for my response.

"Jannia Redmon. Your music was incredible."

"You are most kind. Ms. Redmon, our time is short and what I have to say may seem strange. I realize you know virtually nothing about me or I, you. I feel, however, that our meeting has been prearranged in some way. I would like to talk with you further, if you will allow. There is no opportunity here or now. Would you permit me to meet with you someplace where you feel safe, and we could talk privately? This meeting would require a significant degree of trust for both of us. If you are uncomfortable, I understand."

He waited, and I stood speechless, trying hard to think what I should answer. Such a meeting was certainly out of my comfort zone. He was a stranger, but I had seen this man in the company of his young daughter when he appeared to be in genuine need. I was still deeply curious about that first meeting, and now he had stirred my interest even further. I knew my decision would need to be made quickly, and I breathed a prayer for wisdom.

"My request must seem peculiar and out of order. Please forgive me," and he moved toward the door to see me out as if I had declined his request.

"Wait, please let me think. Maybe we could meet at the front entrance of Riverside Cemetery in downtown Boone's Summit. Tomorrow morning at nine? It's located on..."

"I shall be there," he interrupted. "Thank you."

Had I just lost my mind?

"Ah, there you are, Jannia." This interruption came from Al Lanier while sticking his head in the dressing room doorway. "It seems as if you two have already met. Sir Neville, splendid performance." He extended his hand. "I am Albert Lanier, Cultural Arts and Entertainment editor for our *Daily Summit*. This young lady is my colleague at the paper. If she has not already stolen my interview, may I please have a moment to ask you some questions?"

"Mr. Lanier, your interview is safe. If you will both please excuse me, I will be waiting for you in the lobby, Al. Please take all the time you need. Sir Neville, good evening. It was a lovely concert." I left them.

3

Unusual Request

To say I had trouble sleeping that night would be an understatement. No position was comfortable; I was alternately either too hot or too cold; everything hurt. When I finally dreamed, I saw little Marta's frightened face. At dawn I got up, dizzy and shaken. The black coffee and overly sweet Danish roll in my still darkened kitchen didn't help much, but the long hot shower gave me some hope. At eight I left my apartment, determined to reach the gates of Riverside Cemetery early for my meeting with Sir Neville.

I crossed the broad, scenic river that flowed through the heart of the city on my way to the midtown cemetery located on the river's edge. It occurred to me that I had engaged in a bit of melodrama by suggesting my meeting with Sir Neville take place in a memorial park. Well, at least it would be a cool, sunny Saturday morning encounter and not a fog-shrouded midnight tryst. I wore sunglasses but passed on the trench coat. In the exacting light of day, this whole business was beginning to sound like a bad novel.

I angled my car near the stone entranceway to the cemetery fifteen minutes before our meeting time so I could watch his arrival without being obvious. I needed to gain an advantage. My last offer to help him had been rebuffed. This time he would have to ask for it.

Exactly at nine o'clock a taxi pulled up to the cemetery entranceway, and Sir James Martin Neville, looking very formal and forbidding in a dark suit and tie, stepped out. He stood for a moment looking around and turned to speak to the taxi driver. I knew that driver. He was the same black man who had been driving little Marta twice a week to her fast-food breakfast appointments.

The taxi drove off and left its passenger standing in the street in front of the cemetery entranceway. He again looked around and began walking toward the open gate. It was time to join him, and I hurried from my car in his direction, my high heels clicking on the sidewalk. I had selected my wardrobe with care, wanting to appear somewhat formal and business-like. We matched well, even if I had to pretend that three-inch heels were not unusual for a Saturday morning.

"Good morning, Sir Neville," I greeted as he turned to the sound of my tapping heels.

"Ms. Redmon, indeed it is a lovely day. Thank you for coming."

We began walking into the cemetery grounds. With my challenging footwear and nine-inch shorter stature, I was no match for his initial pace, and he soon slowed to keep me from having to run to keep up.

I decided a frontal attack would work best. "After the unusual circumstances of our initial meeting, I will admit I'm eager to hear why you want to talk to me."

I stood my ground facing him and held his eyes as we paused beneath a spreading and ancient oak. I could already hear the sound of the river in the background, and somehow its steadfastness gave me reassurance. This time he was not covered in blood, and I would not be intimidated by his commanding presence. Or so I told myself.

"Ms. Redmon, I know nothing about you except what I can easily observe. Neither of our previous meetings added much to that history. At the risk of insulting you or invading your privacy, I need to ask you a personal question before I proceed further."

"What do you want to know?"

"How did you come to be with my daughter in the apartment on the afternoon of our first meeting? How did you find us? Why were you there? It is very important that I know."

There was something grave behind his simple question. This man was clearly in no mood for evasion or pretext. I responded accordingly. "It was the taxi. I followed the taxi that takes your daughter twice a week to breakfast."

He seemed puzzled by my response.

"You see, I'm a writer and therefore naturally curious. I'm always searching for story ideas...out of the ordinary events or unusual things that interest me. While having breakfast at McDonald's some weeks ago, I noticed a taxi carrying a young girl and driven by a black driver. Their presence at a fast-food restaurant in a taxi seemed odd, and I was intrigued because I knew there was more to the story. I followed the taxi to see for myself. It appears as if I was right."

I paused, and he waited.

"Keeping up with that taxi proved to be quite a challenge." This brought a flicker of a smile. "It took me two weeks to find out where it was going. When I was finally successful, I was almost knocked down by the little girl from the taxi on the steps of your apartment...or someone's apartment. She was rather distraught and begged me to come and help. I followed her inside, and you know the rest. By the way, I also have about a thousand questions myself related to our encounter, but I'll wait my turn." Again, I noticed the slightest amusement in the face of the man beside of me.

"As you are now aware, the child was my daughter, Marta. She had been warned soundly about talking to strangers; she knew the dangers. She must have been quite upset to speak to you at all."

"Had Marta not been in such obvious distress, I assure you I would not have approached her or tried to talk to her. I don't encourage children to act foolishly. I was there when we met simply because I was curious. You know what they say about curiosity and the cat."

This brought a blank look.

"Never mind. It's just an old expression. But why are you asking me this? Surely you don't believe I intended harm to your daughter?"

"Ms. Redmon," his hand rested on my clenched ones lightly and only for the briefest moment, "I am not accusing you. I simply needed to hear your own account of why you were there. Allow me to explain why I must be vigilant and cautious in all situations. You observed from our meeting that I had been injured. The injury resulted from an assault that occurred as I was leaving the airport to come home to my daughter after having been away for a concert appearance. The attack was not random but calculated, and I was the intended target. I was fortunate that the incident was interrupted, and my injury was limited to the cut on my head. Unfortunately this was not the first such occurrence."

He held up his hands for me to view a line of scars across the backs of both hands. The hair on my neck crawled, and I expected to see men dressed in black swarming over the cemetery ready to strike again.

"Who's doing this to you? Why is this happening?" I heard the beginnings of hysteria in my voice. "Are you in danger here...now?"

"I was not followed here today. My driver takes great precautions. We are safe for the time."

I willed my breathing to slow and my voice to sound calm. "Please, go on."

"As you are aware, I am a musician currently engaged to perform in a series of African benefit concerts. What you may not know is that I am a citizen of one of those countries. My home country is Khutule, which is located in the southern portion of the continent adjacent to South Africa. Two months ago I came to the U.S. on a non-immigrant visitor's visa that will expire soon after our final concert in a few weeks."

Again, I was aware of his distinct accent, only now it was easier to put into context. His African country of citizenship must once have been a British colony because the inflections and intonations of the mother tongue were clearly present in his speech. Still there was something more, a staccato and rhythm that must have their origins in a tribal dialect. Although he spoke English, I had to concentrate to understand all that he was saying. I looked directly into his gray-blue eyes.

"May we sit, Ms. Redmon? I need to tell you of the circumstances that cause me to request a meeting with you today."

I nodded assent, and he led me to a stone bench overlooking the river. I sat, watching the cold water flow by in the ancient river and willing my hands and body to not fidget. I had an uncomfortable feeling that what I was about to hear might somehow change me. The awareness was not reassuring.

"As I stated, I came to America from my country to take part in the benefit concerts. It was only by special arrangement between our embassies that I was allowed to travel. When the concerts are concluded, both the United States and my government will expect me to travel home. My daughter must remain here, as she does not live in Khutule. While she holds dual citizenship, she cannot safely travel with me to my country. She has not been there since infancy. Marta lives here with her great-grandmother, who is devoted to her but whose health is becoming somewhat fragile. The situation could become complex in my absence."

"Your wife?"

"My wife is dead. She died a few months after the child was born. Africa did not agree with her, and the child's birth damaged her health beyond repair. Although she returned alone with our baby to America, she only lived a short time longer."

"And Marta? Didn't you make arrangements to come here to be with your daughter when your wife died? Or at least bring her to Africa to be with you?" I was beginning to sound accusatory. Clearly I didn't understand his position. Surely he hadn't been away from Marta for the seven or eight years of her life?

"You must understand. I tried to come to her many times but was denied exit from my country. I am not free to travel as I wish. I was allowed to come here now only because of the benefit concerts and the American dollars that my artistry might bring back into my country."

"I'm sorry. That must have been awful for you."

He didn't pause to accept my compassion but continued with his story.

"I know virtually no one here except professionally, apart from my daughter's great-grandmother and a close friend from Khutule who immigrated to this area. My wife came from a family of some means, and she was an only child of an only child. Her parents died some time after her death. Marta is well cared for by her great-grandmother, who is a most private lady and also very proud. She has few close friends and will not seek help of any kind unless the situation is desperate. This friend of mine from Khutule does what he can. Any of Marta's trips away from the apartment are due to his insistence on some outings for the child."

"He's the taxi driver. Am I right?"

Sir Neville seemed surprised at my deduction. "You are correct. He is a trusted friend and cares deeply for my daughter's well-being. He watches from afar and does what he can, but again, he is only allowed so close. There is no woman...no female to whom my daughter could turn in the event that her great-grandmother should..." He sighed. "They live nearly as hermits."

"What about Marta's school?"

"She is tutored at home."

I began to feel more anxious and apprehensive the longer he spoke. There was a reason he was relating his family history to me. I had to know. "Why are you telling all of this to me?"

He raised his eyebrows slightly. "I am in a position to need some assistance. Your assistance, I am hoping."

At this point, he asked me a curious question. "Ms. Redmon, are you a religious woman? If so, may I ask what faith you follow? You see, I may be on the verge of making a grave mistake, one that could prove to be very costly. Such a mistake must be avoided if at all possible."

This completely unexpected turn of conversation unnerved me. I was not sure where this line of questioning was headed, but it quickly served to put me on the defensive. While I was certainly not ashamed of my faith, I had never before been questioned so bluntly about it. This subject I considered to be extremely private and one that I was not accustomed to discussing openly, especially with virtual strangers.

I had, however, as a child learned the etiquette trick of turning the unwanted question back on the asker. "Why do you ask?"

He was not to be deterred. "Ms. Redmon, please honor my question if you will. I realize the serious nature of what I am asking."

He wanted an answer; I would give him one.

"I wouldn't characterize myself simply as religious, Sir Neville. I'm a Christian...a follower of Jesus Christ with whom I have a personal relationship and on whom I depend for my salvation. I call myself a believer. Is that a problem?"

"Quite the contrary, Ms. Redmon, and I felt that would be your response. Your forthright answer allows me to speak freely about my situation. But before I proceed, I must ask you one additional...and I am afraid highly personal...question. You may find it invasive, but I am afraid it is necessary."

I waited, watching him closely without response.

"Do you consider yourself a woman of faith?"

He had a way of catching me off guard that left me feeling vulnerable and unsure of myself.

"If you're asking whether I have a faith, I'm sure about the answer to that part, as I told you earlier. I have a deep faith in Jesus Christ, and because of Him my eternal salvation and security are not in question. But I'm thinking you mean whether or not I depend on the source of my faith to help with my everyday actions and decisions. Honestly, probably not nearly enough, Sir Neville.

"I've never been asked that question before now, and it's hard to talk about. Most of the time I depend on my own skills and instincts. Sometimes it works and sometimes not, but that's what I've learned to do. I know God is interested in my well-being, and I find that comforting, but I've just always done all I can for myself and let Him help with the really hard parts. That must not sound very spiritual, but I'm afraid it's true."

I forced myself to make eye contact as I finished my explanation. His question was challenging, and my response didn't leave me overwhelmed with confidence that I was right. But I was truthful.

"I appreciate your candid, honest answer. I am sorry I made you uncomfortable."

He looked away now toward the nearby river, almost hidden by the trees. The cemetery apparently had no other visitors except the birds in the trees overhead and the two of us. The gentleman had acknowledged my discomfort at having to open myself to his queries, but strangely he didn't seem disappointed.

"Ms. Redmon, I am going to make a request that will, no doubt, prove surprising to you. I am fully aware that we have just met. Please know that I am quite serious. I ask that you hear my appeal and consider it carefully and prayerfully. Please know I will understand if you are forced to decline."

I couldn't have imagined what was coming with his next sentence.

"Would you consider becoming Marta's legal guardian, should anything happen to her great-grandmother, who has custody of Marta at present? I must return to Khutule quite soon, and I cannot take Marta to Africa with me. Neither can I stay here with her at this time. I have pressing concerns in Africa of which I have not spoken. While I hope to return to the States as soon as possible, it is not certain when or if I will be able to do so.

"Would you be willing to visit with Marta and her grea- grandmother in my absence to ensure that they are not in need? My friend with the taxi brings them groceries and the things they request. He acts as their driver should they need to go out, as he does when he takes Marta to McDonald's. While my friend has vowed to assist them, as he is able, that still leaves a vulnerable support system should an emergency occur. Ms. Redmon, I know this is most unusual, but I need your assistance."

Sir Neville was correct when he predicted I would be surprised at his words. I would rather have chosen the word *shocked*. What he asked was so unexpected that I could barely speak. "You don't even know me. How could you trust me with such a responsibility? How can you be sure your family would be safe with me? Besides, why do you think I would even be interested, or available, to do what you are asking?"

His incredible and unreadable eyes watched me as I stood to go. He stood also and took me softly by the arm. "It's true that I do not know these things for sure, Ms. Redmon. Unfortunately, I have few options. This may sound to you like something of a...long shot, as I have heard it put? I realize that. But you must understand that I also believe in Divine involvement into the matters of my life, as complicated as it has become. I watched your face and your actions that day you found us in the apartment when I was injured and my daughter was so distraught. What I saw was a woman of character."

He paused and ran his long fingers though his black hair, as if trying to decide how far to go in defending his case. I knew the moment he decided to let me see the reasoning behind his unexpected request.

"Ms. Redmon, I believe our meeting was no random accident. Do you remember the story of Isaac and Rebekah in the Old Testament? The patriarch Abraham sent a trusted servant back to his home country to find a wife for his son Isaac because there was no suitable wife in the land where they were living. God told Abraham that an angel would go ahead of the servant to prepare the way. Abraham believed Him. When the servant arrived back in the homeland, he prayed that God would point out the chosen bride specifically and immediately. God honored his prayer, and Rebekah walked up while he was still praying."

I didn't know how to respond to such an example of pure faith. While I was familiar with the amazing story, I hadn't read it in years. My silence was apparently misunderstood.

"Ms. Redmon, you look so concerned." I could detect a defined twinkle in his eyes. "I am not planning to propose marriage. I merely wanted to illustrate why I believe that some meetings are the result of Divine intervention. I prayed for assistance, Ms. Redmon, and I believe you were...are...the answer to that prayer. You see, I consider myself a man of faith."

He saw my wary look at what could have sounded like supreme arrogance. "I assure you there is no boasting in that statement. It is simply that I have chosen to put my confidence in the power of the same God of Abraham, Isaac and Jacob...in the same God who is sufficient for the troubles of this world today. I believe He can help me protect my family in the same obvious way that God helped Abraham find a bride for his son."

As he spoke, I was aware of a lack of conceit or vanity in his words. There was something clean and simple in this confidence of which he spoke.

"You see, Jannia," he continued, using my given name for the first time, "I prayed when I had a need just like the servant of Abraham did, and you appeared with Marta soon afterward. Of course your coming could have been a coincidence; that is true. But I choose to believe that God Himself brought you into our lives. For what purpose, I am not yet sure. I prayed specifically for someone who could help me with Marta, should I have to leave her."

"If I were sent," I asked, "why did you disappear and leave me standing alone and completely confused in a deserted apartment when I was trying to help you?"

He didn't reply at once but sat in reflection, gazing at something in the distance of the cemetery. "Even a man who tries to live by faith can have second thoughts, Ms. Redmon."

The sound of an insistent car horn from outside the cemetery gates interrupted the quiet between us.

"I am afraid there is more to my story that may further dissuade you, even if you have not already decided to reject my appeal. I will have to explain at our next meeting. I must go now. Please consider what I have said. I know where to find you." He rose and left the cemetery.

I waited until he was out of sight and then walked quickly in his footsteps, but I was no match for his long legs. I reached the gate just in time to see him enter the taxi and be driven away.

4

Sir Neville's Story

It was three days before I heard again from the mysterious Sir James Martin Neville. On Tuesday evening, as I was leaving my downtown office, he fell into step beside me when I reached the sidewalk.

"I regret that I was unable to contact you before now. I thought perhaps we could have dinner. Would that be possible, or do you have another engagement?"

I was amazed at the ease with which he blended his stride with mine, taking my briefcase in hand as we moved along the sidewalk. I was not sure whether to be pleased to see him again, afraid of what he might tell me next, or insulted that he could show up on his terms and obligate my time.

I decided quickly to take the risk. "I'm free; what did you have in mind?"

A light, cool rain had begun to fall reminding me that, while spring was moving in, it would be some time before it brought real warmth.

What he had in mind was a small Italian restaurant offering quaint authenticity in an out-of-the-way neighborhood within walking distance of my work. I had neither eaten there nor seen it previously, but there was a wonderful sense of secreted delight in ducking into the warmth of its candle-lit dining room. We were either early or past the usual dinner rush, if there was one. We shared the room with one other couple and an old man. Seated before a window onto the street, we could both watch the rain and feel the warmth of the fire in the small fireplace.

Sir Neville ordered for us both, antipasto followed by a comforting pasta dish with a glass of red wine to warm us. At first we ate with little conversation. It wasn't uncomfortable to sit quietly, sipping the wine and watching, alternately, the fire and the rain.

Finally, he began to talk. "My given name is James Martin. I am accustomed to using both; I think that would be preferable to Sir Neville, if you please."

"Then I'm Jannia."

"If you permit. It appears as though I spend an inordinate amount of time explaining to you the details of my rather complex circumstances. Perhaps tonight there will be few interruptions. It is important that you understand the risks related to any involvement with my family on your part. That is, of course, if you have not already made up your mind you want no further part of what I am requesting?"

His voice turned the last statement into a question. As he spoke, I watched his face and then turned my eyes toward the window on the street outside and waited. He did the same. He didn't seem to be in his usual hurry this evening.

"Go on," I finally answered.

His response was the fabric of which history is made.

"My grandfather was Sir John Neville of Dawlish on Devon in the south of England. He immigrated to an unfamiliar and isolated territory in the southern part of Africa at the age of twenty-two in 1870. There he lived for the rest of his life. The land was vast and made up of deserts and savannahs, cut through by deep gorges, meandering rivers and a small range of mountains. Sir John survived when other early visitors to the Dark Continent, as it was then called, failed because of keen survival instincts and a penchant for blending with his surroundings. It meant joining a native tribe and living as they lived until he learned enough of the language, landscape, and native savvy to help ensure his continued existence. With this knowledge to keep from making mistakes due to ignorance, he struck out to discover all he could about his new home. In the course of his travels, he came upon a colony of British citizens living near a beautiful inland lake in an area that was to become the first capital of his adopted country.

"Among the families living there, and there were five or six, was a young orphan girl named Magnolia, the cousin of a wealthy merchant who had moved his family to the wilds of Africa to protect them from what he believed to be the evil influences of England in the nineteenth century. She was nineteen, and Sir John was twenty-seven. Their attraction was immediate and undeniable. Fortunately, her guardian appreciated the independent spirit of the newcomer and realized that he would make a better match than most in this secluded place, so he consented to their marriage less than a year later. That marriage lasted for fifty-three years. When he was fifty-eight, my grandfather became the fourth prime minister of his adopted country."

It was an intriguing beginning, but my knowledge of African history was weak.

"Where was your grandfather? What was this country?"

"It used to be known as New Victoria. Today it is called Khutule."

"Please go on," I urged.

"John Neville and his wife had three daughters; all died from the dangers rampant in that part of the world at the time. A son, Marcus James Neville, was born in 1893. That boy was my father. He was to become the seventh and final prime minister of the colonial republic that was formed in New Victoria in 1875. Father served for more than forty years as a loyal servant of the British crown in his adopted country, eighteen of those years as its leader.

"My father was strong in both mind and spirit...a gentleman who respected all honest men, regardless of their race. He was a follower of Christ, having been converted as a young boy by an Irish missionary who brought him the message of Christ. As a leader of his country, he did what he could to further the spread of the gospel of Christ while showing consideration for the native culture of his citizens. My father was highly regarded by people of both British and African descent for raising the standard of living and strengthening the rule of law for all."

James Martin paused to order us coffee, taking the time before it came to twirl his teaspoon between his fingers and stare again out at the rain. He seemed to be far removed from the city where we sat. It was like watching a drama rather than participating in a conversation with him. After the coffee arrived, he began again.

"During the last few years of my father's leadership, unrest over perceived wrongs related to colonial occupation was sweeping the continent. Activist guerillas, most with communist backing, were beginning to stir up fear and hatred among the citizens of Khutule, white and black alike. At first, the rebels were content to cause harassment, delays at border crossings, and intimidation of travelers. There were occasional break-ins and burglaries, but little blood was shed.

"As the anti-colonial movement strengthened, so did the intensity of the guerilla activity. Beatings and murders of non-Africans became common, and many white families made plans to leave the country rather than face such terror tactics. In 1962, there was a coup attempt by a military general, once loyal to my father, but now under the influence of a local rebel group calling itself the African Re-Unification Coalition. In the takeover attempt, my father's first wife and her sister were killed. The coup failed, but it signaled the closing stage of colonial rule in the country."

James Martin paused and looked at me as if deciding whether I was interested or pretending to be out of courtesy.

He needn't have worried. I closed my mouth and waited for him to continue.

"Events over the next few years led my father's government and Britain to sanction national elections in 1975. In 1976, England relinquished the reins of power to a newly formed democratic government in the renamed country of Khutule. My father's last acts as Prime Minister were to welcome the first African president and to arrest the general responsible for the loss of his wife following a long manhunt. The new president outlawed the African Re-Unification Coalition, or ARC as it was commonly called, and arrested many of its members in the name of peace-making in the emerging democracy. Relative quiet prevailed during the imprisonment and trial of the general."

I had to know when his place in this story began.

"And you? How do you fit in to this history? Your father's wife was dead. Who was your mother?"

"His first wife died in 1962. Two years later he met a young nurse who was working at a mission station near his estate. My father was several years her senior, but they soon married, and I was born in 1968, their only child. When my father retired at eighty-two, we moved permanently to his country estate, where we lived quietly and peacefully for two years as a normal family. My only bad memory of that time was when my father left to attend the trial proceedings of the general, and he went as often as he could. I remember how frightened my mother was during that time. The verdict was guilty, and the sentence was death. But when the execution was finally carried out, it seemed to signal an era of renewed coming together in our country. If the story had ended there, we would not be sitting here tonight."

I forced myself not to interrupt. I had a hundred questions, but I knew it wasn't the time. I could read it on his face.

"Unfortunately, the members of the ARC, though now underground, had vowed to continue the fight against my father and his family begun by their general. The group eventually surfaced and re-started their tactics of terror. Three years after my father's retirement, while I was abroad at a private school in England, my father, my mother, his driver, and a bodyguard were murdered as his car was leaving the estate to take them to church on a Sunday morning.

"Although there was widespread outrage among all sectors of the society, no one was ever brought to justice for the killings. There were countless investigations conducted and rewards offered, but no arrests. General opinion and considerable testimony pointed to the ARC, but whether out of fear of further reprisals, corruption, whatever...no real action was ever taken. The blood of my father seemed to satisfy the group, and their activities again declined."

He followed this statement with a small movement of resignation that was painful to watch. The relative safety and ease of my childhood made it hard for me to imagine what living under such circumstances had required of him.

"What about you?" I asked. "How did all of this horror affect you?"

He shrugged. "As a child, I was kept largely out of the spotlight surrounding my father's leadership, sheltering that no doubt came as a result of the early losses in his family. I was not allowed to be shown in family photographs or to make public appearances with him. My schooling came at home with tutors until I was sent out of country to private school as a boy of ten. Except to those close to my family, I hardly existed due to his carefully crafted plans to protect me.

"Father always warned me of the possibility that such an event as caused his death might occur, but I did not believe it possible. I never feared for the safety of my parents or myself. When the attack actually happened, I was shocked and disillusioned that someone who had been revered and loved was now dead at the hands of his own countrymen. It is ironic that my mother died because her fear for my father was so great she rarely left his side. I finally realized, even at such an early age, that I was vulnerable after all. The same could happen to me."

"What did you do? How did you live? Who took care of you?"

"My godparents. They immigrated to England soon after my birth. I remained in England and continued my schooling under their care. We did not even come home for my parents' funeral. Under the direction of my godmother, who was a world-class pianist in her own right, I continued my studies in piano, begun as a young child, throughout high school and university. I returned home to Khutule several times for brief stays with remaining family members and friends, but I was in my early twenties before I came home for good. By then, I was beginning to develop an international reputation as a pianist and composer. I could have stayed in England, but I knew how committed my father's family had been to their country, and I wanted to be a part of that heritage."

"What was left in Africa for you? Who was there for you to come home to?"

"My father's extended family had been looking after the family's business and property in Khutule since his death. The estate where I had been born was now under the watch care of my father's cousin, and I had no desire to return to live where my parents had been murdered. I wanted to be on my own, and I was determined fear would not make me a recluse in my own country.

"Leaving my older cousin to continue in his life at the Neville family estate, I moved to another family property, a cattle farm, located about thirty kilometers from where my father had lived. It suited me well. I kept busy with my duties there and with my music, but with my eyes open and a gun always hidden at my side.

"Although I worked quietly behind the scenes to find my parents' killers, few people knew my real connection with the family. Music provided the focus I needed to re-create my identity. I began to perform internationally as well as in Khutule using the name James Martin without the Neville surname."

I knew him as James Martin Neville. What had brought about the reverse in his connection to the family name?

"The subterfuge continued for some years, until I was about to be knighted in England for services recognized by the royal family. Sufficient time seemed to have passed making it safe to re-assume my real surname. It was also time to come to terms with my family history, so I became Sir James Martin Neville, son of late Sir John Neville, final Prime Minister of Khutule."

He stopped his story, motioned to the restaurant owner, and requested our bill. He talked no more until we walked out into the evening. We strolled without direction and without conversation for some time. Finally, I stopped and faced him under a street lamp so that I could see his eyes.

"Your story isn't finished, is it? There's more, and that's why you're here with me now. Am I correct?"

I wanted him to know that I was ready to hear more if he was ready to tell. We began walking again.

"My wife's name was Elisia. She was the daughter of an American businessman who often visited in Khutule. He owned a number of hotels across Africa and spent considerable time at a home he owned near my father's estate. His only daughter and I met as children and saw each other a number of times through the years during their visits when I was on holiday. We knew even as playmates that one day we would marry. After college she came to Khutule on her own as a humanitarian aid worker.

"Elisia and I married soon after she arrived. She continued her humanitarian efforts for a while, but she wanted children badly. By the time we were expecting Marta, Elisia was already unwell, and Marta's birth was difficult. We sent her for treatment to the States with Marta, but there...."

James Martin stopped abruptly, so I finished his sentence in my mind...*she died.*

After a time, he continued, "I knew after Elisia's death that it was unwise for me to have Marta returned to Africa. After much consideration, I decided she should remain in the States with Elisia's family. The African Re-Unification Coalition, which had been underground and nearly dormant for years, was renewing their activity. The group gained the ear of Khutule's president at the time, who removed the ban on its existence. Because I was now a public figure, my connection with my father was well known. The new leaders of the ARC had not forgotten my father had hanged their founder, who was now considered a folk hero.

"I began to get threats, only a few at first, but enough to know that my child would be in danger if she were with me. I employed bodyguards, and that seemed sufficient for my safety but not hers also. Marta's grandparents cared for her until they died together in an accident. Her great-grandmother became her guardian, and she was insistent that Marta's life not be risked by a return to Africa.

"I will admit I was badly affected by Elisia's death and turned to my music for comfort and solace. It was easier to allow Marta to remain with her great-grandmother. I knew she was well cared for, and I could bury myself in my music. The choice is not one of which I am proud today, but at least she was safe for the time being."

We stopped near a small park and sat on a metal bench near the playground, unmindful of the wet condition of the bench or the misty rain falling around us.

"Didn't you miss her deeply? Didn't you want to come to the States and at least spend time with her here?"

I was not sure of the source of my maternal instincts toward the child, but her virtual abandonment by her father made me uncomfortable.

His response was direct and free of any self-defense. "Travel outside of my country was increasingly difficult for me. As I became better known and connected with my father's memory, I began to be tracked by the Khutulen government whenever I traveled. It seems I was considered a presumed threat. Travel beyond our borders was very difficult to arrange, as I was frequently refused travel privileges to neighboring countries, much less outside of the continent. My prominence may have protected me from bodily harm, in a sense, but my movements were monitored and often restricted.

"The political climate became one of growing distaste for any memory of the colonial period of our history, and my family played a prominent role in that history. Many of the persons who had known and loved my father during his time as prime minister were no longer influential or had died. The younger population seemed only to remember that they had been subject, in their own country, to rule by a foreign power. That fact left a bitter taste in their mouths, although they seemed to know few actual facts about the time or its events.

"The pressure of being part of the Neville heritage became too great for some of the family members. My cousin's family, his son, and daughter-in-law, were afraid for the lives of their children and decided to immigrate to England. The cousin, who had lost his wife by then, made plans to go with them. They were able to leave the country only with the help of a government official who was given a significant sum of money to arrange for their departure. While my parents' home and farm were left in the hands of a trusted caretaker, within a month squatters had overrun the property, and the home was burned.

"During this time, international travel became all but impossible for me. Either I was denied exit from the country outright or I was only allowed to travel with a government representative, ostensibly all for security reasons. I suspected it was to prevent me from building a power base of my own and to ensure my return to Khutule, where my movements could be watched. Even as I began to understand what Marta and I were missing by not having each other, I realized the futility of trying to unite us in Africa."

"How did it become possible for you to do this concert tour?" I asked. It made me wonder if his government handlers were watching us even now.

"This tour is being sponsored by some very high profile organizations, and much of the proceeds are earmarked for the benefit of children and mothers in my country, although corruption remains so rampant many in need will not receive help. Through the joint efforts of the United Nations, the International Red Cross, and some influential donors here in America, the lineup of performers was assembled and the tour made a reality. The U.S. State Department has worked closely through its Embassy in Khutule with the government to allow my travel for this specific tour. I was granted a short-term visa that expires as soon as the concert tour is completed, which is quite soon.

"I do not know what assurances were exchanged in order for me to be allowed to come. Perhaps the brevity of the stay influenced my government. I also suspect that I did not come alone. Strangely enough, I am being allowed a great deal of freedom on this trip, perhaps due to the amount of publicity received by the benefit tour. There are, however, other individuals besides government representatives who are tracking me."

I wondered if this man beside me in the well-cut business suit, now soaking wet, was really suffering an episode of psychotic paranoia. The story unfolding was something you read in novels of international intrigue, not something that happened openly in small southern cities. My expression must have hinted at my skepticism because my companion eyed me and laughed.

"I am not surprised at your reaction. Mine would be the same, were I not at the center of this little drama. Please hear me out. You must understand that the African Re-Unification Coalition movement has grown in recent months. There are a number of cells of ARC members operating here in the United States. Their task is to gain sympathy for their causes, such as the return of all African lands currently owned by non-native Africans or those who are of white colonial descent to ownership by black Africans and the nationalization of all foreign business interests. They are also major fundraisers in the States for the efforts of their followers back in Africa. While living in America, the members of the ARC have lost none of their zeal for their homeland...or their contempt for anything colonial, including me."

"How can you be so sure you're being watched on this trip? What makes you so convinced?" I had to press the point here to see what I could find out about this bizarre story.

"You witnessed for yourself the handiwork of one of these groups on our first meeting. I am just not sure which one, my government or the ARC. I have been physically attacked twice since leaving Khutule. The last time was right before you found me at the apartment.

"It is difficult for me to know whether my life or simply my career as a musician is in danger. They seem especially intent on trying to injure me...my hands. That would be a cruel prelude to taking my life, rendering me unable to perform." James Martin held up his hands again, the scars on the backs of them clearly evident. "I have managed to escape any significant injuries so far, mostly due to the grace of God and the interference of my childhood comrade who now lives here in this city."

"Your taxi driver friend, again!" I responded. "He's a bodyguard helping to watch over both you and your daughter, Marta, isn't he?"

"You are correct. He is Banolo Benadie, my oldest and most trusted friend. He immigrated about five years ago to the States after many years of trying. Even as young boys, we had a bond that was stronger than that of brothers. He has done what he can for Marta and her great-grandmother, what little the proud lady will allow him to do. He has convinced her that Marta needs to begin to experience some of American society, to get out into the city even for small excursions. She has been so continuously sheltered and hidden away, just as I once was."

"That explains the bi-weekly trips in the taxi to get breakfast at McDonalds." Now I understood. "He can keep her safe with him and also let her see a little of the city at the same time. And this is where I came into the picture," I added.

"Yes, as distressing as your discovery was to Banolo, you found us by following his taxi to where Marta and her great-grandmother live."

"In the apartment above where I found you. That's where they live, isn't it? Marta's great-grandmother is the woman I saw in the window of the apartment on the second floor. But whose...?"

"In whose apartment did you find me? It was the apartment in which Elisia grew up with her parents. They lived there when they were not living in Africa or traveling. They both died about two years after Marta's birth. Their apartment has been left as it was when they died except for periodic cleaning. It is magnificent, isn't it? Marta lived there with her grandparents until their death when her great-grandmother closed the apartment and moved the child in with her."

All at once I realized I was freezing, soaked, and exhausted. Furthermore, I was sitting in a park with a stranger listening to a story that had all the earmarks of having been prefabricated by a highly creative, deranged mind. And I was lost. Self-preservation alarm bells began to ring loudly inside my head.

As if he read my mind, my companion slipped a cell phone from his pocket and punched in a number. He spoke a few words into it and returned it to his pocket.

"Banolo will pick us up in a few minutes."

"Sir Neville..."

"James Martin, please."

I hugged my arms around me to keep my teeth from chattering visibly. I was mystified at his revelation of this fantastic tale to me. Why me? Regardless of how he characterized it, suppose we had only met by coincidence? That thought was followed by a mental rerun of our next meeting on the evening of his concert. If it were coincidence, it didn't happen once but twice. Otherwise he wouldn't have known my identity or where to find me. Maybe coincidence was not, after all, the right choice of words.

Again as if he read my thoughts, James Martin stood and faced me, looking down from his considerable height to where I was still sitting on the wet bench.

"I do not believe in happenstance. Coincidence is directed by what some call Providence. I prefer to think of Providence as an omniscient God. Our meeting was no chance. What the outcome will be, I cannot say, but it happened, and now we must see what plays out. I have kept you out in the rain much too long. Come along. Banolo is here for us."

And indeed, Banolo and his ever-present white taxi appeared on the street opposite us. It was as if he were waiting all the time just around the corner. James Martin handed me into the back of the vehicle and stepped in to sit beside me.

"Ms. Redmon, this is my lifelong friend, of whom I spoke. This is Mr. Banolo Benadie. Banolo, Ms. Jannia Redmon."

"I am most pleased and charmed to meet you, Ms. Redmon," Banolo spoke with the same accent as James Martin, only his was more pronounced and his voice was softer. He pulled the taxi away from the curb.

"The pleasure is mine," I responded.

The dark-skinned man's smile was broad, open, and engaging. At first glance, it was not hard to imagine him as a trusted friend.

"We may speak freely before Banolo. He is a brother, and he understands my present situation and concerns," James Martin continued.

"I'm sure that must be reassuring," I answered, feeling response was necessary but not really knowing what to say. The intuition that often keeps us safe if we heed it stirred in the back of my mind, and I had an even stronger awareness that some pieces of this puzzle were still missing. This man, although a gentleman in every word and action so far, was still a relative stranger to me. Here I was, in a taxi, speeding down a dark city street in the company of two...well...foreigners. I edged toward the door on my side of the back seat.

I again saw the flicker of a smile cross Sir Neville's face and watched him exchange a glance in the rearview mirror with Mr. Benadie. Fortunately, it appeared to be an amused exchange, but I was a little too tired to appreciate amusement. I turned what I hoped was a business-like stare toward my companion and waited. He had the honor to lower his head in the face of my stare. I continued to wait, as he shifted on the seat.

"Jannia, you have been most patient with me and most fair to hear my life's story. I wanted you to know the background and circumstances from which I speak. It is time that I clarify my earlier request for you to help with my child. I need for some responsible person...a woman... to watch out for my daughter and her great-grandmother. In the event of my death, I need someone to become Marta's guardian when the need arises."

Sir James Martin Neville's simple restatement of his request for his family unsettled me. I had heard his earlier plea, but it focused that what he was asking was serious business. It would bring with it significant responsibilities. I was an independent woman with few attachments except family members I visited too infrequently. My time and energy were dedicated to my newspaper work. Probably too much so, but that was my choice. I was responsible for no one but me, which suited me fine. My days, my evenings, my weekends were mine to plan and to change those plans at will.

Sir Neville's words replayed in my head: *"I need for some responsible person to watch out for my daughter and her great-grandmother."* What he asked would make me partly, or fully, responsible for a seven-year-old child and an eighty-something-year-old woman. Two ends of the age continuum I knew nothing about. Stranger still: *"In the event of my death, I need someone to become Marta's guardian when the need arises."* I would at that point become a parent. How restrictive would that be?

I had no one to blame but myself for this unbelievable dilemma! My insatiable curiosity and constant search for novel ideas had gotten me into this. Now what would I do to get out?

My self-centered thoughts showed on my face. I could tell by his expression and by the way he turned from me to look at the rain coming harder now against the windows of the taxi.

"I am sorry, Jannia," James Martin whispered. "I am afraid I have misspoken. You must forgive me." And then louder, "Banolo, I see that we have returned to Ms. Redmon's office. Please wait while I walk her safely to her car."

I had been dismissed. His request had been withdrawn, however silently. I understood why, and he was completely justified. He had only *misspoken*, to use his word, because he had misjudged me in the first place. He presumed that because I showed concern for his daughter the day he was hurt...well, he presumed incorrectly.

James Martin's disappointment, as we walked silently to my car, was palpable. My face began to burn hot with embarrassment and then irritation. How dare he be disappointed in me when he had put me in this position by his presumptions? By the time we reached my car, I was angry and defensive.

"Ms. Redmon."

"Sir Neville."

We spoke simultaneously, relapsing into our more formal mode. Our eyes met but couldn't hold. This wasn't easy for either of us. It occurred to me, as our eyes met again, that his contained no look of blame or resentment that he had not gotten his way. He smiled, and the smile was real. Then I remembered his story of Abraham's servant finding Rebekah. I heard again the words he had spoken earlier: *"I am a man of faith."*

"Sir Neville, I'm very tired tonight, and you have given me more information than I can possibly process at once. I need time to think clearly. I can't make decisions of the magnitude you are asking this quickly. The fact is, I may not be able to make promises to you at all. I want you to understand that now. But I would like a little while to think about what you ask."

"Jannia," his voice was soft, "it is not necessary for this to go further. I do not mean to put you under duress. Please forgive me."

"Thank you. I understand, but I would still like some time, if you will." I got into my car and drove away, leaving him standing on the sidewalk.

It was true that I was exhausted. I longed to fall into my bed and forget, for the time being, all about Sir James Martin Neville and his predicament and my responsibility until I rested for about twelve hours. What actually happened was very different.

5

The Dilemma

As it was quite late when I finally got home, I raced through the door to my apartment, dropping shoes, briefcase, and clothes as I went. I was desperate for a quick shower and my bed. The bedroom was quiet and inviting; the clean, lilac-smelling sheets soothed me. I shut my eyes, breathed a quick prayer of gratitude to be home, and prepared for oblivion.

It did not come. I fluffed my pillows and turned over. My hip hurt. I turned back over. A police car raced down the street with its siren on. The light from the alarm clock made the room too light. I punched my pillows again and tried lying on my back, but that made my neck hurt. My eyes burned, and my head began to ache.

Finally, I slept but awakened an hour later after dreaming I saw Marta being chased by men with machine guns in a jeep who were trying to kill her.

In the next hour, I awoke running up the steps to the apartment where I met James Martin, only to be knocked backwards again and again by Marta's great-grandmother, who was pushing me from the top of the steps. I recognized her even though she had a lace curtain over her head.

The third time I awoke, the dream was too horrible to talk about it even now, and it left me shaking and terrified. I lay perfectly still and prayed until my breathing slowed and I calmed enough to reach for the bedside light. It was 3:00 a.m., and sleep was now out of the question.

The TV in my den provided some companionship, although the movie choices at that time of the morning were dubious. I left the sound off so I could think. Thinking had been the last thing on my mind earlier, and now I was frantic to organize my thoughts and find some logical way to put the events of the last few weeks into perspective.

It was hard to believe that just recently my life had been uncomplicated by comparison. My worries had been few and usually minor. I preferred a quiet, predictable, calm lifestyle. Living from one drama to another, as I had seen others do, held no interest for me. Now it seemed drama had found me, drama of the life-changing sort.

I refused to believe I had brought this on myself. How much could one small act of following a taxi across town be responsible for the events that followed? How much of what came next was chance, and how much was God's intervention? How much was God involved in the everyday lives of his followers? I hadn't given much thought to the subject before. The memory of a verse learned in Sunday school, something from Romans, floated across the screen of my mind.

I turned on a lamp and pulled the Bible I had owned since I was twelve off the shelf behind my chair. The verse, Romans 8:28, was marked with what looked like green magic marker: *"And we know that in all things God works for the good of those who love him, who have been called according to his purpose."*

In all things? In following a taxi across town on a Saturday morning? Had I simply stumbled into a strange set of circumstances that morning or was something more significant happening to me? Something beyond me? Something I could also miss out on because of my own selfishness if I were not careful?

Dawn was beginning to appear as a faint orange light in the sky outside my kitchen window when I made my way back to the still darkened bedroom to sleep....

When I finally awoke, Saturday morning had come and gone and most of Saturday afternoon with it. I expected to feel refreshed by my long sleep, but instead I felt anxious and ill at ease. After fighting the feeling until dark and dreading another night of unrest, I did what I had often considered a weakness in others. I called the pastor of the little church I had been attending for the time I had been in the city.

Pouring out my troubles to others had never been a practice of mine. I usually pretended to any watchers that my life was under such control I had no troubles to speak of. In most matters, I considered myself to be self-sufficient. Prayer was important, of course, but usually after I trying everything I knew to do and becoming desperate. I was nearing desperate now, as my uncharacteristic action showed. Certainly bothering a pastor on a Saturday night when he had a sermon to deliver in a few hours was unheard of for me.

Pastor Terry was home, and he was patient. He listened quietly as I briefly outlined my strange dilemma. Should I become involved in a situation of this magnitude with someone I had just met under such peculiar circumstances? Even as I voiced my question, I knew what advice I would have given, had I been in his shoes.

His response shocked me.

"Jannia," he said calmly, "from the point of view of human wisdom, what you're telling me about this gentleman's request raises a lot of questions. To agree might even be a great mistake. However, sometimes God's business and man's wisdom don't match. We're going to have to seek God's insight into this situation. Let's take at least a week to do so, earnestly, and see what God is telling us then."

When I didn't hear from Sir Neville for a week, I was convinced that he had reconsidered the request for help with his daughter based upon my rather disappointing reaction to it at our last meeting. It never occurred to me that God might be giving me my week, unhindered, to seek His will in this quandary.

Even so, it seemed strange that the man had not at least called or sent word that I was off the hook and free to go on with life, as I knew it. That's what I had tried to do in the intervening week, become so absorbed in my work that memories of Marta's face or his eyes did not distract me.

Still, I can't report that my reaction was completely dispassionate when the telephone rang on the following Thursday evening. I was surprised to hear, instead of Sir Neville, another distinctly accented voice on the other end of the line.

"Ms. Redmon? Banolo Benadie speaking. I have been asked by Sir Neville to inform you that he requests to meet with you as soon as possible. Would it be convenient for me to arrive at your home within the half hour so that I might deliver you to the meeting site?"

This was strange. Why was Banolo, however formal and polite, acting as a go-between?

"Mr. Benadie, no offense please, but why did Sir Neville not call me himself to make the arrangements?"

"Ms. Redmon, you must understand that these circumstances are most unusual. Sir Neville has met with...another accident, and I am afraid he is in hospital at the moment. My apologies for speaking in his stead."

Chastened by my arrogance and presumption, I responded quickly to his explanation. "Certainly, I will be ready."

Had James Martin not given up on me and my involvement with his child after all? I had prayed sincerely during the past week that I would know the answer to give him, when or if the need arose. Now might be the time, and where was the answer?

The ever-present white taxi arrived in twenty minutes, and Banolo met me at the front door.

"Mr. Benadie, I'm sorry for my rude question on the telephone just now."

"Ms. Redmon, you had no way of knowing what had happened, which Sir Neville will explain himself. Please, it is of no concern."

Sensing that he wanted to take me to the hospital as soon as possible and was not eager to talk about the details of the situation, Banolo and I rode in silence to Mountain Memorial Hospital located on a hill above the downtown area of the city. He left me at the front entrance with directions for how to find the correct room. He specifically requested that I not ask for directions at the visitors' desk.

The hospital was old, a little worn but highly reputable. Unlike newer facilities, it still smelled strongly of antiseptic, and the nursing staff even now wore starched white uniforms and moved with no-nonsense determination.

The door to Sir Neville's room was closed, and I knocked lightly. When I heard his curt, "Come," I entered slowly as my eyes adjusted to the dimly lit room with its closed blinds and low bedside lamp.

I could see no overt injuries as I glanced first at his face and then scanned for a view of his hands, those powerful musical instruments that he feared were a target for harm.

"Jannia, thank you for coming. Is it too dark for you? I am afraid my medication causes the light to bother my eyes."

I got directly to the point. "What has happened to you? Why are you here?"

"I was assaulted two or three days ago; I am not sure exactly when. It caused a concussion that has resulted in some rather severe headaches. That is why I am still in hospital."

"James Martin, I'm so sorry. Were you hurt otherwise? Your hands?"

"No, as you can see," and he held them up for my appraisal, "they are fine. But please, sit down. I am sure there is a seat somewhere..." He tried to prop himself up but lay back down in obvious pain.

I pulled a chair nearer to the bed and sat at an angle that allowed me to view his face. I didn't know where to go from there.

"Banolo said that you wanted to speak with me. Is he the one who saved your life this time?"

A short laugh came from the bed. "I am pleased to state that this time I rather managed for myself. Although I strongly suspect I had angelic assistance. I was rehearsing at the old theatre downtown. I like to practice as if before an audience. I was alone and heard a noise backstage. When I went to investigate, someone struck me and ran. I managed to alert the theatre caretaker before I blacked out."

"Isn't this attack number three? Who's doing this and why? Have you called the police? At what point are you going to ask for help?"

I was beginning to sound strident. I really don't like strident sounding women and worked to control my voice and manner. I stood and walked to the window to put some distance between the gentleman and me. I needed to regain my composure and hide my concern. The view of a darkened sky above the city offered little consolation.

"You must understand that my position here in the States is precarious, at best. As I told you at our last meeting, I have reason to believe I may be in the crosshairs of two opposing groups who mean me no good, although I certainly do not consider myself to be of any inherent value to either group. I think, rather, that my family heritage seems to be working against me."

I sat back down opposite him, determined to listen impassively without either doubting or believing his story. I wanted information to decide whether he really needed my help or was a mad man. I didn't doubt his musical genius ran deep, but the possibility existed that his delusions ran just as deep. I waited.

"I have told you before that I do not believe I came to America for this tour unaccompanied. I was meant to believe that I am free and unobserved by members of my government, but my own intelligence source tells me that representatives from our secret police traveled here soon after I arrived and are even now near and watchful."

"Banolo."

"If you mean that he is the main source of my intelligence, you are right. Very observant, Ms. Redmon. You must certainly be aware of how much I have come to depend on him and his loyalty."

"Why is your government so particular about your whereabouts and actions? Surely your talent can only be an asset to your country, not a threat."

"You are engaging in logical thinking, Ms. Redmon. Those are not the sorts of conclusions the leaders of my country are making. I have told you of my father's former status and position in Khutule. His political influence ran deep and remains viable, even though he represented colonialism. While this was not a popular period in our history, still it was a time of relative calm and prosperity for the young nation. There are not a few who would like to see a return to such a time and under the direction of someone who was close to their colonial leaders. Certainly there are factions vehemently opposed to such an idea, but a surprisingly large cross-section of citizens representing various groups has urged me to seek political office, even that of president of our nation."

I was shocked by this revelation. I had heard him tell how both his grandfather and father had served as colonial prime ministers of their country. I will admit I had even done some preliminary Internet browsing about the history of the former British colony now known as Khutule. What I discovered was a model evident in Sir Neville's homeland that was the polar opposite to that of many other African countries. Khutule's history reflected a pattern of beloved colonial leaders who led well and fairly and who attempted to build up all aspects of the country and its people groups within their influence.

"I hasten to add," he continued, "that I have no desire whatsoever to participate in politics or achieve political power of any sort. I am a musician, and that is how I have chosen to live my life. I have repeatedly tried to make that clearly understood. I regret that there are those in current leadership who doubt my sincerity and consider me a grave political threat, despite my best efforts to dissuade them."

"Why, then, would they follow you here?" I asked. "Why would those in power in your government not be overjoyed that you have left the continent?"

"Have you not heard that the unwatched enemy is the most dangerous? Besides, time I spend here might be time I am acquiring financial and political backing to stage some kind of coup, even if it is a bloodless one at the polls. I could even now be meeting with powerful allies to plan the overthrow of those in power back home."

"If you are considered such a threat, then why don't they...?" I obviously had not thought this line of questioning out before I spoke. I closed my mouth and dropped my eyes. He was not fooled.

"Why do they not just have me killed? Why indeed? You are correct to raise the possibility. I have considered the prospect carefully."

He must have noticed my eyebrows rose in question, for he continued. "My worth as a fund-raiser for my country is considerable. Even my private concerts back in Khutule bring revenue from taxes and from fees amounting to little more than extortion that must be paid for official assistance at large group gatherings."

"So you are too valuable an asset to lose? They like the money you attract?"

"That seems to be the case; however, I believe the current president and his immediate followers would even be willing to sacrifice the revenue I represent to see me removed as a political threat. I could even be eliminated, were there not fears that my unexplained death might result in considerable unrest among my countrymen. This could add further turmoil to the general instability that already exists in Khutule, and this must be avoided at all cost."

"Then I don't understand what's behind these multiple attacks, each one brutal enough to wound but not kill you. If your government fears reprisals at home for harming you, surely it can't be responsible for what keeps occurring." The position of Sir Neville was becoming more confusing and ominous by the minute.

"I agree with your reasoning. I do not think my government is conducting the current attacks. I believe they are part of a plan being executed by members of the African Re-Unification Coalition—the same ARC that killed my father's first wife and her sister. I believe these are revenge attacks being carried out by the followers of the general who was executed for these murders just before my father left office. This same group eventually killed my father and my mother. They will not rest until I am dead also."

"Then why do they hit and run, leaving you obviously wounded but alive?" If he were targeted, as he believed, what would stop them from reaching their goal?

"I think the attacks so far have been intended to injure and alarm me, possibly preventing me from performing. Ultimately, they are planning my demise, of that I am convinced. They intend to disrupt my life first. Killing me outright would not accomplish their purpose of making me suffer."

"And this last attack has left you hospitalized," I finished for him. "Am I to understand that you, then, are involved in some sort of strange cat-and-mouse game being played by a dangerous group that eventually would love to have you assassinated, but for the time being has its own twisted reasons for keeping you alive?" I was horrified by the very words I was speaking.

"I am afraid you are correct. And time may be running out on my reprieve. I have been informed that the political conditions are deteriorating within my country. At any time the government could impose extreme restrictions on all aspects of life in Khutule. Those actions could prompt radical moves on the part of my enemies." Sir Neville's face was grave and raw.

We sat in silence for several minutes. He rested with his eyes closed and his head on his pillow while I gazed again at the dark sky and shadow silhouettes of trees outside of his hospital window.

Sir Neville broke our silence.

"Perhaps now you see the nature and urgency of my request. I feel I must make arrangements for Marta in the event of my death. Should I escape that end, I will be leaving her soon to return to Khutule, and I cannot take her with me. Surely you understand why."

"How long do you plan on being gone this time? Are you speaking of permanent separation from her? From what I have heard and seen for myself (I was remembering the face of the old woman at the apartment window), GranJuel is...old. How long will she be able to continue to care for Marta?"

I knew he couldn't answer that. I was being blunt, but I was also grasping for time to deal with the enormity of what James Martin was asking me to do.

"Jannia, my hope is to take care of important unfinished business back home and return as soon as I am able. But that is the crucial question, is it not? How soon will I be able? Allow me also to be straightforward. What I am asking of you must not be dependent upon a time limit. I am asking you to agree to oversee the well-being of my family in my absence, regardless of how long, and to step into my place in the event that I am unable to return for whatever reason. The request is simple enough; the tasks it entails may be another matter."

I stood by the bed of the wounded man and regarded his situation as unemotionally as I could. If I agreed to his stipulations, I might well be undertaking the most difficult and long-lasting mission of my life. If I did not, how could I continue living in relative ease and self-absorption without seeing Marta's face constantly before me? What was my reasonable responsibility to her or to this man? Sufficient unanswered questions remained to raise logical concerns about the entire situation.

I could face real physical dangers myself, either from those who wanted to harm this man...or from this man himself, should he not prove to be who he claimed. Then again, I remembered the story of Abraham's servant, and of how he had found Rebekah as a bride for Isaac. The servant had prayed, as I had, for Divine guidance. Logic alone would not have worked so well in the servant's circumstances either. Faith did.

"I will agree to what you ask," I said, "under one condition. There is someone...the pastor of my church...who is praying for me about this decision. I'm sure that you will understand why he must be involved on my behalf. I have no one else here to whom I can go for counsel, and this is a very big step. I've shared the story with him in confidence. He has agreed to meet with you, if you will allow it. I must have his approval before I can proceed."

I've not seen such instant relief on any face before or since. It was as if he already knew what Pastor Terry's answer would be.

"Of course. That is most wise, and I regret I did not suggest it from the beginning. If you can arrange to have him visit with me here, I would be most grateful. I am sure, as a pastor, he is not opposed to making hospital visits."

After promising I would arrange the meeting as soon as possible, one further question nagged at my confidence. "James Martin, how can I be sure that my help would be received and accepted by Marta and GranJuel? Of Marta, I'm not so worried, but GranJuel...?"

"They will do as I ask. I have been assured. They understand, as much as they are able, the gravity of the circumstances." He spoke with authority, even lying on his back in a hospital bed.

"And what of Banolo?"

"He will continue to assist them, and you, as he is able."

6

The Decision

The meeting between Pastor Terry and Sir Neville was arranged for the next evening. I decided not to accompany my pastor to Sir Neville's room, but to remain in the waiting area and let their interaction proceed naturally, however it was to happen. I would know the outcome soon enough.

My wait was a lengthy one, and I was restless and out of dated magazines when Pastor Terry entered the waiting room. I watched his eyes as he approached me, sure that I could always read eye messages before words were spoken.

"Jannia," he took my hand and spoke in the caring, kind way many good pastors have toward the members of their flocks, "my mind tells me this is an honest man. His words convince me his story is true and he means you no harm. This, coupled with my own communion with God, gives me comfort that Sir Neville is a man who loves God and has placed his faith in Christ. What have your prayers taught you?"

"That I should offer him my help."

After saying a brief prayer of thanksgiving, Pastor Terry left for home, and I went up to give the news to James Martin. He was smiling as I entered his room and did not appear to be surprised at my news.

"Your pastor is a wonderful shepherd. He brought me great encouragement. Thank you for sending him to me."

I was eager to proceed before my own courage weakened. "What is my next step?"

"Please allow Banolo to take you to GranJuel and Marta's apartment. It is time you made your first real visit with them. I am sure you remember that Banolo acts as a bodyguard of sorts for us. I depend upon him to take me to and from my family's home without being followed. His ability to do this is reassuring. It is important, of course, that no one connect me with them and the apartment. So far, no one has...except you, of course."

He smiled. His eyes when he smiled did not match the seriousness of his words, and I wondered at his ability to find amusement in the midst of such alarming circumstances. I heard again the echo of his voice telling me, *"I am a man of faith."*

Banolo and I left immediately in his taxi to wind up and down the hilly streets, ensuring we were not followed before he turned onto the now familiar old boulevard leading to the apartment where Marta and GranJuel lived. He accompanied me to their door and disappeared into the night to wait while I visited.

I knocked at the entrance to the upstairs apartment—the one where I had seen the face of GranJuel on the day I met Sir Neville. This time, both Marta and her great-grandmother met me at their door, Marta shyly holding out her hand to be shaken when I introduced myself and GranJuel greeting me with barely polite and reserved dignity, as she invited me to enter. We sat in the formal guest parlor. It was large and adorned with grand but slightly tattered old Victorian furniture. I could make out a dark and ornate grand piano at the far end of the dimly lit room.

The somewhat threadbare elegance of the room was a fit setting for GranJuel, who was herself a picture of faded grace and beauty. Her ankle-length gray dress bore a striking rhinestone (or real diamond) pin at the throat, and that was the only adornment she wore or needed.

Marta, on the other hand, seemed to be out of place in the room lit only by two crystal table lamps. Her hair and eyes caught what little light there was, and although she did not speak unless directly addressed, her eyes showed that she missed little that happened in her presence. She was like a tiny fairy child in the castle of an aged and foreboding queen. The part of my heart Marta didn't already own became hers immediately.

"Mrs. Everston," as I had learned GranJuel's surname to be, "thank you for agreeing to see me this evening. As you know, I've just had a conversation with Sir James Martin Neville. He asked me to come and visit with you for a short while."

The grand lady nodded solemnly. "And how did you find Sir Neville's health?" she asked carefully.

"He appears to be resting comfortably enough." I wanted to give her some comfort without alarming the child. "And you are Marta." I addressed the child, wanting to pull her into the conversation further. "How nice to see you again."

"Thank you, Ms. Redmon," the child spoke almost in a whisper. She was a good listener and a quick study, as my name had not been repeated.

Silence followed, and I heard the ticking of a grandfather clock somewhere nearby.

"Mrs. Everston, I realize I'm a stranger to you and you know nothing about me. I'm here solely at the request of Sir Neville."

"Of that, I am quite aware, Ms. Redmon, if you please." Her voice was cold, brittle, unyielding. Such a response failed to bolster my confidence, but the face of the child watching me expectantly did.

"I also understand a little of your present situation here..."

This time she interrupted me rudely. "I doubt that you do, in all reality. We are quite self-sufficient, you know. Please be sure that I am in reluctant agreement with whatever you have been told by my grandson-in-law. Marta and I carry on quite well, do we not, my dear?"

"Yes, ma'am. GranJuel takes good care of me." Again the child's voice was near to a whisper.

I tried another tact. "Marta, your father has asked me to help GranJuel look after you, in case you should need me. You would like that, wouldn't you?" I was gambling and unsure of my hand.

Marta turned to her great-grandmother, read her face, and looked down. Then she surprised us both. "Yes, ma'am. I would like that. I need some new friends." She did not raise her eyes to either of us but studied her little tennis shoes.

That left GrandJuel and me to study each other's eyes. Hers were bright blue, like the child's. She was a beautiful woman even now. I supposed her to be well into eighty, but her skin and her posture suggested much younger.

"I have no desire to interfere in any way, Mrs. Everston, but I'm sure Sir Neville has explained his concerns to you in the light of his...current state of affairs. He asked that I come because he is concerned..."

Again she interrupted me. This time not so rudely. "Please, he has certainly discussed his plans with me. There is no need to go further at the present time." She arched her brows pointedly toward Marta. "I will honor Sir Neville's wishes, as I have little choice. But be clear that while I am alive and able," again she glanced at Marta as if wanting to protect her from talk that might prove upsetting, "I will continue with our current arrangement as it suits the two of us very well." She nodded at Marta, and the child nodded back, although I suspect she had no idea of what she was affirming.

"Of course." I could give her that. "If you will excuse me, now that we understand each other, I will say good night. It's getting late. Thank you for seeing me." I arose and reached to shake her hand. She gave it grudgingly, and it was cold and unresponsive. I reached for Marta's hand, and it was warm and touched my heart.

The white taxi was waiting, and I entered without talking. When he stopped before my apartment, Banolo turned to face me as I sat behind him.

"Ms. Redmon, we have a saying in my former country: *The gazelle can run towards safety as swiftly as he runs from danger.* I am not a man of many words, Ms. Redmon, but I need to thank you for what you are about to do. In doing so, you may truly be running towards safe ground rather than away from the dangers you so fear."

These were strange words from a man I hardly knew. They were also surprisingly comforting. I had been on my own for years and rarely felt lonely. The encounters of the past several weeks awakened a feeling of isolation inside that I wouldn't have thought possible. It was unfamiliar and unsettling.

I stepped onto the sidewalk in front of my apartment with only a brief, "Thank you, and good night." I watched the taxi drive away through the window of my darkened sitting room.

I had only two days to wonder what would happen next in the continuing drama that had become my life. My cell phone rang at work on Monday morning, and GranJuel's voice greeted me. She minced no words.

"Ms. Redmon, I assume?"

"It is. Good morning, Mrs. Everston."

"I think that under the circumstances, you should call me GranJuel. You appear to be somewhat of a permanent presence in our lives. What I am about to request is entirely against my better judgment. It is clear to me, however, that my wishes are no longer the main consideration."

How to respond to this less-than-subtle challenge by the formidable lady escaped me. I chose the evasive route as the only safe approach, since I had no idea of the direction this conversation would take.

"How so, GranJuel? I am not at all sure I am following you." It was an understatement of my position at best.

"As you may be aware, James Martin will be performing at a final benefit concert..."

"Should we be talking openly over the telephone about his plans?" I couldn't take a chance that we had listeners, even at the expense of insulting the grand lady.

"I assure you, we have taken all precautions on this end, although I am sure your cell phone must be quite vulnerable to eavesdropping."

I was not going to be put on the defensive so easily. "Then I am quite sure we are safe. Please proceed." I could also be direct.

"As I was stating, you might be aware that James Martin will be performing at the final benefit concert in Atlanta, Georgia. He has requested that Marta and I attend."

Silence followed. What was my cue?

"In your company, Ms. Redmon. He insists that it be in your company." GranJuel made it sound as if my company were some new strain of flu about to cause a pandemic.

"Are you suggesting that I am to travel to Atlanta with you and Marta for the performance? When exactly is the concert, GranJuel?"

"Well, yes, I believe that is exactly what James Martin wishes to happen. The concert is Saturday evening. It is not as if we can travel with him, is it? He would never risk that. Very explicit instructions were left for you. Shall I relay them to you now? I am afraid that I do not use email, Ms. Redmon," she said with a sniff of disapproval.

How interesting that Sir James Martin Neville had interpreted my acquiescence to his request as the freedom to order my life. The word *astounding* seemed appropriate. But my argument was not with Marta's great-grandmother, I struggled briefly to remind myself. He and I obviously required an understanding. In the meantime, I had no weekend plans and seeing another performance by the touring artists appealed to me.

"If I may, I'll stop by on my way home this evening and collect the information in person."

7

GranJuel's Revelation

It occurred to me that there might be some risk in going again to GranJuel's apartment so soon. Suppose I was being followed? I would have to resort again to the hazardous driving that had gotten me into this situation in the first place. I would just pretend to be following Banolo in his taxi.

Apparently I was either good at losing followers, or I was traveling alone. After thirty extra minutes of weaving in and out of traffic and up and down unfamiliar streets lost, I happened onto the right street and parked just down from the apartment. When I rang the bell, it was not GranJuel who met me but James Martin.

I was surprised and a bit unnerved. When I last saw him, he was lying in a hospital bed. That was a far cry from his dignified presence before me now. I was uncomfortable with the nervousness that threatened my ability to be professional in my greeting. I opened my mouth to see if anything would come forth, but he solved my problem for me.

"Did I startle you, Jannia? Come in, please," and he ushered me inside but not before I noticed that he glanced out at the street below us. "Apparently I arrived just after GranJuel telephoned you. I was rather surprised that she complied with my wishes on this matter." His smile was short and pleased.

All the while we were moving through a dark hallway, and we came into a small, elegant sitting room where I found that we were alone. I still had not spoken.

"Please, sit down. Perhaps you will have tea with us, but first, I would like to discuss the trip to Atlanta with you. There are a few details I must explain to you."

I agreed wholeheartedly. I remained standing in the middle of the room, and my face and manner must have mirrored my wonder at his audacity. This tall man with his aristocratic demeanor and gray-blue eyes was now about to commandeer my life. At this thought I almost laughed out loud at my over-dramatization of the situation.

"You seem amused, Jannia. Perhaps I have said something..."

My resentment was fast fading, and with that came the return of my voice. "I was a bit taken aback by your assumption that I could leave town at little more than a moment's notice. After all, I do have a job, other responsibilities, a life."

"Yes, of course. I see. If you need to decline my invitation, naturally I will understand. I assure you, I never meant to dictate your actions. I never thought...please forgive me." He was looking at me as if he had no idea why he was apologizing, only that he must.

"No, I've already agreed to go, and I'll certainly enjoy the concert. Maybe Marta and I will get to know each other better. But I'm not so certain about GranJuel." I needed to let him know my fears, even if the grand lady herself were listening from somewhere near, which surely did not appear to be her style.

"But that is precisely why I asked you to accompany them. They both need to feel more comfortable in your presence, and you in theirs. You must understand that Marta has never heard her father perform, except on compact disk. My concert appearance in this city came on the heels of one of the attacks, and I was reluctant to expose her to the possibility of another one. Security will be more tight in Atlanta, both for the entire concert and for me."

"GranJuel seems uncomfortable with me and with the whole idea of my intrusion into their lives. Surely you are aware of that." I met his eyes directly, to be sure my point was made. He had to realize the seriousness of the barriers GranJuel could place in the way of my relationship with Marta, especially should he not be in the picture. GranJuel might be old and frail, but there was an iron will behind those blue eyes and a determination to protect her own.

"Please, sit down, Jannia." James Martin indicated a brocaded chair. I sat and faced him as he rested on a small sofa nearby. "Surely you also are aware"—he was sending my own words back to me—"that this agreement into which you have entered will be filled with difficulties on all sides. What I have asked you to do will not be easily accomplished. I should have made that more clear from the beginning."

He waited and watched me, as if I would bolt and run. I didn't answer but also didn't break eye contact with him, although I wanted to do all three. I had my pride.

"Jannia, I have been with my daughter for less than three months, actually much less, for I have been traveling constantly until these last weeks. I barely knew GranJuel when I married Marta's mother, Elisia, and then she watched her granddaughter come home with a newborn infant to die without me by her side. I have only seen my child a handful of times in her life, each time in the face of GranJuel's begrudging presence. Why would the lady not resent my place in my daughter's life? I have only brought her pain and now danger besides."

"And you have introduced me into this situation because it's time she understood she won't live forever," I responded. "Of course she will resent me too. That possibility hadn't occurred to me. I thought she might welcome the support, but I'm a stranger. At least you are family."

"That is true, but if something should happen to me, or if I should not be able to return from Khutule, you would become a substitute parent for Marta. I realize that would further threaten GranJuel's possession of the child, in her eyes." James Martin spoke quietly and firmly, looking directly into my eyes to ensure that he was understood clearly.

"GranJuel has given me a wonderful gift by rearing and protecting my daughter when I could not. She has done it unselfishly and very well. It is not difficult to see what a delight the child is, even though her shyness worries me a little. GranJuel has given a good part of her later life, when she could have been free to travel, enjoy friends, and pursue her own interests, to the care of my little girl. I have chosen to forgive her attitude towards me and to overlook her apparent coldness on my behalf, for Marta's sake. I would ask you to do the same. She is devoted to the child, and Marta to her. We must do nothing to shorten their time together."

"I am honored to hear that you understand the nature of my feelings for my Marta," GranJuel spoke quietly as she entered the room, ignoring the fact that her response indicated she had been listening from the hallway. "I thought perhaps you would join us for tea in the dining room."

This was directed at me, as I rose from my seat when she entered the room. She turned to go, and Sir Neville indicated that I was to follow. Somewhere a melodious old clock struck seven times.

The dining room of GranJuel's apartment was small, formal and elegant, although faded and slightly worn. The furniture in this room was antique, heavy and dark, but the china service, in contrast, was fragile and the lightest robin's egg blue.

The menu was true high tea and consisted of buttered meat sandwiches, a salad, fruit and cheese, and the most tempting miniature iced cakes. An aromatic almond tea accompanied the meal, being poured from a matching robin's egg blue teapot by GranJuel, who was dressed in a long, simple gown of the same color. She was a master at dramatic presentation, and I had a lot to learn.

Our conversation included Marta and was light, positive, and filled with

56

questions she could answer and anecdotes she could understand. GranJuel managed all of this, and James Martin was an able participant. I contributed when I was included. Marta wore a simple yellow dress with a ribbon in her hair, and she looked lively and merry, unlike I had seen her in the past. She was obviously becoming used to family gatherings and was learning how to take part appropriately.

Marta appeared to be at ease with her father; although still a little shy, she smiled at him in appreciation each time he addressed her. Even GranJuel seemed to enjoy herself. When the child had finished her meal, GranJuel excused her for the evening, and she politely said her good nights to each of us in turn. She kissed her great-grandmother and father on the cheek and put her little hand in mine for a shake, flashing me a timid smile.

GranJuel led James Martin and me into the same formal sitting room where she had greeted me at our first meeting. She left the room and soon returned with a coffee service, which James Martin used to pour us each a chocolate-flavored after-dinner coffee. I felt as if I were suspended in the middle of a fairy tale, tasting goodies between the wicked queen and prince charming. I normally had a pleasant life, but certainly not like this.

I waited to see what would happen next, wondering if I were supposed to heed some unspoken signal to take my leave.

"James Martin, will you play for us, please?" GranJuel stood as soon as we had quietly finished sipping our dessert coffee.

"I think I really should be...," I began to say as I arose, still afraid I was overstaying my welcome and being unsure of the rules of etiquette that would apply here. The strange dynamics among the members of this household were beginning to wear on me. While it was clear that both of these adults were devoted to Marta, their relationship with each other appeared strained and uneasy. My presence could only add further discomfort to GranJuel, as she grappled with the reason I was in her life.

"No, please stay." The warmth of James Martin's voice and of his hand on my arm urging me to sit back down on the rose brocade chair from which I had arisen made leaving not seem such a good idea.

I was further surprised when GranJuel added quietly, "Yes, I'm sure you would like to hear James Martin play for us. James Martin, if you will?"

He walked to the far end of the room and switched on a small light on the top of the piano. The light cast a haunting glow over the old wood as he sat down at the keyboard and paused for a long minute before he began to play. The music was "Clair de Lune," which had always been one of my favorites. I had never heard it played with the beauty and feeling of Sir

Neville's interpretation. This musical interlude only added to the surreal nature of the evening, and I was captivated as he moved flawlessly into a composition by Rachmaninoff.

"Ms. Redmon." I jumped at the sound of GranJuel's voice low and gentle at my side. "I am old, but I am not in the least senile. I am aware that my grandson-in-law, Sir Neville, feels he must make plans for my replacement with Marta. I suppose he is wise, in that I will not live forever." She placed a thin but strong hand on my arm and gave a forceful squeeze.

"There are things that you do not know, both about me and about him," and she indicated with a blue veined and diamonded hand in the direction of the man who was still playing an evocative melody at the other end of the room. "I will not give up my place in Marta's life until I am ready. The two of you should not underestimate me nor try to force her from me. I am a strong woman yet. I do not take my responsibility for the child lightly nor will I share much of my remaining time with her with a stranger." She left me little doubt about whom she spoke.

I was speechless. I barely knew Marta's great-grandmother, had only met her on two occasions, yet she appeared to hold me in such contempt already.

"There's more, much more," she was almost whispering now, although there was no chance we were being overheard by James Martin. "He hasn't told you everything. You may regret your involvement yet, as you may be prevented from reaching your goal." She smiled at me then, and the vision of the wicked queen came clearly back to me as she stood and turned to leave the room. I still had not spoken.

"Oh, Ms. Redmon, if you will notify me of your exact plans regarding our upcoming trip to Atlanta, Marta and I will be ready at your request. Good evening." And she was gone.

Instantly the verse from Ephesians warning me not to sin when I became angry flashed before my mind. I was both deeply annoyed and hurt—a dangerous combination—at my treatment by Mrs. Everston. I wasn't a child to be talked to in such a patronizing manner. And there seemed to be something more. She seemed to be insinuating that I had ulterior motives for agreeing to help James Martin with his child.

I stood and reached for my purse, accidentally dropping my empty coffee cup on the pastel oriental underfoot. It failed to break, and I was almost sorry as I bent to retrieve it. How dare she treat a guest in her home the way she had treated me? How dare she malign my intentions for being involved at all in this increasingly bizarre situation? I began to shake as I searched for a way to leave the apartment without appearing to be rude to Sir Neville.

Just as I had given up hope of finding an easy exit and was turning to execute an undignified flight, James Martin ended his playing, rose abruptly from the piano bench, and walked toward me.

"Has GranJuel bid you good night?" His voice showed surprise and his eyes, as he drew closer, seemed to take in my shaken state.

"Yes, I believe...perhaps she...thank you for the lovely performance," I finished unconvincingly. I turned away, opening my purse to search for my keys to cover my embarrassment as hot tears stung my eyes. "Please express my gratitude for the meal, and now I..."

"Jannia, please look at me." I was unused to obeying the commands of my acquaintances or of anyone for that matter, but I turned to meet his eyes as bravely as I was able. My eyes were tearing, but I would not let him see that my feelings were hurt like a helpless child.

"What has happened?" He watched my face. I fought to appear calm, in spite of my tears. "What has she said to you?"

Sometimes strength comes in the nick of time and when least expected. "Nothing important. I simply think she is wary of the unknown and frightened of losing Marta. I can understand such a reaction. She told me they would be ready when I am for the trip to Atlanta. Everything will be fine. Thank you for the evening, and now I really must go." I turned in the direction I thought led to the door.

"I have made all of the travel arrangements for the three of you. I will make sure that your itinerary is delivered to you tomorrow by Banolo." He spoke all of this to my back.

"Thank you," was all I could manage.

"You are a brave woman, Jannia. I am quite relieved to have someone like you I can trust."

I remembered GranJuel's hurtful remarks of a few minutes past. *There's more, much more... He hasn't told you everything.* Trust had always been a frightening concept to me. How did he know I was someone he could trust? And was he worthy of my trust?

8

Trial By Fire in Atlanta

The final concert for the Please and Thank You Southern African Benefit Tour would be held the following Saturday evening amidst the glitter and glamour accompanying the support of the Atlanta social scene. While I was greatly looking forward to seeing James Martin and the other Africans perform their magic music again, I was not eager to participate in the surrounding festivities. I was determined to shelter Marta from publicity related to the concert, and I knew James Martin would support me on that account. GranJuel, I was also sure, had no desire to be part of any personal exposure.

Our plane left the Boone's Summit city airport on Friday morning for a flight that would take us to Atlanta in less than two hours. I took comp time for an all-nighter I had pulled some weeks earlier at the newspaper office. James Martin had gone ahead to meet the other performers and rehearse. Banolo, minus his taxi, would meet us at the airport and ensure we were safely settled in a fine old downtown hotel that was both small and a little out of fashion, just to my liking.

Marta fared well on the plane ride and timidly asked constant questions about everything new she encountered. I was pleased to see her so communicative and tried hard to give appealing responses to her questions. GranJuel, on the other hand, clearly tired easily but assumed the stoic stance of a martyr and refused all offers of nourishment or assistance that would have made her more comfortable. I had begun to question the wisdom of exposing her to such strain.

By the time we arrived, I had juggled Marta's constant inquisitiveness and GranJuel's unfriendly demeanor until my head ached and my hands were shaking. I welcomed Banolo's friendly smile and competent assistance as we gathered our luggage, and he commandeered a taxi. After seating us, he hopped into the front seat to share insider stories with the driver while we raced to our destination.

I felt more confident following our check-in to a suite of adjoining rooms with a small sitting area. I shared space with Marta, allowing GranJuel to have her own privacy, which I felt was vital to her ability to rest. A light meal at the hotel restaurant refreshed us, and we completed it by watching Marta devour a bowl of vanilla ice cream. Her eyes danced as she questioned me about what we would do next.

Knowing that she needed anything but an afternoon cooped up in a hotel room, even with TV to keep her company, I began to form a plan. This trip should be one that she would long think back on with pleasant memories.

Apparently Banolo was thinking in the same direction, and he answered for me. "Little Ms. Marta," he began, using an expression of fondness, "would you and Ms. Redmon care to join me on a trip to a zoo? There is a very fine one right here in the city. What is your pleasure?"

I looked at Marta and knew her answer, but the child stole a glance at her great-grandmother. GranJuel was watching Marta also. With a resigned expression she gave a nod of permission, and the child's face gave the older lady her reward.

After assuring GranJuel we would return in plenty of time to meet James Martin for dinner, Banolo again hailed a cab and off we went. The weather was beautiful, and the outing met all of our expectations.

A thousand steps and almost as many animals later, a weary Banolo carried a sleeping Marta in his arms from the taxi up to our room. She had skipped and eaten and drunk her way through almost the entire zoo, and I was sure she would not come to until morning. Banolo was almost as exhausted as she, and he begged off of any evening activities.

James Martin was sitting with GranJuel when we returned, and he slipped in to kiss his sleeping daughter good night. GranJuel, looking rested and in better spirits than at lunch, had already ordered room service for an early supper. She insisted that she would watch over Marta while James Martin and I dined.

Although I was also feeling a bit weary and worn, a shower and change of clothes made me presentable enough to appear in public again. At his request, I rejoined James Martin in the sitting room where we bid good night to GranJuel and caught the elevator to the street level.

James Martin had made dinner reservations within walking distance of the hotel. The night was warm; a gentle wind blew the folds of my gauze dress as he took my arm to cross the street. He was strong and confident. At that moment, he was someone I desperately wanted to trust.

At a small, quiet restaurant, which we entered by way of a door almost hidden near the mouth of a darkened alley, we were shown to a private dining room. The table was set with white linens, fine silver, and red roses. I had never been in such a place. We ordered and were served course after course with impeccable and unobtrusive service.

James Martin put me at ease by asking me to tell him about our trip to the zoo. He wanted to see all of the sights through Marta's eyes, and it was my pleasure to share them with him.

From there our conversation wandered...drifted...naturally and easily through topic after intriguing topic, revealing mutual interests and a recognition of shared values and faith far beyond my expectations. I had preconceived him as lofty, distant—a bit arrogant. In fact, on this evening he was warm, approachable...funny.

He talked and I laughed. The time went by too quickly.

Over a final cup of coffee we still lingered as he told me of his anticipations for the coming concert. James Martin took my hand and thanked me for bringing his family to the city. He held my eyes with his astonishing blue-gray ones and told me how pleased he was that I had come and would be with Marta and GranJuel in the audience for his final American performance.

I believed him. A new emotion was beginning to stir that I had not recognized before; it must have influenced me to believe him. Perhaps I should have been more cautious.

As we walked out onto the street, I could smell his cologne on the breeze and the scent, combined with his presence and the absolute romance of the lights of Atlanta in the late evening, fanned the quiet new feelings deep within me. It was a slight little alarm in an otherwise enchanting evening. That small new sensation I would remember with longing in the darker days to come.

It was past midnight when we arrived back at the hotel, and he bid me a quick good night at the door to my suite with the assurance he would meet us tomorrow just before the concert.

Always the complete gentleman, he once more took my hand, kissed it lightly, and turned away down the hall to the suite he shared with his friend and bodyguard, Banolo.

I would love to report I considered the events of the lovely evening with Sir Neville as merely an extension of the role I agreed to undertake for his family. I wish I could testify I believed his kindness and attentiveness was simply gratitude toward me for helping with Marta and GranJuel. Unfortunately, that was not the case.

The magic of the few hours I had spent in James Martin's company that evening in Atlanta inexplicably altered my thinking about him permanently. I ceased to consider him as a man who desperately needed my help to care for his family. Rather, as part of the mystery of life, he became someone I was beginning to love. That realization came as a shock as I examined my emotions after he left and I returned to my room and Marta, who was sleeping soundly.

While I had experienced a few romantic interests in my years of moving from one job to another, I never seriously considered any of them to be made of the substance from which a lasting relationship is built. In fact, I was so enmeshed in pursuing my career there was hardly the time or energy to consider what love, in the permanent sense, might involve. I had heard it described as a *you'll-know-it-when-you-see-it* phenomena, but it had taken on no personal shape...until now.

My hours with James Martin over the preceding weeks, and especially the past evening, threatened to change my perspective on the subject. The vulnerability of my emotions at that time frightens me, even now. My thinking was impressionable, naïve, and adolescent. I was also unprepared for what would follow.

As it turned out, James Martin's time was not his own on the day of the final benefit concert. We received word early in the day that, due to rehearsals and public appearances, he wouldn't be able to join us until after the event itself. Security for James Martin, we were assured, was ample, and therefore Banolo would be free to see to any needs of our little entourage.

Banolo proved to be a master at finding ways to keep us all entertained and refreshed. He found a wonderful park for a morning walk and an early afternoon movie Marta declared to be delightful. GranJuel accompanied us on the walk but declined the movie for a nap.

After an early dinner, which Marta was too excited to eat, we dressed for the concert. Because it was the high point of the benefit tour and its grand finale, the concert was to be a fine and formal affair attended by both the glitterati and serious philanthropists of Atlanta.

GranJuel was delicate and lovely in a long gown of soft violet. For Marta, she chose a bright yellow "dress up" gown, which served to make the child look tiny, frail, and beautiful.

I had hurriedly shopped for a new formal myself, and now was more than a bit self-conscious in its long, soft, silvery folds. Although I may have appeared more sophisticated and worldly-wise than in my usual casual look, I felt like a child myself, ready to play dress-up with Marta.

To boost my confidence, I silently took pleasure in reliving my dinner with James Martin and looked forward to the possibility of spending more time with him after the concert. I prayed for his safety and for his freedom of mind and spirit to perform at his best.

Those prayers were answered. The Boisfeuillet Jones Center where the concert would be held was nearly full when Banolo escorted us to our reserved seats near the stage. Marta was beside herself with expectation and grasped my hand tightly from the time we exited the taxi, refusing to let go even after we were seated. Even GranJuel appeared to be pleased, as she sat watching the audience and waiting to hear her grandson-in-law perform with his fellow African musicians.

While the concert program was long and the time was late when it ended, I was never conscious of anything but the glorious music. We were all completely transfixed by the magic of the performers who transported us to their native homelands through the rhythms and sounds of their music. As they performed, scenes from their countries—both beautiful and poignantly tragic—were flashed upon large screens behind the performers and to both sides. I felt as if I were on safari to the lands being depicted in the music.

James Martin's performances literally took my breath. Marta applauded him until her palms were red, and I felt tears cooling my face more than once while we listened. After he played for the final time, even GranJuel rose to her feet in appreciation of his musical genius. I was completely emotionally full at that moment. As he made his bows, I knew he could see us. I worked to keep my composure while Marta had no such intentions, and she jumped up and down to show her delight.

The finale featured a musical tribute to America, as their host country, by all of the musicians from the three participating African countries. It served as a final *Please and Thank You*, as the name of the tour suggested, for the hospitality and contributions given to the group over the past few months. I've never heard a more moving musical experience before or since that evening. We sat drained in our seats, waiting to be taken backstage to congratulate James Martin, as the other patrons slowly left the auditorium.

Banolo suggested we wait until most of the backstage greeters had cleared away to find our way back. There was also to be an after-concert party later in the evening. I didn't think Marta or GranJuel would be up to attending, but I will admit, I hoped...expected...to be asked to attend with James Martin. In any case, I wanted to see him and found waiting patiently to do so difficult, as did Marta.

Banolo escorted us backstage when he felt it would be comfortable and less crowded. I don't think I can describe, even years afterwards, the shock and disillusionment that were in store for me when we were finally taken to James Martin's dressing room. James Martin was standing in the center of the small room, greeting the last of his well-wishers. The space around him was filled with breathtaking floral tributes, and at his side stood the most beautiful woman imaginable.

She was tall, nearly as tall as he, and slender. Long blond hair with exquisite curls cascaded around her shoulders and framed her striking features. This lovely woman was dressed in a simple gown of emerald green. Her right hand held a beaded evening purse, and her left hand rested possessively on James Martin's shoulder.

In my eagerness to see him, it took me awhile to comprehend the significance of the scene before me. I felt Marta let go of my hand and rush to her father, unheeding anything but his presence. He bent down to hold her close and then straightened to introduce Marta to the woman. The lady bent to greet the child at eye level, and as she did, the place of importance the woman must hold began to dawn on me.

James Martin greeted GranJuel warmly and introduced her, as well, then finally turned to me. I was unable to speak. It's impossible to put into words the near-physical pain I was feeling.

"Jannia, I would like to introduce you to Ms. Branda VanderCross. Branda," and I watched him meet her beautiful eyes as he gestured toward me, "Jannia Redmon is the young woman of whom I spoke in relation to my daughter."

I don't think I ever spoke to either of them. I must have smiled or nodded or done whatever I had to do to appear normal, but my face was stiff, and even my hearing seemed impaired. I never registered who the lady was or any explanation of why she was there. My reactions were so bizarre that I was afraid I might actually faint. I honestly didn't know I was capable of such strong disappointment and hurt. The ache in my midsection was totally disproportionate to the circumstances, and it left me feeling exposed and off balance.

Banolo must have sensed something was wrong because I felt his presence behind me, his hand on my elbow.

"Ms. Redmon," he whispered close to my ear, "shall we make ready to take Mrs. Everston and Marta back to the hotel now? Perhaps they will become overtired?"

Banolo, my rescuer.

"I think that's wise." I managed a smile and turned to leave as he quietly suggested our exit.

"Thank you for your presence here this evening," I heard Sir Neville say to us collectively as he walked us toward the door. "I regret I have been detained by unexpected circumstances. I will join you for breakfast." While his voice was warm and affectionate as he bid us good night and kissed his daughter, he seemed guarded in his manner. I didn't even risk eye contact.

The hallway was now deserted, except for a pair of Atlanta policemen lingering the corridor who watched us make our exit. I'm ashamed to say I couldn't keep from turning back once more as GranJuel and Marta followed Banolo down the quiet hallway. I saw the beautiful woman reach out to close the dressing room door firmly behind us.

Back in our hotel room, Marta was asleep within minutes, the concert program tucked under her pillow and a smile on her face. I, however, slept little, alternating between profound embarrassment over misinterpreting James Martin's interest in me and intense annoyance at him for setting me up for such humiliation, though I doubted he was even aware of my dilemma. Mostly I was angry with myself for being vulnerable and incredibly sad for vanished hopes. The only logical, sensible conclusion was that any personal interest Marta's father had in me, beyond being a stand-in guardian for his daughter, was most certainly my own fabrication. There was actually no one to blame but myself.

I rested for a while in the early hours of the morning by meditating on words that came to me from 2 Corinthians about being bewildered but not in despair. Finally, exhausted, I prayed that His strength would be made perfect in my weakness, and I slept....

It was later than usual for a Monday morning when I awoke in the hotel room with Marta still asleep in the next bed. A heavy rain beat against the windows. Feeling unwell but fit enough to begin packing for our trip home, I was sad but also comforted by my prayers from the previous night. The force of my emotions alarmed me, and I wondered how I had let my guard down so entirely. It was uncharacteristic for me, and I determined to protect against such an invitation to pain in the future.

I roused Marta and helped her dress for breakfast with her father and GranJuel. She chattered with excitement built up from the busy weekend and the attention she had received. After delivering her to GranJeul's room, where room service was already setting out breakfast, I begged off of dining with them in favor of the coffee shop on the ground floor. Facing James Martin just yet was out of the question.

Our plane home left at noon. At 9:30, James Martin knocked on my door. The luggage was ready; I was more than ready to put this weekend behind me and return to the safety of my life. I had on my professional game face.

"Good morning." My voice sounded almost normal, even to me who knew better.

His smile threatened my resolve until I remembered the humiliation I had felt the night before when faced with his beautiful companion.

"Good morning to you also. I trust you are feeling better?" His eyes were warm and held a question. "I...we missed you at breakfast."

"Thank you. I'm fine...merely a little worn around the edges. Are we ready to leave for the airport?"

"We are, and the porter is here to collect the luggage. Marta's belongings are...?"

"Ready, as well." I turned to gather up my raincoat, pocketbook, and hand luggage.

"Jannia," and he waited for me to turn to face him, "I feel I need to...there is something that...you must understand..."

I smiled a costly smile. "Sir Neville, what a wonderful weekend this has been for your daughter and for GranJuel." I used my brightest and most engaging voice. "I want to thank you for them and for inviting me to come along. You were magnificent last night. I wouldn't have missed it for anything. And now it's time to fly back to the real world."

"It's Sir Neville now?" My use of his surname seemed to surprise him.

"Sometimes you just seem like Sir Neville to me. This is one of those times."

He raised his eyebrows in question, but Banolo entered to help with the luggage, and the moment passed.

I noticed a pair of police officers again in evidence, this time in the lobby, similar to those outside James Martin's dressing room the evening before. They accompanied us outside as we were met by the limousine and saw us safely inside.

I overheard one officer say quietly to James Martin, "We'll be right behind you, sir." I thought these were routine safety measures.

Both Banolo and James Martin rode with us to the airport. As GranJuel, Marta, and I prepared to enter the security clearance area, one of the officers accompanied us and one stayed behind with James Martin.

Marta turned to wave good-bye to her father once more. We knew he'd be staying a few extra days in Atlanta, and I was not surprised when his new lady friend joined him. She stood close by his side, looking around at the crowd of travelers as if our departure were inconsequential.

To my surprise, Banolo had accompanied us through security and onto the airplane. I didn't realize he was going to fly home when we did, but I was glad for his company.

The police officer stayed near us until we boarded the plane, but when I tried to question Banolo about his presence, now too obvious to ignore, Banolo shook his head slightly, glanced at Marta, and answered softly, "James Martin is a famous personality, Jannia. One can never be too careful."

As the plane ascended for the short trip back to North Carolina, Marta made a little nest in her seat, rested her head on her great-grandmother's shoulder, and fell asleep. GranJuel followed her lead and closed her eyes, making conversation with her unnecessary. Banolo sat across the aisle and appeared to be immersed in a travel magazine he plucked from the seat back in front of him.

Relieved to have some quiet time to reflect, I also shut my eyes. The weekend's events flickered past my closed eyelids, bringing a collage of conflicting emotions. It was true I had loved spending more time with Marta. We had progressed significantly in our relationship, maybe too much so, as she seemed to be attaching herself to me more and more. I was certain this fact was not lost on her great-grandmother, but she had said or done nothing to indicate Marta's actions bothered her.

GranJuel was civil to me, nothing more. We shared no confidences, and she asked nothing of me. While I took a lead in the care of Marta in Atlanta, GranJuel subtly resumed the parental role on the trip home, as Marta's drooping head on her arm affirmed.

My visits to the zoo and the park with Marta and Banolo were satisfying highlights. The concert and its music were poignant memories that would forever imprint lovely and tragic scenes on my conscience. The weekend had brought me some of the highest and lowest points in my life.

What was behind James Martin's overnight change of behavior toward me? Who was the new lady in his life, and when had he met her? Was it she who had kept him from spending promised time with his family? Why had we suddenly been joined by what appeared to be a police escort when the weekend had begun so peacefully? These and countless other questions about my experiences in Atlanta desperately needed answers, but there seemed to be no satisfactory way of getting them.

I wanted to examine more closely the feelings that had encroached on my previously calm existence before this weekend, but each time I thought about my time alone with James Martin, the film of my reflections broke and left me with the sounds of the airplane and the movements of my fellow passengers. I prayed fervently for wisdom and strength, and again I was able to rest.

9

Unexpected Discovery

T he ensuing week was refreshing in its springtime glory and in the fact that my ordeal, my *trial by fire* in Atlanta, as I had come to think of it, was over. Time was now my own again, and my work provided its usual refuge. In the middle of the week, I made a socially obligatory telephone call to GranJuel to tell her I enjoyed the trip to Atlanta and to check on Marta's well-being. She was characteristically distant but polite and assured me that Marta had not stopped talking about the trip. GranJuel was also careful to inform me of Sir Neville and Ms. VanderCross's arrival from Atlanta just that afternoon. It seemed as if Branda would be visiting with the family for several days, and I would be most welcome to call.

I refused to let myself believe her invitation was an intentional challenge. I'm pleased to say that I graciously declined, using work as an excuse, but promised to arrange a time soon to visit with Marta. I would stick to the script I had agreed to perform with Sir Neville's family and leave it at that. I'd allow myself no more improvisations.

It proved impossible, however, to erase James Martin entirely from my thoughts in the intervening days after Atlanta. The time left on his temporary visa should be quite short now. Soon he would be leaving for his home in Africa. While he had discussed his plans to come back to the States as soon as possible for Marta's sake, I was aware that complications were probable, given the state of politics in Khutule. In the event his return to the States was delayed...or prevented, I would need to become a major participant in his little family. That is, unless he had made alternate plans that now involved Branda VanderCross. I remembered how GranJuel had slyly waved her name at me.

At the least, I hoped James Martin would let me know when his departure was imminent so I could prepare myself for whatever was to come. Thinking about what might be the outcome of his return to Khutule left a continual knot in my stomach, but apart from prayer there was little remedy until his plans, and perhaps his future, emerged. In the meantime, I would need to remain patient and occupied.

At the end of the week, no word had come from Sir Neville. Refusing to be tied down for a weekend of waiting, I planned to drive to a quaint old mountain town nearby for sightseeing and shopping...alone. I had been on the road for about thirty minutes when my cell phone rang. I was tempted to ignore it, but remembering that others might be depending on me, I answered.

"Jannia, James Martin here. I would like to see you as soon as you are able, if I may. I am afraid there has been somewhat of a problem, and I really must discuss the situation with you."

James Martin usually sounded in control and confidant, regardless of the circumstances, and I'd seen him in some less than optimal situations. But this time his voice sounded tense, strained. His serious tone caused me to check the joking response I almost made about checking my schedule to fit him in. Although I'd planned to spend the night away from home, I immediately began looking for a place to turn around for the trip back to the city.

"I was on my way out of town. I'm about thirty minutes from Boone's Summit, but I'm turning back now and will meet you at GranJuel's apartment as soon as I can. You sound serious."

"No, Jannia, we will come to you. Please give me your location and a moment to speak with Banolo. I believe it will be safer this way."

I did as he asked, and we made plans to meet at a small state park just off of my route. I drove directly there and waited not so patiently for Banolo's taxi to appear. When it did, after about an hour, the two men were not alone.

Branda VanderCross sat in the rear of the vehicle with James Martin. She got out, spoke to me briefly, then leaned against the taxi in the sunshine as I greeted Banolo and James Martin. James Martin took my arm and steered me toward an empty picnic shelter at the far side of the park while Banolo followed us at a distance, as if on guard.

Their behavior confused me, but James Martin's rather forceful actions concerned me more, and I loosened my arm from his grip as we walked into the shadowed shelter. When I looked closely at his face, it was grave and unsmiling. This was not a social visit. Whatever the problem, I figured it to be ominous and tried to prepare myself for what might follow.

When we arrived at the picnic shelter, James Martin came directly to the point. "Ms. Redmon"—now it was his turn to be formal—"I have been far less than candid and forthcoming with you, and for that I ask your forgiveness. I have done you an injustice by misleading you. If you wish to renege on your agreement with me following this conversation, you may do so with my sorrow and my blessing." As he said these words, he looked me straight in the eyes, giving himself no quarter.

Foolishly, all I could think was that he was about to apologize for and explain the presence of Ms. VanderCross. It was all a misunderstanding. In what other way could he have possibly misled me? Unless...oh unless she had just become his wife, or worse yet, had been all along?

At that point my heart started pounding at the same pace that my mind was racing. It took all my strength to return his direct gaze and say primly, "James Martin, I'm sure I can't imagine what you mean. I can think of no injustice you have committed toward me."

I was taken aback when this normally formidable, confident man slumped down on a bench beside me and put his head in his hands. I stood by wordless and at a loss about what to do.

After a long, helpless moment on my part, he straightened and gestured for me to sit also. "Please listen carefully as I will admit this is most difficult. I truly felt God had sent you to help with Marta and GranJuel when I was feeling quite concerned for their future. You do remember I compared your sudden appearance to the miraculous story of Abraham's servant finding Rebekah, the future wife of Isaac?"

I nodded.

"What I told you about myself, my life, and my daughter was all true, as far as it went. I regret to admit that I did not give you the complete story. There is more, and the implications for any obligation on your part are much greater. That is why you must hear me out and, afterwards, if you wish, I will relieve you of your promise to me. I am very sorry I did not have the courage to tell you the whole truth from the beginning."

The thought of James Martin being without courage was not one I could integrate with what I'd come to know of this talented man of the world so far.

"Marta is not my only child. I have a son who is still in Africa. His name is Jack, and he is twelve years old. Jack is Marta's brother. He was five when his mother gave birth to Marta. When it became apparent that she was very ill and must return to America, Jack remained in Africa with me. I felt the situation with my wife was too serious to send both children with her. She was so ill when she left Africa that I had great fears I would not see her alive again. When she died a short time after coming here, I thought I had done the right thing by keeping Jack with me. One baby was enough for her family to handle. While I had lost my wife forever and my baby girl for the time being, at least I still had my son."

As he talked, I sat quietly. I didn't know what else to do.

"About three years after Elisia died, it became clear that I could not keep Jack with me. I had not realized the danger in which I had placed my son by keeping him close to me. Elisia and I had always tried to shelter him from public scrutiny, and few people knew I even had a son. As the political situation in Khutule worsened, it became apparent that Jack's life would be at risk if he were associated with me."

"Why was he in danger? He was just a child."

"The enemies of my father, and now of me, from the African Re-Unification Coalition would have taken my son, had they known about him, to get to me. Some government officials were also becoming uneasy because they considered me a political threat. I already discussed these facts with you."

"What about the U.S.? Couldn't he have come to be with his sister here?"

"By then it was not safe to risk trying to get him out of Khutule. I was under increasing surveillance, and without a parent to accompany him, how was he to travel? What would happen if someone I trusted were discovered trying to leave Khutule with my son?"

Again I nodded, already shocked by his revelation and wondering what else he could disclose. "Then, where is Jack now?"

"He has been in safe hands, at least up until now. My solution to a worsening situation was for Jack to go to a missionary friend whose compound is far out in the country where there was little political activity at the time. My friend's name is Bertram Wallace. He operates a small orphanage and day school for boys, mostly African youths. Some of the children at the school, however, were white like Jack, the sons of other missionaries or of white citizens in the area. The addition of another child, even a white one, would not be cause for notice."

"But that would mean that you and Jack were separated. He was a baby himself, James Martin. He must have been only eight years old."

"Yes. By the time I realized the gravity of my dilemma and made the arrangements, Jack was almost nine. Living with me required him to be sheltered far beyond what is healthy for a boy his age. When he moved to the compound, he was, in effect, freed from prison. He could finally have friends, attend the mission school, play out of doors. We gave him another identity, a new last name. My missionary friend, Bert, became Jack's legal guardian."

"Were you able to see him? Could you still act as his father?"

"My visits with Jack have been infrequent and naturally secretive. I became somewhat obsessed with his safety. Jack is a bright young man. He has been carefully coached not to discuss his background openly. He seems happy, and my friend considers him a son."

"When was the last time you saw him?" I had to ask.

The pain in his eyes warned me of the length of the separation before he answered. "I have not seen my son in almost two years. As I said, he is now twelve, almost thirteen. I might even have trouble recognizing him in a crowd. Jannia, I have two children, and both of them are now being reared by someone else whose last names they use."

"Oh, how tragic" was all I could say. I could only think of the years the children had missed their parents...and the time this father had already lost with them forever. These immediate thoughts overshadowed, for the time being, the fact Sir Neville had not entrusted me with information about the existence of his son before now. In spite of his usual confident manner and charming demeanor, it occurred to me that this man might hold many more secrets.

"What will you do now?" I asked. The dread I had felt earlier over his impending return to Africa and the risks it brought returned now in a darker, more convincing form.

"I will go for my son. I have just received word that the mission is closing and the school and orphanage with it. There is increased ARC and military activity in the region, and the children and workers are no longer safe. It appears the area that was once isolated and relatively secure has now become a refuge for disenfranchised groups, such as the ARC, that oppose the sitting government. The time has come for me to make arrangements, if I am able, for my son and my friend leave the country. Jack is an American citizen with an American passport. My friend holds permanent citizenship in a neighboring country where he can safely resume his work."

"When do you leave? When does your visa expire?"

"The visa expires in three days. I fly the day after tomorrow to New York to begin the journey home. Jannia, I need for you to understand how real the possibility is that I will not return soon, if at all. My energies must now be put solely on getting Jack to safety. When I arrive in Khutule, and as soon as Jack is safe, I will immediately request to be allowed to return to the U.S.; however the political situation in my country is quite serious now. I fear that I have already overstayed my welcome here.

Nothing prepared me for this. No previous experience in my life told me how to act or what to say as I looked at the face of this man I was beginning to love and realized these might be my last minutes with him on this earth. My determination not to pursue a relationship with him that I feared wouldn't be welcomed was of no help to me now. Even the thought that his lovely new friend might also be losing him didn't give me comfort.

All of the pat answers and glib clichés simply vanished in the truth of the moment. Despite my best efforts, and I tried valiantly, tears slid down my face. I wanted to ask him what to tell Marta about him. I wished I were brave enough to ask him about Branda VanderCross and what she meant to him. I wished a thousand things, but my voice was numb.

He mistook my reticence to speak or move as misgivings about my promise to him over the responsibility for Marta.

"Jannia, should you feel you cannot go through with our agreement, you are released from it now, with my blessings and understanding. The likelihood that you will have to step into my place on behalf of Marta and GranJuel, and now maybe even Jack, is great. Banolo will manage until he is able to find someone else suitable. Please tell me you understand what I am saying."

"I understand." It was a whisper, but it was all I could manage.

"Would you like to be released?" I knew he was deadly serious because I could see it in his eyes and hear it in his tone.

"No." It was barely a whisper.

"Pardon me? I'm sorry. I didn't..."

"No." I was stronger now, and he heard me clearly.

"Are you sure? Absolutely sure?"

"I'm sure."

"Banolo will keep you as informed as he is able."

James Martin didn't touch me or say anything more. It was sealed. And then he was gone, striding back to the taxi alone, leaving me to walk slowly behind him to my car.

I watched him as he took the arm of Branda VanderCross and helped her into the back seat with him. He must have said something to Banolo, because his friend moved toward me to see me to my car. While he didn't linger after I got behind the wheel, Banolo did make one strange remark so quickly and casually that I knew more was behind it than he could say at the time.

"Ms. Redmon." He smiled broadly. (I now understand it was a cover for what he was telling me.) "May I telephone you this evening? It is of utmost importance. You must stop Sir Neville from making this trip. I will explain later."

His parting smile and wave were open and friendly as if we were old and close friends parting only for a brief while. I knew he didn't want James Martin to know he had confided in me. I forced an equal smile and wave in return.

10

Jannia's Gift

I watched the taxi move out of the parking area, and with it went my plans for a relaxing getaway. I wondered when I would ever feel tranquil again, as I turned my own car back toward the city. The winding road home was a familiar one, and it failed to keep me so occupied with my driving that I couldn't think about what had just occurred. A thousand questions assaulted me from all directions, each one begging to be answered before I had analyzed the one before it.

Why had James Martin kept the existence of Jack a secret from me? What was his plan to get Jack out of Africa safely? What part in all of this, if any, did Branda VanderCross play? Why did he never mention her to me, except upon introduction, yet she was with him and his family even now? How would I proceed if my worst fears were realized and James Martin didn't soon, or ever, return to the U.S.? What was I to do to fulfill my promise to him and his family?

As I crested the final hill and viewed the city lights now shining in the darkened valley before me, one final question pushed all of the others out of my mind for the moment. How would I ever be able to live in outward peace until this drama played out and I knew for Marta...and for myself...whether James Martin and his son would be safe?

As surely as if written across the face of the moon shining low on the far horizon came the familiar words of Psalm 56:3: *"Whenever I am afraid, I will trust in You."* Little was I aware then of how often I would need those words in the coming days.

Banolo didn't call that evening; rather he came in person soon after I arrived home. With little by way of greeting, he quietly entered. We had just sat down with a cup of coffee at my kitchen table when he came directly to the point, and both his tone and his manner left no room for doubt as to the gravity of his mission.

"I am not given to dramatics, Jannia Redmon," he said. "I have seen a lot of things I had rather not have seen and been in many situations I would have chosen to avoid. I tell you this so you will not think I exaggerate the situation I bring to your attention."

I am generally more comfortable making eye contact when I converse, and the look in his eyes frightened me. "Please go on," I prompted unnecessarily.

"James Martin must not go to Africa at this time. He must certainly not go home to Khutule now. If he does, I have every reason to believe that his life will be lost. Surely he has told you of the political conflicts stirring within the country at this time. The government finds itself more and more at odds with the rebel African Re-Unification Coalition. Both are very powerful, strong-armed and ruthless. Both groups have tasted power, found it to be a seductive fruit, and wish for more. The common people and many of the once-powerful landowners alike are caught in the whirlwind between the two factions."

"Yes, he has explained this to me."

"He may not have explained that we have learned both groups now wish him dead. For a while, the ARC threatened him because of the actions of his father, but now the vendetta is more personal as his fame grows and his popularity in the eyes of his countrymen rises due to his music. Much the same is happening on the part of government leaders. Jealousy is a hateful attribute in one's enemies, I am afraid."

"But, Banolo, I understood that the government watched James Martin closely but only at a distance, because he and his ancestors are held in such high esteem in Khutule. I thought that harming him would be stirring up trouble with many of his countrymen."

"As you say in America, the cards of my government are now on the table. It can no longer tolerate James Martin and his growing popularity among the people. The madman who is now in power has taken James Martin's status as a personal affront and political challenge. There is a death warrant on his head the moment he enters the country."

I don't think I answered in words, but with an audible gasp.

"I will admit I mean to frighten you, Jannia." This was the first time he had called me by only my first name. It was an indication that he had set all niceties aside to make his point. "I hope to frighten you into finding a way to prevent James Martin from going home. He will not be able to return to America; he will not live out his first week in Khutule."

I am not a fainter, yet I distinctly felt my blood rush from my head and my vision begin to blur. I lowered my head to rest it on my arms on the table. "Wait, what about his missionary friend who has Jack now? Mr. Wallace. Surely he can get the child out without James Martin's help? He is the legal guardian, isn't he?"

"He is, but he is also now being closely watched. He has not been ill-treated as yet, but his contacts inform him that government officials are tracking all of his moves and those of other foreign missionaries. He must soon leave the country; he will be forced out if he does not leave on his own. What he doesn't know is whether anyone suspects whose son he guards. He was already keeping Jack out of the public eye as much as possible, and now the boy is nearly a captive in Wallace's mission compound for safety's sake. Bert Wallace is arranging alternative care for his orphans and making plans to leave the country with Jack, but at any moment he may be detained or forced out and made to leave all of his charges, including Jack, behind, regardless of his guardianship. The rule of law no longer can be counted upon, I am afraid."

Banolo's fear was nothing to match mine. I could barely think from wanting to hold my breath lest we be overheard half a world away in Khutule. I half expected my own door to be crashed open at any moment.

It was then that I remembered once more the calming advice of Psalm 56:3: *"Whenever I am afraid, I will trust in You."*

Oh, God, I hope so. I hope I can.

I didn't speak the words aloud; I don't believe I did. But I wanted to in hopes the comforting words would become real to me.

"Jannia, I have told James Martin I will go in his place. He has refused, as he knows that I am also well known back in our country as his friend. He is afraid my presence will endanger not only me but also his son. He argues that if one of us is to be sacrificed trying to save his son, he will be the one. I also have no current passport. I no longer travel outside of the U.S. and have not kept mine current since gaining U.S. citizenship."

A passport. I had a current passport. I always kept mine up to date because of occasional travel for pleasure or work. Once in a while, our editor at the paper would select one of his employees to visit places in the U.S. or abroad as personal fact-finding investigations for a travel column on extreme vacations he liked to write himself. I had a current passport...and an idea.

"Banolo, I have one day before James Martin leaves for New York. By tomorrow noon, I hope to have a plan. You must not tell James Martin we are arranging anything or he will leave early, and we will not be able to stop him."

"What is this plan of yours? Can you explain it now?"

"Not yet, not until I'm sure. But this I do know; you're right in that James Martin must not leave for Khutule. His visa will expire before the end of this week. I can tell you that a part of my plan will require him to request official political asylum here in the U.S. We will need some forms of proof, some substantial indications that his life will be worthless if he returns to Africa now. Can you help with that and quickly?"

"What kind of proof will you need? What is the nature of the proof?"

"I'm not sure myself," I said, sounding much more confident than I felt. "But I think it will have to be more than say so...more than merely rumor that James Martin's life is in danger. We will need testimony, spoken or written, like affidavits, or letters or emails, or...you begin to see what you can do through any contacts you have, and I will investigate the process of political asylum. We have to be fast and quiet, because his enemies on this side of the Atlantic have already attacked him three times. Banolo, can you help with this?"

"I can help. But what about the rest of your plan, Jannia?"

"I'll know whether my idea will even be feasible by noon tomorrow. You will have to wait, and say a prayer for me until then."

"Bless you, Ms. Redmon. I will." He shook my hand and was gone.

The managing editor for the midsize daily newspaper for which I worked was Jake Bean, a man I had known for about ten years. Mr. Bean had managed the city paper for over twice that long, and although I had just joined his staff three years ago, his daughter had been my roommate in college. This connection had given me a leg up for my current job, but I worked hard and never took advantage of our relationship to promote myself. Even so, I knew I was a favorite at the office with him, and now I needed this benefit.

I was in front of his desk at seven o'clock the next morning.

"Good morning, Jannia. I knew you were an early riser, but this is a bit early even for you. Would you like coffee?"

"No, sir. Thank you for seeing me, Mr. Bean. I have something serious to discuss with you. I won't take much of your time. If you can't help me, I'll certainly understand, but I ask you to please hear me out. I assure you, if this weren't important to me, I wouldn't ask."

"What is it?" His voice and eyes showed he knew I was serious. "Is something wrong at home? Is someone ill? Is it a coworker?"

"No, sir, but I do have a rather unlikely story for you and a bit of a strange proposition to make." I proceeded to tell him, in the briefest of terms, about my initial meeting with James Martin under such out of the ordinary circumstances. I outlined the succeeding events, omitting my personal feelings, leading up to his determination to return to Khutule for his son despite the known dangers to both of their lives. I concluded with my bizarre plan to help.

78

"Mr. Bean, this whole situation may sound improbable and probably even suspect to you. I assure you that I am telling it just as I experienced it. Now that I'm in the middle of it, I feel like I have to do something. That's why I'm appealing to you as both my boss and as my best friend's father. I cannot simply do nothing, knowing that if Sir Neville returns to his country, both he and his son may well die."

"What are you proposing?" He came directly to the point, as I knew he would.

"I'd like for the paper to sponsor me to travel officially to Sir Neville's country, Khutule, as soon as possible. I will, of course, pay my expenses, but I need to go as an official member of the press. Maybe I could gather information for one of your extreme safari getaway features for your column or some such official assignment. I need the cover as a news correspondent to be able to travel without suspicion. I want to go to Khutule in Sir Neville's place. I could be ready to leave almost immediately, as soon as I make the arrangements. Travel to the country is not restricted, although there are some problems. I have to try to get his son out before it's too late. I can't just do nothing. I assure you, I haven't made any promises to Sir Neville or even spoken to him about my plan, although I know in advance what he will say. I wanted to see if I could put the plan together first, then worry about persuading him to allow my interference. What do you think, Mr. Bean?"

By the time I finished speaking, Mr. Bean was on his feet behind his desk and scowling at me darkly. "Ms. Redmon, I think of you as a daughter, and I am going to speak straight to you like I would to my own Jill. This story and your plan constitute two of the most unrealistic and preposterous ideas I have encountered, and I've heard them all in this business. If I let you proceed with my permission in this direction, I might be responsible for you spending the rest of your life in some third world prison at best and for burying you at the worst."

He stopped and stared at me. I was determined not to be the first to back down, nor would I cry, as close to it as I was. He seemed unaware of my tenuous hold on my emotions. Although he was angry at being put in this position, his eyes held the look of a father. I just stood there and waited.

"Jannia, if I were a smarter man, I would stop now with those final words and send you packing to your desk. I might even call your family to warn them of your misguided thinking. I'm not a very smart man, but I do seek to be a wise man, Jannia. I pray for that daily. I'm going to give you my answer in two hours. I need some time. If you need an answer now, my response is *No.* I'm not promising anything. Asking for time does not mean you have convinced me. I simply need time to do some checking of my own. I strongly suspect that you are planning to go ahead with your plan, as much of it as you can, even without me. In the place of your father, I am asking you not to do that. Give me two hours to seek wisdom and some further information on this proposal, and I will have an answer for you one way or the other. I need your assurance you will follow my advice and honor my answer."

He was right. I knew that he would give me godly counsel that would be balanced and based on having considered the whole situation.

"Thank you, Mr. Bean. I will be at my desk." I left his office.

I went to my desk and immediately began preparing for my trip to Sir Neville's Khutule, should Jake Bean agree to sponsor me. I downloaded information related to travel to the country, including information about acquisition of a visa and a temporary work permit to work as a journalist within the country. I also investigated what might be needed in order to escort a minor out of Khutule without a parent. Thank goodness for the Internet.

In addition, I downloaded critical information I would need for another part of my proposed plan, to persuade James Martin to apply immediately for political asylum. I soon learned that the bar for who could be granted such asylum had been raised post 9-11 when the Immigration and Naturalization Service became part of the Department of Homeland Security. Regardless, I was convinced that he had sufficient grounds for throwing himself upon the mercy of the U.S. government for protection, especially in light of the dual citizenship status of his children and the U.S. citizenship of his deceased wife. There were also the three attacks that occurred while he was on tour here.

By eight o'clock, I had my homework done and threw myself headlong into the day's work responsibilities, resting on the promise of Jake Bean that by 9:30 I would have my response from him.

Oh God, please give him wisdom, and help me to trust him and You to work through him. And please help James Martin to go along, if I am to take his place in Africa.

I prayed as I wrote up a story on the philanthropic activities of a local group of Daughter's of the Confederacy.

At 9:30 precisely, I sensed someone's presence behind me and turned to see Mr. Bean standing in the doorway to my office. I could tell nothing from his face.

"Ms. Redmon," he spoke quietly for the sake of those around me, "may I see you in my office please?"

Immediately upon my entry into his office, he closed the door behind me and turned to speak. "I have made a number of phone calls, including to some friends in the State Department. While I still have grave misgivings on a personal level, I will agree to sponsor your trip to Khutule as a representative of the newspaper. I have already inquired as to what credentials and documents you will need. It will take at least three days for you to receive a permit to allow you to enter Khutule as a journalist, but you must pick it up in person at the Khutulen embassy in Washington. That should give you sufficient time to make all of your other arrangements. I'll help you map out an itinerary that includes the vacation sites in Khutule, where you will collect extreme travel information for me to legitimize your stay. The newspaper will foot all expenses for travel to and from the country and for expenses incurred while pursuing your research for me. For all other expenses, you are responsible. It's important that I not know too much about any other plans for deniability purposes, so as not to implicate the newspaper unnecessarily."

This was an uncharacteristically long speech for Jake Bean, and I listened carefully. He was not finished.

"Jannia, I ask three things of you. Number 1, you must agree to take no unnecessary chances. Number 2, you must talk at length with my State Department contact who will fill you in on travel conditions in Khutule. There is currently no ban on travel to your destination, but there is a serious travel advisory I want you to discuss with him. You will need to register with the Embassy there before you travel beyond the capital. Number 3, you must ensure that someone has complete knowledge of all of your plans, including your personal ones, and will be willing to share it with me and whomever else might require it, should the need arise. Are you in agreement?"

His tone invited no disagreement, but I could live with his conditions. They were far better than I had imagined. This step must be unimaginably hard for him; supporting this idea of mine was risky at best and at worst...? Best left unanswered.

My most difficult task would likely not be found in Africa. Convincing Sir James Martin Neville to allow me to go in his place to aid in bringing his son to America would be far more delicate. He would not easily send a female into danger instead of going himself, of that I was sure.

And then there was the matter of his request for political asylum. I wasn't sure he would be in favor of such an action, but what were his choices? Stand in line with the US INS Office for a slot to re-enter the U.S. legally and permanently? Even with his growing celebrity status, that might take months or years. He could attempt to enter the U.S. illegally and live below the radar in some obscure place where he could secure unlawful work or live on any savings he or GranJuel had, which I suspected in her case were substantial. This would require sacrificing both his music and his freedom of movement, to speak nothing of his ethics. Of course, he could always go home to Khutule to stay, sending Jack to the U.S. alone to live with Marta and GranJuel or me— if he could get the boy out of the country.

To chose this last option meant he would sacrifice more valuable years of his children's lives without his company. While he held the final choice, I hoped it would not be this last option for their sake and for his.

I was out of time. Tomorrow he would leave for New York. The next day, on the very day that his visa expired, he would leave on an airplane for the long ride home to Africa. Not only might tonight be my last time to see him alive if he left, more importantly it might be his last evening with Marta. This was unacceptable to me, and I had no choice but to act.

11

Sir Neville's Acceptance

I knew he had already told me good-bye and therefore would not come to me...so I went to him. Knowing I had to be sure I was not followed, I drove around for an hour after work, up and down the streets, doubling back and even resorting to taking one-way streets the wrong way. When I was sure I was alone, I parked four blocks from GranJuel's apartment and walked the rest of the way, looking over my shoulder all the way.

GranJuel herself answered my knock, as she often did. I could tell I surprised her and she was not pleased to see me. I could also tell she had been crying. That fact, in turn, astonished me. I had never seen the grand lady show that type of emotion. She could be arrogant and cold. She could also be stoic and grave. I didn't think she was capable of tears.

"GranJuel, I need to see Sir Neville right away. I know the timing isn't convenient, as he is saying his good-byes to you and Marta. I'm sorry, but what I have to speak to him about can't wait. This is critical. Please tell him I need to meet him in private for a few minutes."

She didn't appear willing to grant my request. Only her impeccable social training forced her to allow me into the foyer. She left me standing there as she turned with an abrupt, "Please wait here."

I did as asked, and the wait was brief. James Martin walked rapidly out to meet me, his face a study in severity. Seeing his gravity did nothing for my confidence or for my ability to remember the speech I had prepared to convince him to agree with my plan. To my horror, I felt my eyes well up with hot tears as a sense of panic threatened to overwhelm me.

No, I would not play the emotion card. I desperately wanted my conversation with James Martin to be based upon strength and not emotions, as important as they can be. And then from somewhere deep within me, I heard the words from 2 Timothy 1:7: *"For God has not given us the spirit of fear, but of power, and of love, and of a sound mind."* The memory of that verse steadied me and gave me confidence. I had been praying continuously since setting my course last evening, praying for strength and courage and confirmation that the direction I had chosen was a wise one.

"James Martin, I won't be here long. I only ask that you give me a few minutes and all of your attention with an open mind for that time. What I have to say is not impulsive or rash. Please, just hear me out."

He took my hand, led me into the sitting room off of the foyer, and we sat together on the small settee. His face was no longer severe, but gentle and calm. "Of course I will listen to you, Jannia. What can be of such importance as to make you this insistent?"

It seemed that the best approach was the most direct one, so that's the line of attack I took with absolutely God-given clarity and cool. I made it clear that I knew the current danger he would face upon returning to Khutule. I quietly outlined the plan for having me go in his place, including the plans already underway, should he agree. I informed him of the conversation I had earlier in the afternoon with the State Department representative who affirmed that Khutule was in political unrest, but also advised that visiting U.S. citizens careful not to dabble in local affairs had been generally left alone. Finally, I reviewed the facts I had learned about the political asylum process and why I felt that this was his only safe course of action.

As I talked, I tried to make constant eye contact with Sir Neville so that he could sense the sincerity of my motives and read my determination to be taken seriously. For his part, I can say that he did as I asked; he heard me out quietly and without interruption. When I was almost finished, I used some of my strongest ammunition remaining to tell him of the support for my plans on the part of his friend Banolo, of my managing editor Jake Bean, and of Pastor Terry from my church. While I didn't try to conceal their expressions of concern for my safety, all were in agreement that for Sir Neville to go home would mean almost certain death for himself and possibly for his son.

When I was through with all that I had to say, and no more than half an hour had passed so I had also kept my word, James Martin stood and walked away from me to the other side of the small room. He kept his back to me for several minutes, standing quietly with his head bowed. Just as I was growing concerned and wondering what my next move should be, he turned to face me, and I also stood.

"Jannia, what you have offered to me tonight is more than any man deserves. You are, in a sense, offering your life for mine, should it come to that. For that offer, I am moved beyond words. There is no greater show of friendship. It is clear that you are serious about what you propose, so I will respond in kind. Were it only my life at stake, there is no way I would ever consider such a gift on your part, no matter how well intended."

Here he paused again, as if struggling with his own inner emotions.

"As you know, it is not only my life that is in question, but that of my son, whom I have already kept away from me far too long trying to protect. I have heard...word has just come from reliable sources that Khutule's political disquiet is growing more precarious daily. Word has also come that there is now a bounty on my life placed there by a high-ranking government official, perhaps ordered by Khutule's president himself. These are things I have learned in the last twenty-four hours. I have been strongly advised by my sources not to attempt to return home for any reason. They have assured me that my presence would seriously endanger Jack's survival, as well."

I had not expected to have an unknown ally who was advising James Martin in the direction that I had feared I must beg him to go.

"Then you will agree to my plan?" He began to shake his head in the negative.

"I don't think I have a choice but to abandon my plans and seek asylum here. For Marta's sake, I don't think there is any other course to take. It may be that my missionary friend will find a way to get Jack to freedom, to get them both out of the country. As for allowing you to go in my place," again he shook his head, "you know that I cannot allow..."

"James Martin, I mean no disrespect to you by this announcement, and I hope you will understand, but I am going to your country. I have decided it is something that I must do for your son. The plans are being made, as we speak. I am seeking entry as a foreign journalist there to investigate Khutule as an extreme vacation site. I have requested a visa to that effect, which I will pick up in Washington in three days, and my editor has presented me with an itinerary to support my mission. That part is true and will take place. What else I may pursue while in your country remains my own business, although I truly hope you will assist me in preparing for what I need to do. It will make my way much easier than feeling about in the dark for the details I need to help Jack."

I'm afraid I ended my conversation with James Martin on a less noble plane than I had begun, but I was now tired of hearing myself talk. I was weary of choosing my words carefully and of watching for how to read each of his reactions. I wanted his blessing to make this journey, and I wanted to go home and rest. And so I told him that, as well.

His reaction startled me but broke the strain I was beginning to feel. He laughed, the wholesome and hearty laugh I had come to associate with him, the one that I had only heard on a few occasions.

"My dear Jannia, what a delightfully direct young woman you are. You spare me no feelings, I fear." And then he became more sober. "I will give you my blessings and my prayers, my constant and continuous prayers, although I cannot say how godly I feel in agreeing to this idea you have presented to me. If it were not for Jack, and if it were not that I feel you have sought godly counsel before coming to me, I would send you on your way with my wrath for wanting to endanger your life. However, you are not a child, and I will not treat you as one. Thank you, Jannia, for the greatest gift any person has ever given me. Now let me pray with you before you go," and he did.

I left then, and just as I turned to bid him good night at his door before slipping away to my car four blocks down the street (a fact I hadn't shared with him), a door off of the foyer into another part of the apartment opened slightly. Whoever was there didn't linger, but before the door closed quietly again, I caught a glimpse of long, golden hair and a flowing dress.

This was not about me at all, I reminded myself, and steeled my reactions to continue the same quiet calm I had maintained up until that point. While the tears threatened to burn my eyelids again, and did so as soon as the door shut behind me, I gained enough of a reprieve to bid James Martin good night and good-bye.

12

Khutule

The next three days were a blur of preparations and travel to secure my journalist visa for Khutule. When I finally boarded the plane for the transcontinental trip that would take me to James Martin's home country, I was already beginning to feel the strain of what lay ahead.

The flight from Washington D.C. to Johannesburg was a long one. I had traveled on long flights before and knew the tricks for keeping myself hydrated, rested and occupied. While my previous destinations had usually been vacation spots picked out far in advance and anticipated for months, my coworkers and I were occasionally commandeered into one of our editor, Jake Bean's, "working vacations." During these expense-paid excursions, we were expected to do on-site research for his extreme vacation newspaper column. If we were too cowardly to actually try the extreme activity under research at the moment, such as sky diving out of a hot air balloon in California, bear hunting in Alaska, or studying elephant training in Thailand, we could at least interview those who were more brave and had done the feat. This trip was far different.

In truth, I would be pursuing on-site extreme vacation information in southern Africa, specifically Khutule, the political hotspot of the region. Regardless of what it might look like on paper, this would be no vacation. While confident I was doing the right thing by going, I couldn't help but feel that the *extreme* part would be defined merely by making my way in and out of the country safely, especially since that involved bringing James Martin's son home with me.

I had been granted a journalist visa that would allow me to be in country for up to three months. The understanding was that I would be reporting strictly on vacation destinations and not political or other controversial topics. Acquiring the visa quickly had not been a problem as Khutule tourism was in a decline due to unstable conditions in the country. The government reacted favorably to any efforts to promote the tourist trade in the outside world. I would be a most welcome visitor, at least for a while.

Three months would be far more time than I needed to accomplish my objectives in Khutule...surely. Even three weeks was longer than I anticipated staying. Prior to a week ago, I knew little to nothing about this somewhat obscure country in southern Africa surrounded by larger and better-known countries like South Africa, Botswana, and Zimbabwe. I had, however, stocked up on travel and history information about the country to get acquainted with my destination. I would be well versed by the time I landed in Johannesburg in preparation for the final leg of my journey into Khutule itself.

In some ways, Khutule appeared to be like my current home in North Carolina—somewhat of a variety vacationland with geography and climate that ranged widely. That was where the similarities ended, as Khutule was trapped in a third-world class of nations, despite its affirmed beauty and offerings of breathtaking adventures.

Almost as if a line were drawn in pencil down the middle of Khutule, the western half of the country consists of small mountain ranges and highland plateaus, which fall away to the east in low lying, grassy savannahs. These savannahs are dotted throughout with shrubs and low growing trees, and they border the several major rivers flowing out of the mountains and highlands. The major river flowing from the highest peak in the Khutule range is the Tandebuto. It spills its cold waters into the large and shallow bowl of Lake Albert on a great plateau, where it wanders broadly and lazily before crashing, in the middle of the country, over the Albert cataracts, boiling through the Katarna gorges in a dramatic drop to the floor of the savannah lowlands.

The Internet information I had gathered hastily before leaving told me that the Greater Lake Albert region, the cataracts and the gorges below were the site of some of the most challenging extreme sport and expedition adventures on the planet, and, the information claimed, these sites have remained pristine and virtually unchanged by outside influences for hundreds of years. Within the span of a few miles, I could view the lake and cataracts from above in a plane or motorized hang glider, bungee jump over the cataracts, or raft in the butter-churn pool below the turbulent falls. One could, if brave enough and possessing the strength to fight the growing current, canoe or kayak above the cataracts, coming as close as thirty feet to the brink. Or one could put in a raft below the cataracts and brave levels 4 and 5 whitewater rafting for the next twenty miles until the river tamed and spread out into a gentle flat expanse.

The highlands themselves, as well as the savannahs, featured large and strangely shaped outcroppings of rocks called koppies, some having served as homes and forts during the early history of the country. These areas were the sites of intriguing geological, archaeological, and paleontological expeditions designed to give the novice or veteran alike a working knowledge of the craft while exploring these strange and mysterious phenomena.

If this were not enough, three large (and questionably run, it seemed) game preserves in the south west of the country offered walking or riding safaris, conducted either during the day or by night. While a variety of game could be seen, the most dangerous were the elephants, famous for their dislike of people.

For less adventuresome travelers there were the usual sites of historical and cultural significance around the country, some in rather remote areas, such as the mountains, but many nearer the towns or cities.

The plan, which Jake Bean and I had worked out, called for me to begin my research into extreme vacation spots with a visit to the Lake Albert site, which had the best accumulation of thrilling adventures. Jake had hastily arranged for me to engage in a series of short excursions involving planes and rafts. I drew the line at bungee jumping and hang-gliding for the time being. This taste of adventure would yield both legitimate information for the travel column and cover for me as I established my bearings in the country.

After five days in the Greater Lake Albert region, I would go far down country to the southwestern part of Khutule for a four-day taste of safari adventure, two days by foot and the next two by Range Rover. This way I would hit the largest and the smallest game preserves, again collect inside travel information and further acquaint myself with Khutule and its peoples. If my movements were being observed in any way, this ambitious schedule was designed to show that I had a real interest in out-of-the-ordinary vacation packages to push to our readers back home.

My third destination would be the capital city of Limbarne for a brief rest of three or four days and, I hoped, a chance to make the contacts I needed with James Martin's missionary friend. Limbarne is located downriver and east of Lake Albert and can be found at about the middle of the map of the country. Khutule only has five cities with populations over 100,000, and the capital is the only city with over a million people.

My next, and hopefully final, destination in Khutule was to be the northeast savannah region of the state between the moderate sized cities of Kore and Mazuru. Located north and east of the capital, these cities are the historical seats of the once vast and rich farming plantations in Khutule, some of which have been in operation since the mid 1800s, even before the formal days of colonization by Great Britain.

In the area between the two cities is located a strange plateau that rises out of the surrounding savannah almost to the height of the plateaus near the highlands of the northwest. The plateau is small in size but more than makes up for it in height. Rising uncharacteristically straight up from the surrounding flatlands, it can be seen from miles around and is called the Soku Mount. The plateau is the site of an ancient trade route city, the ruins of which are constantly under archaeological exploration by universities and institutes from around the world. As part of my assignment, I was to join the current archaeological dig for as much time as I desired. We had left the dates open ended for a reason.

The northeastern part of Khutule was once its breadbasket and was the home of most of the great cattle, grain, coffee, and vegetable plantations that fed the country and imported products to the world. This area was where the two Neville family estates were located, the one where James Martin and Elisia lived, and the older one pioneered by his grandfather—the same estate where James Martin's father was murdered. A more remote location further north was the location of Bertram Wallace's mission station and orphanage, the adopted home of James Martin's son, Jack.

As I leafed through my printed itinerary and my copies of the information about Khutule, I realized that in less than two weeks I might be face to face with Sir James Martin Neville's son. This was why I had come, or rather to bring him home was why I had come. Anticipating my mission and what I might encounter during it made my heart beat faster.

I would be met at the airport in the largely tourist area of Lake Albert by a representative of Southern Africa Ultimate Escape, the extreme vacation specialists who would guide my trip while in Khutule. Under the auspices of this respected tourist franchise, I wouldn't be traveling alone in a country that warns visitors, especially females, against traveling singly. I would remain under the agency's care as I traveled to the safari region and then on to the archaeological dig. Jake Bean, through his contacts, had even made special arrangements for a guide to remain with me during my rest days in the capital and to be at my disposal for whatever I chose to do after the dig, this time at my own expense.

The words from one of the travel sites I had downloaded from the Internet seemed to stick and take root in my brain as my flight neared its destination.

Khutule is a hauntingly beautiful and mysterious place, the unforgettable kind of escape about which most of us dream and never realize. To experience Khutule is to partake of a veritable feast of the senses designed to leave you satisfied, peaceful, and at rest.*

The small asterisk following this copy referred the reader to very fine print at the bottom of the page that read,

*While Khutule has usually been a safe and secure country for visitors, please be aware that it is currently in a semi-state of turmoil due to political and economic factors beyond the control of this tour agency, who will not be responsible for acts of war or violence conducted to or against its patrons while in country.

This statement was in black print that was all but obscured by blackened silhouette images of animals against an orange and red sunset over the savannah. No one but the most observant reader would notice the warning. I was an observant reader. The peculiar pull and push of this country was beginning to have an effect on me, and I had not yet exited the airplane.

13

Lake Albert

I finally disembarked at the Lake Albert International Airport (recently renamed, I read, the Lloyd Pfungwa Zikhali International Airport by the current president in honor of himself) and found I was in a state of imbalance between the world from which I had come and the third world of Khutule. My view from the window of the Airways Khutule plane as we prepared to land showed well-kept runways and a beautiful airport terminal about the size of the one from which I had departed back in North Carolina.

Once on the ground, as I walked from the gate area to where my luggage and customs were located, I saw an interior design and decorations so sleek, modern, and sophisticated that I began to question the information I had just been reading about the dire straits of Khutule's political and financial circumstances. How could any place this beautiful and well maintained be representative of a country in apparent chaos? The discrepancy between what I had read and what I was seeing was significant.

Suffice it to say that I was ill at ease during my pass through customs. My papers were in order, but I knew this government was guilty of sometimes disregarding credentials and accusing visitors, at will, of a variety of violations of Khutulen procedures, sometimes to extort money and sometimes for no apparent reason other than to refuse the visitor admittance to the country. Would my cover, even though it was genuine, be enough to excuse me from suspicion of some supposed (or real) clandestine behavior?

As I handed over my documents to the customs agent, I was sure he noticed the tremor in my hand and voice as I responded to his questions about my destinations, length of stay, and other usual queries. The presence of armed and uniformed guards stationed conspicuously around the airport did nothing to slow my breathing, especially since the uniforms seemed to be military in nature rather than regular airport security. I tried to dismiss my concerns by remembering that this was a post 9-11 world, but I could feel the cold and frank stares, even when sunshades worn inside of the building covered the eyes.

Despite my fears, as I moved away from the customs side of the airport into Khutule proper, no uniformed hand reached for my arm and no voice called for me to step out of line for further questioning. I had entered Khutule without international incident.

True to its agreement, an agent of the Southern Africa Ultimate Escape agency was holding up a sign with my name on it as soon as I could move about freely. He introduced himself as Jamul Legassi, and his dark-skinned face was open, friendly, and welcoming as I was given a handshake and an invitation to enter a van to begin my research into extreme vacations, Khutule style.

Lulled by the beauty and order of the airport, I was not ready for what I saw as I was driven away toward my lakeside holiday hotel. Although this popular tourist city tried valiantly to keep its face made up for tourists, all was clearly not as well in this country as whoever maintained the airport would have us believe. My driver had mentioned that we would be taking a short cut to reach the resort area. I couldn't understand at the time why anyone genuinely trying to impress vacationing visitors or a journalist intending to inform prospective vacationers would have chosen the route he did.

Two blocks from the airport brought us past the first signs of what I can only call a state of poverty, disorder, and decline I was to encounter again and again throughout this otherwise visually spectacular country. Once off of the main airport highway, the back streets, roads, bridges, and other parts of the infrastructure were in a noticeable state of disrepair.

Ill-clad children played in undesirable surroundings before dwellings that were as squalid as the airport had been upscale. We passed such scenes of abject poverty that I began to suspect I was surely seeing the slums of the city, but I later found these living conditions were common for much of Khutule's population. It was as if the most prominent structures and sights had been whitewashed while the rest of the country looked something like the recently abandoned set of a war movie.

As we drove, it was not uncommon to view derelict or burned-out vehicles on the sides of the streets, deserted and apparently uninhabitable buildings covered with graffiti, and small congregations of young people lounging on the street corners in the middle of the day.

Just as my first impressions of Khutule gained from viewing the lavish airport were surprisingly positive, my second impressions from the vantage point of the city streets were disheartening. Surely this was a country in critical decline unless something dramatic occurred to change its course.

By the time we arrived at the lakeside resort, with its heart being an ancient and outwardly immaculate old Victorian hotel built in the late 1800s, I was beginning to feel like a time traveler whisked among different eras with little transition. The resort could only be described with words such as *grand* and *stunning*, as it rambled along on a slight hillside above the water. It had additions sprawling in both directions from the main structure, all showing off their up and downstairs porches like fine ladies in crisp white layers of starched petticoats.

Starched also described the resort staff that appeared out of nowhere to meet guests' every need in immaculate white uniforms reminiscent of days long gone. Once more, I could not reconcile this Khutule with that which I had viewed from my seat in the van on the trip here. I sensed a dissonance in this country that defied explanation, and I had only been here for about an hour. It was as if parts of Khutule were put on display for outsiders like a beautiful wedding cake, while other less desirable parts were carefully cloaked from view. I became an uneasy observer to the deception.

I wish I could have compartmentalized my thinking in Khutule to concentrate separately on my two reasons for being there. That was impossible for me. During the time I was scheduled to experience a vacationer's paradise, collecting impressions to record for our readers back home in search of new adventures, all I could think about was finding James Martin's son and getting him out of the country.

Granted, my surroundings in the several days I spent in the Lake Albert area defied easy description. The lake itself is vast, covering about 23,000 square miles, making it one of the largest in the world, according to my vacation guides. The sunrises and sunsets alone provide reason enough to visit and linger, rising early and dining late. The animals still gather there as they have for centuries, wildebeest, antelope, rhinoceros, even though their numbers are greatly reduced due to poaching. The birds are glorious and abundant. Personally, watching the animals, birds, and tourists provided sufficient extreme amusement for me, never mind the more glamorously advertised activities.

I arose early each morning, had my breakfast and coffee on a second-floor dining porch overlooking the top of the falls, and then dutifully trudged off to experience whatever *extreme* experience in flying, rafting, hiking, or whatever was scheduled for me during the day. All the while my mind was preoccupied with the real reason I had come to Africa.

I dosed myself daily with the admonition from Philippians about whatever my circumstances are, I should be content in them. While it helped as long as I obeyed, I found myself quick to stray back to a state of uneasy anxiety and urgency over my charge to rescue Jack Neville.

Each night I would return to my room exhausted to record my impressions and the information gleaned from the day's experiences for Jake Bean. When I would stop for even a minute, Jack's face would appear on whatever lap top screen or travel brochure I was looking at. James Martin had given me several pictures of Jack before I left on the trip, and he had warned me to study them carefully but not to bring them on the trip. Jack's face could travel in my mind, but not in my luggage for his safety and mine.

I had also been cautioned to be wary of anyone who tried to become too familiar with me on this journey. For many obvious reasons, a woman traveling alone might appear to be easy prey anywhere, but Khutule's recent history of petty crimes against tourists required extra caution. As long as I was in the company of my tour guide, Jamul, I was relatively safe on that count.

For me, however, there was an even greater reason to be concerned over anyone showing undue interest in my affairs or me. James Martin had warned, because of the threats he had experienced from his Khutulen countrymen even while stateside, that my connection to him might be known even in Khutule.

14

Initial Contact

Being aware of the potential dangers around me and wanting to make contact with Jack as soon as possible, my days of enforced vacation in Khutule were akin to having nightmares. With dogged determination, I completed my extreme fun in the Lake area and boarded a small plane for the southern game preserve regions of Khutule and the safari phase of my journey with my trusty guide, Jamul Legassi, in tow. I found this portion of my fact-finding even more physically taxing than the lake activities, and I welcomed the strenuous and busy days on various safari treks to keep my mind as occupied as possible.

The terrain and climate in the southwestern part of Khutule were nothing like that in the Lake Albert area; there was a rugged and untamed quality in this region that was more appealing to me. North Carolina was also known for its beautiful shorelines, but apart from the Asheboro Zoo, there was nothing back at home remotely like what I experienced in the Khutule game preserves.

The game parks offered a vast sampling of animals and ways of viewing them. Elephants, lions, water buffalo, rhinoceros, hippotamuses, gorillas, chimpanzees, baboons, giraffes, zebras, warthogs, foxes, otters, hares, bats, shrew, and anteaters could be accessed by riding, trekking on foot, canoeing, flying or simply sitting in a lodge above a watering hole waiting for them to come to you. The lodges were as exotic as the animals they exhibited.

On my final evening at the guest lodge of the remote Lukani Game Preserve, I sat on a high veranda overlooking a grassy plain where I could just make out in the twilight a herd of waterbuck moving lazily across the horizon. The air was cool, and I pulled my jacket more closely around me for comfort, not wanting to stir yet to return to my room. I felt the presence of the stranger only a second before he spoke to me from behind my chair.

"Lovely, isn't it? The evening I mean."

His voice caused me to jump in my seat and become instantly on guard. I had been expressly warned against the intervention of strangers.

"Forgive me. I did not mean to startle you."

It would be rude not to reply and more highly suspicious to retreat without acknowledging the stranger's presence. I decided that the direct approach was best. "Yes, it's not only extraordinarily beautiful but also remarkable peaceful."

I could sense a hesitation as he answered. "I am afraid falsely so."

Was this a double meaning? Was this an innocent interchange between fellow guests...or maybe a garden-variety come-on? Or something more sinister?

Suddenly I was cold. Against my better judgment, I played along. "Why so? What could endanger the peace of those animals, Mr...?

"DeSoto. Fredric DeSoto, at your service." The man actually did a slight bow as he reached to shake my hand, which I had not extended in welcome. I was still on the offense, although I backed slightly away.

"Packs of free-ranging wild and domestic dogs, lions, leopards, hyenas, cheetahs...one never knows what might be lurking nearby in the dark, Ms. Redmon."

Ms. Redmon? I decided to go for broke; I hoped not foolishly so. I stood to face him on his level. We were the only ones occupying the dimly lit veranda.

"Mr. DeSoto, are you on safari here? Perhaps I missed seeing you on our outing today. And however do you know my name?"

His smile, to my surprise, was open and friendly, and his response came quickly. "I asked the management. Does that offend you? I specifically needed to find you. I believe you and I have a mutual friend." I could see him gauging my reaction. At the same time, I was trying to gauge my level of exposure.

"You must be mistaken, sir. Except for the guides and fellow travelers I've met on vacation, and now you, I don't know anyone in Khutule. This is my first visit to Africa, actually."

This time he paused before speaking, and I forced myself not to fill the silence with chatter or movement.

"I think perhaps it may be a friend you have yet to encounter on this trip," he finally said, without further explanation.

This clearly fell within the danger zone, and I prayed silently for instant wisdom as so much depended upon my reaction. Should I risk one more question? Should I wait and see if he offered to explain? Or should I innocently reaffirm that he was mistaken and excuse myself to my room?

As if sensing my quandary, this man who called himself Fredric DeSoto continued quietly, "I am a friend of Bertram Wallace. I understand that you

might be interested in meeting Mr. Wallace for the purpose of exchanging"—
he looked casually around us—"essential goods?"

Essential goods? Could that be a euphemism for a child? It certainly could
be to the child's father. I decided to proceed.

"Mr. DeSoto, I'm a newspaper journalist here for the purpose of exploring
the topic of unusual or extreme vacation spots for my editor back home in the
States. I've visited the Lake Albert area and am just completing my stay here in
the game preserves. I'm planning on spending a couple of rest days in the
capital before moving on to participate in an archaeological dig. While my
stay in Khutule is quite busy, I do hear that Mr. Wallace has some interesting
goods I wouldn't mind looking over. Is his appointment schedule open at all
during the next couple of weeks? I don't anticipate being in the country much
longer than that."

There, the ball was back in his court.

"I am at liberty, Ms. Redmon, to say that Mr. Wallace also plans to travel
to the capital in the next few days on vital business. I might be able to arrange
some time for you to discuss what goods you are looking for with him to see if
he can accommodate. If you would be so kind as to scribble your hotel on my
card and the dates of your stay in Limbarne, I will be most happy to contact
Mr. Wallace on your behalf." His smile seemed genuine as he handed me his
card and a pen.

"Thank you, Mr. DeSoto, for your interest in our transactions." I
scribbled as I spoke. "Please thank Mr. Wallace for being so kind as to
accommodate me. Now I will bid you good evening," and I turned to go.

"No, Ms. Redmon, the pleasure is mine," I heard him say quietly as I left
the balcony.

It appeared as if the real extreme vacation I had come to experience in
Khutule had finally begun. The contact with DeSoto, as mysterious and vague
as it remained, told me that someone knew I was in the country. I could only
hope and pray that it was the right someone and not the mastermind behind a
trap being laid for me somewhere down the road. I really hadn't much choice
at this point but to play along. At least I hadn't been arrested on the spot.

The thought that within a week I might be face-to-face with Jack's
guardian and on my way to completing my mission in Khutule left me
apprehensive but elated. On the other hand, the thought of spending days on a
dig studying the paleontology or archaeology of even the most interesting
geological and historical area of Khutule left me frustrated when normally
such an expedition would hold great appeal.

It was only my loyalty to my boss and my fear of jeopardizing my cover that kept me dedicated to completing the whole of my itinerary. As eager as I was to find Jack and see him safely out of the country, I had to be as cautious as possible not to endanger both of us any more than necessary.

I was to leave my hotel at the game preserve at a leisurely hour the next morning for my few days of R and R in the capital city of Limbarne. Traveling to and from the capital city would have been tricky for me alone. Again, my constant touring companion, Jamul Legassi, was with me as my escort, driver, and guide to the city and to the savannah beyond where we would find the great plateau and the Soku Mount.

Jamul I found to be amiable and amusing. Those characteristics made for more relaxing travel conditions. I was beginning to feel comfortable in his presence and safe in his care. Without openly discussing it, I suspected that we shared a faith.

By this time, both my mind and body longed for a brief respite from adventuring. I needed to work on my travel notes for Jake Bean, but more I wanted to contact Jack's guardian about plans to meet Jack and get him out of the country as soon as my upcoming expedition was completed. I was still convinced that this job was mine to do, but I was feeling the weight of it and a concern over whether all would go well.

The trip from the Lukani Game Preserve to Limbarne was about one hundred miles, which in America would have taken two hours or less. In Khutule, the trip took twice as long due to the unpredictable road conditions, government checkpoints, and sporadic gasoline supplies. Both the physical beauty of the country and the acute poverty of its population continued to leave me stunned. We passed dwellings that were little more than hovels stretched out along the roadway, either by themselves or in the small settlements we passed. In stark contrast, we also glimpsed elaborate mansions barely visible behind security fences and curtains of landscaped greenery hinting at the incongruent presence of great wealth.

There were, thankfully, no major obstacles on the trip to the capital, unless you count two flat tires and five roadblocks, which seemed to be less than Jamul expected. I was just beginning to feel smug about how easy the trip had been when we entered the outskirts of the city. The self-satisfied feeling came to a gradual but decided halt as I began to get a sense of the city we were entering.

The highway entering Limbarne was lined with increasingly more densely populated shanties pieced together from old corrugated tin, miscellaneous pieces of wood, and cardboard. Children and animals wandered or played along the sides of the roadway breathtakingly close to the movement of the vehicles. Mud and standing water acted as an artist's palette to paint everything a reddish brown. It was a depressing early view of the city.

The shanties gave way to more substantial cement structures, but they too seemed desperately in need of attention as many were rundown or abandoned and some had no windows or roofs. More than once I caught sight of what looked like armed and uniformed militia on patrol, sometimes in pickup trucks with manned mounted machine guns in the truck beds. The more I saw, the greater my sense of apprehension grew about the wisdom of visiting this city, especially under my current circumstances.

As we neared the heart of the capital, and I knew we were because of the running comments of Jamul, there was such a drastic mixture of old and new world, prosperity and poverty, elegance and garishness that my senses were in constant overload. Striking modern architecture stood side by side with near-medieval construction. Buildings looking as if they had scarcely survived aerial bombings sat next to smartly appointed palace-like structures. Men and women in western attire of the latest fashions moved in the streets side by side with others in traditional tribal dress or worn and tattered rags.

There was such a dissonance in the scenes before me that my senses refused to compute the disparities. It was as if something ominous and threatening was just beyond my sight. I could feel it but couldn't see it. This was decidedly not a friendly place. The glances from bystanders and fellow travelers we passed were either hostile or hollow. I didn't like this city and surely did not relish spending several days within its limits.

I struggled to shake off the near despair that was clouding my mind and my spirit. It was as if unseen evil loitered in the crowded and cluttered city streets. As the sense of darkness and fear began to smother me, I prayed in earnest for protection, strength, and discernment to keep my focus on why I had come and what I needed to do. As clearly as if I had been handed a letter, the words of 2 Timothy 1:7 came, reminding me that the spirit of fear doesn't come from God, but rather a spirit *"of power, and of love, and of a sound mind."*

Immediately after repeating those words to myself several times and claiming their promise, I began to feel more hopeful and optimistic about the task that lay ahead. The faces of little Marta and her father paraded before me, and I wanted desperately to see Jack, safe in America, standing with them.

15

Bertram Wallace

The lodging where I was to spend my rest days in Limbarne was a small inn located on a side street about three blocks from the large capitol plaza of the government buildings, offices, and President's Palace. My hotel, one like it, and a handful of small shops clustered around a small, green park-like space covering about two acres. I could see people gathered in the well-kept park, but it and the street in front of my hotel were surprisingly quiet for midday in the city. It was as if this little oasis gave respite from the crowded and untidy conditions I had viewed while entering the city.

My spirits lifted even more as I helped Jamul gather my luggage to enter the hotel. The innkeeper, Mr. Graham St. James, was from some middle European country and welcomed me profusely as if my expected arrival marked the high point of his day. Surely here I would be safe and have a quiet spot to work for my remaining days in the city.

It was with some relief that I signed the registration forms and received my room key. I was tired and more than ready for a long soak and a rest. When the innkeeper summoned a bellhop lounging nearby to take my luggage to my room, Jamul intervened immediately, commandeering my luggage himself and starting off toward the elevator. After thanking the innkeeper for his kindness, I hurried off to follow my luggage and Jamul to my assigned quarters.

Once inside my room, Jamul placed my baggage in a neat row beside the door. My room was on the second floor with a view of a pleasant inner courtyard vibrant with greenery or native plants. The room was large and, though not luxurious, adequately appointed with a cool, relaxing décor. A door led to a small balcony overlooking the courtyard. As I entered the room, Jamul walked directly to the balcony door, opened it, and turned back to me.

"Ms. Redmon, may I have a word with you...outside, please?" His tone was formal and insistent, and he stepped out onto the balcony. I followed him.

"Yes, Jamul, what is it?"

"Ms. Redmon, you have been kind to me and generous as well," he began, his voice low but firm.

So, that was it. I had forgotten his tip or some other extra charge. I was reaching into my purse for my wallet when he interrupted my movement by placing his hand lightly and briefly on my arm.

"Ms. Redmon, you misunderstand. You owe me nothing. I am afraid I must warn you to be most careful during your stay in this city. I fear I have brought you here in error, even though this is what I was requested to do. Please do not be fooled by the beauty of your present surroundings. There is great vice in Limbarne." He looked carefully around him, as if to be sure we were not overheard.

"Jamul, what are you trying to tell me? Please be more clear about the nature of the danger. Everything appears to be in order here at the hotel."

"Yes, that is why you were brought to this exact place. But please understand that the mood of the city changes quite quickly. You might call Limbarne and its peoples unpredictable. Quiet can quickly change to riot. Safe can fast become perilous. Our present government can be..." He looked down and appeared reluctant to continue.

"What do you suggest that I do? I have work I must do here before going on to the archaeological expedition at the Soku Mount. I can't leave now when I have only just arrived."

"I understand." He spoke as if he really did not but was humoring me. "I must ask that you not go out into the city, even into the park or to a restaurant, alone. There is a small café inside the hotel for your convenience. I will be most happy to accompany you anywhere else you need to go. I am staying nearby with relatives while I am here. You must tell the innkeeper of any travel needs, and he will call me to escort you. You must be careful to keep all of your current business most private. There are few who can be trusted."

"My current business, Jamul? Why would anyone care that I am here to report on vacation places? Why would that be a problem to anyone? I have a permit." Something was strange about this conversation.

"Ms. Redmon, I am hopeful that no one will have a problem with your visit to Khutule. While you are here, it is my responsibility to see that you are protected, as best I can do so. You can trust me. We will speak later, but now I must go."

"I understand. Thank you, Jamul." I gave him my handshake. I wondered if he somehow knew about my real reason for being here. His words offered the promise of comfort, and I needed to trust someone. I needed to ask him who else could be trusted. What about Fredric DeSoto? While I did feel a bond with Jamul Legassi, I realized I was still left with a deep uneasiness that everything in this country would become wearying before my time in Khutule was over.

After Jamul left, I walked back into my pleasant room and looked around. I noticed a telephone, a television, a worktable, and a small garden tub. A brochure on the bureau stated that a café on the first floor served three meals daily, and there was a small pool at the basement level for exercise and relaxation. I would be comfortable here, as long as the electricity remained stable.

I had just arranged my belongings for comfortable access and removed my travel clothes in favor of a robe when the room phone rang. I was sure it was the innkeeper with some bit of information he had failed to relate. I was mistaken.

"Yes?"

"Ms. Redmon, Fredric DeSoto at your service."

I wish I had Jamul's assurance that this man was a friend.

"Mr. DeSoto, it's nice to hear from you again. To what do I owe this pleasure?"

"I have a message for you from a mutual friend. He would like to meet with you as soon as possible, if that is convenient for you."

"Yes, Mr. DeSoto, I am available and eager to meet with our friend."

"I will let him know at once, and he will be in contact. Thank you, and have a pleasant visit in Limbarne." I could hear the click as he hung up his phone.

My heart was beating rapidly as I sat down on the edge of the bed, and I felt as if I had been holding my breath for a long time.

I certainly hadn't had to wait long for the contact, but I still didn't have any specifics. When would the meeting take place? Where? How would I know it was Bertram Wallace whom I was meeting, the missionary who had guardianship of Jack Neville? Would he bring Jack with him?

No sooner had I run through a mental list of my questions than a knock sounded at my door. I had bolted it and put the safety latch on, as well, when I entered. I was not about to open it to just anyone.

"May I help you?" I called through the door panel.

"It is your innkeeper, Mr. St. James, Ms. Redmon. There is a message for you."

According to Jamul, the inn had been selected for me as a place of relative safety, and I had felt comfortable in the presence of the innkeeper upon my arrival. I opened the door.

"I am sorry to bother you so soon after your arrival. I know you must need your rest. However, you have a visitor who is waiting for you in the terrace garden within the patio. He asked that I deliver this note to you. I will also vouch, Ms. Redmon, that this gentleman is the man he claims to be." He handed me the folded notepaper on which were written these words.

Greetings and welcome to Khutule. I would request that you join me for tea in the terrace garden at this time, if it is convenient with you.

It was sighed *B. Wallace.*

Mr. St. James waited for me to read the note, then looked at me questioningly for my response.

"Thank you, Mr. St. James. Please tell the gentleman I will join him for tea in fifteen minutes. Will it be possible for you to serve us in the terrace garden?"

"Of course. I will inform him at once," and he was gone.

It was a long fifteen minutes. I changed quickly and spent the rest of the time sitting on the edge of my bed in prayer. So much rested on what Mr. Wallace and I would be able to accomplish in the next several minutes. I needed Divine guidance and strength. I needed not to rely on my own wisdom and understanding of the serious situation that faced us, that of getting Jack out of the country safely, not to speak of Mr. Wallace and myself.

I left my room with two minutes to spare and easily found a way down to the first floor and out the exit to the terrace garden. It was a multi-colored haven of cultivated flowers and greenery surrounding a cement and rock terrace and fish pool. The afternoon was warm, but a gazebo beside of the pool complete with ceiling fan provided respite from the heat.

Seated in the gazebo with his back to me was a short and somewhat rotund man dressed in a blue and white seersucker suit. He arose and turned toward me as soon as I spoke.

"Mr. Wallace?" I stretched out my hand in greeting and he took it warmly, returning my greeting with a smile both friendly and reassuring.

"Ms. Redmon, how do you do? And I am Bert to those who know me."

"And I'm Jannia. Please, be seated." I sat down at a small bistro table as he sat across from me, placing his broad brimmed straw hat on the side of the table.

We were alone in the garden except for a waiter who appeared, as if on cue, with our tea and sweets tray as soon as we were seated.

104

I poured from the dainty floral pot, and we both selected a tantalizing sweet from the tray. I was neither hungry nor thirsty, but there is great normalcy in food. We both took sips and bites before either of us spoke again.

I began. "May I ask you about Mr. DeSoto? Who is he, and how did he know how to find me at the game preserve?"

Bert Wallace laughed heartily as he wiped crumbs of sweet off of his short beard. "I was warned that you get right to the point. Our friend in America, I'm sure you know the one, has told me how delightfully serious and straightforward you are. Mr. DeSoto is a professor of religion at the University of Khutule, located here in Limbarne. He also happens to be a former student at the Mission School where I have been headmaster for thirty years. He is a fellow follower of Jesus Christ and a loyal friend. He knew about you and your whereabouts because I have been communicating with our American friend. Although it is a bit risky, thank the Lord for email."

I hadn't thought of that approach as a means of sidestepping the dangers of regular mail, which might or might not arrive in an untampered state, or at all, in a country like Khutule.

"I must tell you how relieved I am to meet you." I lowered my voice. "When will I meet Jack? What do you think our best approach should be to...accomplish our goal?"

He laughed again, infectiously, and reached across the table to pat my hand. Surprisingly, I was not offended by his familiar manner, which was somewhat fatherly rather than forward. He looked directly into my eyes with his own light blue ones.

"Jannia, I am grateful to God that you have agreed to undertake this task. I see your eagerness to be about it. I, too, am ready for this to come to an end." He also lowered his voice and leaned toward me. "I love James Martin as a brother and Jack as if he were my son. I truly wish he were so, as now my time with him is short."

He paused for several seconds, as if to compose himself, and wiped his eyes briefly with a white handkerchief. "Are you quite sure that you comprehend the inherent risks and dangers involved in this undertaking, not just to your health but to your very life?" Both his expression and tone showed that he had turned deadly serious.

"I can't say that I understand everything, due to the complexity of the problem and my naiveté about this country, but I do think I'm ready to do what must be done." I realized that sounded a bit heroically vague, but I made up in determination what I lacked in bravado.

"May I ask why you are agreeing to do this thing? Why involve yourself with strangers and risk your life to carry out a task for people you hardly know?"

I could see that he too could be straightforward. Again I was not offended. It was a reasonable question under the circumstances. Now what was the answer?

I returned his gaze eyes for eyes. "Mr. Wallace...Bert, I've not been famous for putting the concerns of others before my own. The situation in which I found little Marta Nev...Everston and her father defied anything I had previously encountered. When I understood about Jack and about the risks his father would face returning here...I had no..." To my surprise and embarrassment I choked on my words, and my vision blurred with tears. I couldn't complete my explanation.

To Bert Wallace's credit, he did not patronize me but rather turned and focused on our surroundings while I composed myself. I didn't want his sympathy but rather his vote of confidence that I was up to the job before us. After some time of sitting in silence, he continued.

"Jack is somewhat confused by this whole situation. He is not thrilled with the idea of leaving his home here, my home that is, where he has lived for so many years. He has been loved, well cared for, and educated. He has many close companions among the orphans at the mission school. I have never forbidden him the close friendship of these children, some of whom were abandoned, some orphaned by hostilities, AIDS, or other dreadful diseases and some rescued from forced service in the African Re-Unification Coalition or similar rebel militia. I wanted him to be at ease with many sorts of friends, as long as they did not wield detrimental influence over him. I keep a close watch for that.

"I've been most particular to inform Jack of his heritage and of why he was with me at the mission school for so long. Jack is very proud of his father; in fact he nearly idolizes him. The boy is well aware of the political circumstances prompting his long separation from his father. He even says he understands his father's inability to return for him now. Still, I sense he feels somewhat betrayed by having to leave what is familiar to him. I'm afraid he has come to consider me more of a father than James Martin; I'm the one upon whom he depends. Jack is a young man in significant conflict. But then, he is nearly thirteen."

"Jack will still have you with him when he leaves Khutule, won't he?" I was sure he would be coming with us.

Bert's swift look told me otherwise. "I will not be returning to America with you both. I have made Jack's father aware of my decision, although he wasn't surprised. My heart...my work...are in Africa. When this is over, I will not be welcome in Khutule; the mission school is even now closing. As soon as my affairs here are completed, I hope to travel overland to the border, cross at some remote checkpoint, and make my way on to another mission assignment in South Africa. This fact should not affect our plans for departure, just how cooperative Jack may be. He knows of my intentions. I love the boy as my own, but now he needs to be with his real father. My presence would cloud the issue."

There was obvious pain in his voice and face. I was mystified by the amount of self-sacrifice his choice to part from his semi-adopted son must have taken. My decision to help Sir Neville required temporary discomfort, but his separation from Jack might well be permanent.

"Do you have other children, children of your own, I mean?"

"No, I'm a dedicated bachelor. I long ago decided it was better for me to remain single, as the Apostle Paul seemed to be, to concentrate on the job God set before me. Not that I'll ever reach Paul's single-mindedness toward doing the work of Christ, but God has confirmed my decision again and again over the years. I will admit," and he looked away again for several seconds out over the garden in front of us, "this time has been the hardest yet."

He smiled broadly at me and the somber mood was broken as he announced heartily, "My God promised that His grace would be sufficient for me, and thus far He is still faithful; so there's no room for despair!"

How I hoped and prayed he was right! My mind rewound words that I had heard weeks before on another continent, words that James Martin had spoken that sounded much like what I was hearing now. *"I am a man of faith."*

Was I up to that challenge? Was I...or could I become such a *woman of faith?*

Bert Wallace then told me that airline tickets would be arranged for Jack and me to fly out of the northeastern city of Mazuru for Cape Town in South Africa two weeks from that day. I would act as Jack's guardian from the point of departure until our arrival in the States when he would be delivered to his father. Bert and I would not meet again in Khutule until we were at the airport and then only as casual fellow travelers when we unobtrusively passed Jack from his care into mine.

If any plans changed, I would be notified through the tour company or otherwise. He gave me papers giving me authorization to act as Jack's guardian and escort, something required for international travel with a minor. Finally, he had me memorize emergency contact information should I need to reach him. Then, with a brief prayer and quick embrace, he was gone through the door to the inn and presumably out into the dusk of the African evening.

I sat for some time in the growing darkness trying to absorb the events of the past hour and praying for strength to be found trustworthy to carry out my end of the endeavor. When the small garden lights of the terrace came on around me, I made my way back to my room.

16

The Soku Mount

The remainder of my time in Limbarne went quickly. Except in two instances for which I called Jamul to accompany me on a driving tour of the city and later on a walking junket to the vast bazaar, my time was spent entirely in the inn resting and working on my notes for the vacation articles for the newspaper back home.

The tour of the city again evoked the memory of the earlier warning that sinister forces were at work within the place. The bazaar visit ended abruptly when I almost became overwhelmed by aggressive street vendors and had to be whisked away down a series of dark alleys by Jamul, who knew the city intimately from years of visiting relatives there.

It was a considerable relief when my time in the capital city came to an end, and it was time to move north to the savannah country and the expedition at the Soku Mount. I was grateful to Mr. St. James, the innkeeper, for his careful attention to my needs and safety at his establishment, but I rested much easier when I found myself settled in Jamul's van ready to head out of the crowded city. The feeling of relief was premature.

One city block from the inn toward the main artery leading out of Limbarne, traffic slowed. It took us fifteen minutes to go another block, where traffic halted for good. Already anxious, I knew there was real trouble when Jamul turned to me (I was sitting in the back seat of the van) and told me to reach down between the parts of the seat and carefully pull out a small box. I did and found in it a loaded gun.

I knew a little about how to use a gun but had never had to do so in self-defense. Jamul must have sensed imminent danger as he told me to put the gun on the floor at my feet and cover it with a jacket. He also told me to be ready to use it if necessary.

We waited. Perspiration trickled down my back as we sat, unable to move. It wasn't long before we heard, before we saw, the source of the traffic jam. Moving toward us from across an area of previously burned-out apartments about a block away came a loud, disorderly group of people.

Mostly young men, they were armed with a variety of chance weapons. As they drew nearer, I could see bats, metal pipes, rocks...whatever they had picked up along the way. And they were angry.

"Jannia, pick up your gun and find the safety. Take it off and be ready to fire it if you must."

I could now see that he too was holding a handgun. He put it on the seat beside of him and revved the engine of the van as the first of the youths reached the street several vehicles in front of us. This was the first wave of a larger gang that must have numbered at least two to three hundred.

We saw passengers flee from the doors of one car in our line of traffic seconds before we heard the blows of wood and metal on shattering glass. The youths moved closer, shaking a small car nearer to us back and forth until it rolled on its side. At that point, I began to fear for our lives.

I heard Jamul yell above the noise of the growing crowd, "Get on the floor, Jannia, and hold your gun ready!"

I often refused to comply with orders given harshly, just as a matter of protest, but in this case I made an immediate exception. There was something deadly authoritative in Jamul's voice.

I crouched low on the van's floor and prayed. A woman screamed above the noise of the crowd somewhere close by. The van suddenly reversed, forcefully throwing me forward against the back of the front seat. It then jumped forward, slamming my head on the bottom of the metal door.

"Jamul!" I yelled, expecting at any second to feel the van roll over and nothing after that. I think I was too frightened to pray as I lay there askew on the floor of the back seat expecting to die.

But the van didn't roll over; in fact, it kept rolling forward.

"Stay down," I heard as we picked up speed. I was tossed around wildly as we swerved from side to side. There were no more words exchanged until several minutes later when I felt the van pull to a stop with the motor still running.

Jamul jumped out and jerked open the back door to the van, reaching inside to help me back onto the seat.

"I'm fine, I'm fine, let's just go, please. I want to leave this city now."

He immediately closed my door, re-entered the front seat, and sped away down a side street. In a few more twists and turns, we came out on the highway that would take us north and east of Limbarne toward the site of my final official stop in Khutule, the high plateau and the Soku Mount.

Without talking, we traveled on endless miles of pitted blacktop through the tough grass and scrub flora that was the savannah. I think I slept out of exhaustion following the adrenaline rush of our escape. It was not until we stopped at a little roadside shop for gas and cold drinks to eat with the lunch that had been packed for us by the café at the inn that I finally learned how Jamul had managed our escape.

"I had begun slowly moving forward and backward as much as I could, trying to position the van to move toward an opening in the traffic to our right that seemed wide enough for us to pass through. Many drivers and passengers around us had abandoned their vehicles and fled in panic and there was confusion all around. The car directly in front of us was rolled over in the direction away from the street, and there was just enough room to maneuver out of line, through the other line of vehicles, and across an abandoned lot to the next street. It was rough going for a while, would you not agree?"

I did, I surely did.

Upon close examination, all we had suffered during our miraculous, in my opinion, escape with our lives was a broken mirror on the passenger side and a cracked rear one.

"What was happening back there? What was going on?"

Jamul's voice was grave as he reminded me of the evil he had warned existed in the city. "This was not an isolated experience. Frustrations build over the political situation. Young people find no work. They have no money. Food is sometimes scarce, even in the city. The ingredients for disaster are always there. Something ignites it; tempers flare; people are injured or die. The police can do little to stop it."

"God help them," was all I could say.

We finished our sandwiches and prepared to move out onto the highway.

Jamul drove us through countless small settlements, too tiny to be called towns, clustered near large farms or what had once been successful cattle ranches before the current government's land re-distribution program.

Under the land redistribution program, many of the large privately owned farms were seized from landholders who had farmed them successfully for as long as two hundred years and turned over to friends and relatives of the President. Smaller sections were redistributed from their white owner-farmers to black Khutulen nationals with little or no previous farming experience or know-how. In either case, the results were too often failed crops, dilapidated structures, and bleached bones of dead livestock. Despite the dismal state of these once fertile and productive operations, there was still a lingering beauty and presence to the landscape itself.

Suddenly, after miles and miles of savannah, it was shocking to get a first glimpse of the strange rock formation that formed a plateau rising from the floor of the surrounding area to a height of about one thousand feet above sea level. The place was called the Soku Mount.

The Soku Mount was believed to have been the site of an ancient city located directly in the pathway of a well-traveled trade route. To reach the city, determined travelers must have had an arduous and sometimes steep journey on a narrow trail cut out of the rock from which the plateau was formed. The city was believed to have served as some sort of medieval resort, drawing both weary travelers from the trade route and those who came specifically to visit the alleged magic waters of the spring flowing from somewhere deep within the plateau and pooling in natural bathing areas along the sides of the slopes.

Universities from around the world vied for opportunities to excavate near these pools where ancient hotel-like structures and bathhouses were carved out of the stone of the plateau. I was to join such an excavation expedition sponsored by a California institution for as long as I wished. The expedition welcomed volunteers seeking extreme leisure pursuits and quickly trained them to act as lesser members of more experienced archaeological or paleontological teams digging for the secrets of the past under the watchful eyes of the Khutulen government. Such programs served the unique excitement needs of the volunteers and provided pay-your-own-way help for the institutions.

This chance to work side by side with real investigators of Africa's past interested me much more than the rafting and stalking I had been engaged in earlier. It was unfortunate that this unique opportunity had to compete with my intense focus on getting Jack out of Africa. Still, I had a few days to kill before making my way up to the northern city of Mazuru to meet Bert Wallace at the airport to take over Jack's protection as we left Khutule. I would try to make good use of my stay on the plateau, both to keep me occupied and to complete the work for my editor.

While my other vacation research destinations had been extreme, by definition, the accommodations had all been on the slightly worn but luxurious side. The accommodations at the plateau reminded me of high class camping. The sleeping was all done in large segregated tents, men's and women's, on either side of a huge wooden structure with no walls that served as a meeting/dining hall. When it rained or was cold, tent flaps were let down all around to keep the elements outside. The bathhouses were corrugated tin with no roofs. One could bathe under the stars or, on rainy days, wash one's hair in rainwater simultaneously with bathing in the tepid, piped-in running water. This was MASH or summer camp at its finest.

My fellow *extremers*—there were four of us—were jovial and eager to learn the ropes. Two were retired history teachers from a New Jersey high school and one was a seminary student who loved anything archaeological. After introducing myself as a journalist, accompanied by a little background on why I was participating that made no mention of my real purpose for being in Africa, we were ready to take the short course on archaeological exploration. We were all assigned to buddy with a more experienced university graduate student and given a low-level task that would provide the flavor of participating in the dig without disrupting the work at the same time. Anyone participating for more than a week could then switch to a new job with a different grad student and so on for as long as the vacationer cared to stay on a pay-to-participate basis.

I loved it with half of my mind and body while the other half kept an eye out for my driver, Jamul, in case there was a need for me to make a quick disappearance. Jamul, in turn, hovered close at hand, making himself both useful and unobtrusive by finding work in the open-air kitchen.

Jamul and I had formed a bond during our weeks together as tourist and personal driver/guide. He looked out for me, and I kept him supplied with stories about life in America. It became clear that he was a committed Christian who had a great love for his country and considerable concern for what was happening to it under the current political leadership.

Our days began early and ended late, as the real archaeologists driving the excavation wanted to get as much done as possible during their digging season. Our particular assignment was excavating the spa or bathhouse areas of the ancient resort, most of which were ruins, although a handful are usable even today, more than five to six hundred years after their origin. The work was slow-going, hot, physically taxing, and fascinating. It was amazing what artifacts the ancient users left in and around their bathing areas, much like what might be found under the sands at Myrtle Beach after a Fourth of July celebration.

I had been hard at work for four days when word came that I had a special visitor. One of the cooks came in search of me, and when I made my way cautiously up to the dining hall, which doubled as a meeting room, I was surprised and concerned to find the gentleman who had served as a messenger previously for Bertram Wallace waiting for me.

"Mr. DeSoto," I said, extending a dirt stained and gritty hand to him; only to draw it back before he felt obligated to take it.

"Ms. Redmon." He nodded in greeting and immediately began to usher me to the back of the open-frame shelter, away from the kitchen workers. "I am sorry to interrupt your...vacation," he continued, "but I am afraid a problem has arisen. As you are aware, Mr. Wallace requested that you meet him at the appointed place to exchange the...goods... to be delivered in exactly four days. Unfortunately, there has been a change in plans. Representatives of the Minister of Information in the Khutulen government are detaining Mr. Wallace at his mission compound. He was just able to get a message to me. He is not sure how long his confinement will last."

The news took my breath away. "And Ja...the goods? Are they safe?" I managed to ask.

"For the time being. The goods have been sent by a trusted coworker to the Khutulen home of your friend who is presently in America. Do you know what I mean?"

I knew he was speaking of James Martin's estate located somewhere further north from where we were meeting. It was the home where he and Elisia had lived, where Jack and Marta had been born and where James Martin had continued to live after Marta and Elisia's departure for America just before Elisia's death.

"I believe so, although I don't know the exact location. Should I go there to collect my goods?" I despised referring to Jack in this way, but apparently Mr. DeSoto felt caution was in order during our conversation.

"I believe you must. Mr. Wallace still hopes to be able to join you for your departure, but in the event that he cannot...you must make your way alone with your charge."

"Mr. DeSoto, about Mr. Wallace, is there anything that can be done for him? Is he being mistreated?"

"Nothing can be done, except for your prayers. I believe that he is not being mistreated at this time, simply detained for questioning. You are aware that the mission school has recently closed, and he has certain plans for his future of which you are aware?" He stated this as a question to me, and I nodded in response. I knew that Bertram Wallace was planning to leave Khutule for good at the same time as Jack and I.

"Of course," he continued, "one cannot be sure just what level of interest the government has in Mr. Wallace. He has not yet been charged with a crime. We are not sure how much they know about his involvement with your friend in America and with the reason you are here. If that were known, one cannot be confident for his safety. At this time," and he lowered his voice considerably, "we are simply hoping that this is one of the government's terror tactics to intimidate him into leaving the compound so that the government might easily take over the area. Mr. Wallace is greatly respected throughout the country for the work he has done for the last thirty years for the orphan children and among the people of the area. If he is openly forced to leave against his will or his compound is overrun, it will reflect badly on the government. The Minister of Information may be trying to avoid that. We simply do not know at this time. We must wait and see. God will protect him, if it is His divine will."

"Will you take me to the place where I can pick up...my package?"

"I am afraid that I cannot, to my great regret. I am a public figure, and it would arouse much suspicion if I were to be seen at that particular estate. I must remain in this country and therefore must also do what I can to protect my family and myself. I will be happy to arrange a way for you to go."

At that moment, I caught a glimpse of Jamul peeking around the door at the side of the building. When he knew that I saw him, he looked at me sheepishly but didn't try to hide further. He acted as if he was looking out for my well-being rather than simply spying on me. I now realized he must have been sent on this journey to help protect me. I was aware there could be other—more sinister—possibilities, but because both his treatment of me and his expression of faith seemed genuine, I was beginning to trust him. I motioned for him to join us.

Fredric DeSoto was introduced to Jamul Legassi. It was obvious that, although the two men probably were from different socioeconomic backgrounds, they met easily and openly. In fact, it was almost as if each knew the other from somewhere in the past but was unsure if the other remembered. They seemed, in some way, to connect.

Suddenly it dawned on me. From the time that I cleared customs in the airport until now, I had always traveled in the presence of someone who knew about my situation and was sympathetic to my cause. Without my foreknowledge, someone...most likely Sir James Martin Neville...had arranged for me to have contacts that he knew or knew him or in some way understood the need for my mission. First Jamul, then Fredric DeSoto, followed by the innkeeper Graham St. James, not to speak of Bert Wallace. Rather like a small band of angels, I had been passed from one to the other—safely so far.

But then I remembered Bert Wallace was in trouble, and Jack was stranded at his father's estate. I had to get to him and immediately. Again, I decided to come to the point.

"Gentlemen, how very grateful I am for your care and for the one who arranged for me to have such comforting contacts. At last I think I understand how I came to be in the company of each of you. Someday we will talk more of just how this all came about, but now we must do what we can for Jack."

My voice was now very low, and I looked straight at Jamul, praying that I was not wrong about his loyalties. As I spoke so quietly the men could hardly hear me, I now dropped all pretense and euphemisms.

"You do know about Jack, don't you, Jamul?"

"I do, Ms. Redmon, and how may I assist you now?"

Marcus DeSoto quickly reviewed for Jamul the unexpected turn of events detaining Bert Wallace indefinitely and leaving Jack in a dangerous position.

"I need to go to James Martin Neville's estate at once, Jamul. Can you take me there? There may be danger, and I understand if you cannot agree to go or if it would endanger your job. After all, you are an employee of the tour company, are you not?"

"I am, Miss, but my current assignment is to do whatever I can and need to do to assure your safety and that of Sir Neville's son. I will take you there at once."

Fredric DeSoto informed us that Jack was currently in the care of his old nanny, Obana, who had remained with her husband, Gele Milward, at James Martin's estate after Jack had been sent to Bert Wallace at the orphanage school. She and her husband lived in small quarters near the estate great house, and Jack might be hidden there or anywhere on the estate. Our task to find him could be easy or hard, depending on the circumstances we found when we arrived there.

"I will make excuses for you with the excavation team," Mr. DeSoto offered. "You will want to gather your belongings and be on your way as quickly as possible. May God be with you and protect you."

17

Disturbing Journey

The estate of the younger Sir Neville, the Sir Neville I knew, was located about two hours further north from the Soku Mount in a region once rich with coffee, vegetable, and cattle plantations. This fertile area had, at one time, fed much of Khutule and exported welcome food goods to neighboring countries. As we wound our way in Jamul's van down off of the plateau and back into flat savannah land once more, I began to see why the demise of this region was mourned worldwide.

We passed estate after estate that appeared to be unoccupied and in a state of ruin. It was also clear that some of the estates were not abandoned. A few appeared to prosper, in fact. I had heard that landowners sometimes made bargains with the government to keep their land by agreeing to pay high fees for the privilege of staying. While the farming operations were saved at these plantations, there was little or no profit left for the landholders and no lasting security.

There were other occupied estates appearing to be in as bad or worse condition as those left forsaken. Their decline was evident in the crumbling buildings, the unkempt grounds, the fallow fields, and the emaciated livestock. These were the outward signs I could see. Heaven help what was hidden.

These farms, according to Jamul, were inhabited by members of the notorious African Re-Unification Coalition, the same ARC that was making James Martin's life dangerous back in the States. It was this group that had killed James Martin's father and his father's second wife as they were leaving the gentleman's estate for church that Sunday morning more than twenty-five years ago.

I had read that the ARC was a loosely organized group made up of gangs of thugs and criminals mingled with enough self-proclaimed veterans of the war between Khutule and one of its neighboring countries in the early 1980s over boundaries and rich natural resources as to be considered slightly patriotic. They were not loyal to the existing government; indeed they were considered rebels and rivals for the allegiance of the people of Khutule.

ARC members also had the reputation of being indolent, calloused, dangerous, and above the rule of law. Properties that fell under their control—and there was an increasing number of estates to meet the fate—were sure to become sites of environmental and moral decay. Not only were the coalition's members not farmers and ranchers, but also they were, as a whole, infamous spreaders of waste and ruin. This group had contributed significantly to the failure of the government's land redistribution program.

We were an hour into our journey when we were slowed to a crawl behind a line of vehicles barely moving along the uncharacteristically busy highway. As the crawl turned into a stall, which turned into long minutes between movements at all, drivers emerged from their vehicles to exchange theories about the source of the delays. From information exchanged with oncoming cars we learned there was a roadblock up ahead manned by members of the ARC for the purpose of questioning or searching vehicles from both directions. The motive for the search was a mystery.

Not again. Please not again when I was getting so close.

Jamul turned to speak to me before our next slow move forward. "Ms. Redmon, I want you to climb over the seat quickly and sit very near to me in the front. You must not appear to be under the care of a chauffeur. We want it to appear as if you and I are in a close relationship. Please do not misunderstand me. I mean you no disrespect. But in the event that this search is in any way connected with your mission or for the purposes of harming foreigners, we want to lessen suspicion about your presence. Fortunately, there are sufficient instances of mixed-race couples today as to make our charade somewhat believable. Please hurry over, as I am beginning to see the source of the roadblock now."

I, of course, obeyed. I was not at all happy with this deception but less happy with the consequences that might arise if Jamul's suspicions about the roadblock were correct. I wasn't sure praying that a deception would work was appropriate, but I remembered David's act of feigned insanity before the Philistines in the Old Testament and figured if it was good enough for David it was good enough for me. I curled my legs under me casually, snuggled close to Jamul, resting my head on his shoulder, and closed my eyes as if napping.

"Good afternoon, sir." The voice was deceptively pleasant, but the eyes were hidden behind reflective sunglasses, and the gun was real. "What is your name, please?"

"Good afternoon," Jamul responded in his most agreeable tone. "I am Jamul Legassi from Lake Albert." Even though my eyes were closed, I could tell when he turned to me and took my hand. "And this is my companion, Ms.

Redmon." He patted my face lovingly.

I stirred a little but did not open my eyes.

"Your papers, sir," the voice ordered.

"Of course." I heard and felt Jamul scrambling in the glove box.

I pretended I was in contention for an Academy Award. "Darling," I murmured and stirred restlessly again, still without opening my eyes, "What is it? Why have we stopped?" My voice was delicately petulant. "Is something the matter? Is it time for dinner?"

"No, no, shhh, shhh," Jamul responded lovingly, patting my hand, which I had rested on his arm. "Everything is fine, my dear. Go back to sleep."

"What is your present destination?"

Jamul was skillfully nonchalant. "We are on holiday. We have been touring around Khutule, just enjoying the scenery. We have recently come from the Lukani Game Preserve. Quite exciting this time of year. Thought we would explore a bit around the savannah area. Are there any good cafés about, sir? We are a bit done in, I am afraid."

There was a pregnant pause, followed at last by, "There is a small inn north of here about twenty kilometers. Not a bad spot. Have a nice journey. You may pull away slowly."

We must have driven for about ten minutes before either of us moved or said anything. Finally, I felt Jamul relax, and I opened my eyes and sat upright. When I looked at him, sweat was pouring off of his face, which shone a glistening black.

When he spoke, his mouth sounded dry. "It was a miracle your papers were not required. I have no human explanation for why they were not. I had to give your real name in the anticipation that he would ask for them. We have been spared once more."

We both knew Who had spared us. Recognizing that, we chose to take a lighter slant.

"Jamul, you were magnificent."

"And the winner of the award for best actress goes to Ms. Jannia Redmon. Congratulations, Ms. Redmon!"

We laughed out of sheer nervous energy until we cried.

I moved to my side of the front seat and sat quietly as the kilometers ticked by, watching the late afternoon sun play off of the grasses of the savannah. We had just passed a particularly ravaged estate when a sudden jolt went through me, causing me to grasp the dash in front of me. I had seen something shocking.

"Jamul, please stop. Stop right here, now please," I pleaded with him.

"What is it? Are you ill?"

Jamul pulled over to the side of the roadway and halted the van.

"Now, please reverse until I tell you to halt." Something in my tone must have cued him to comply without question.

"Stop, stop here!"

Opening my door, I stepped out of the van. I stumbled over rutted ground as I made my way across what was the entrance to the wrecked estate. The once imposing decorative pillars on either side of the drive were thrown down and their stones scattered in the overgrown ditches nearby. I could still see well enough in the growing dusk to make out the dim outlines of a partially burned-out great house in the distance, one wing completely destroyed and the other partially caved in. The windows in the main section of the house were missing, and there was a black space where the front door had been.

I stood riveted by the scene before me while Jamul called my name in the background, urging me to return to the van. The desolation of this place affected me so profoundly that I couldn't remember why I wanted to stop so suddenly. Jamul's voice finally reached my consciousness, and I turned back toward the van. My foot hit something hard, and I almost fell. When I looked down to see what had caused my near mishap, there was a large flat stone lying partially in the ditch and jutting toward the shoulder of the road. It was jagged and broken but appeared to have something engraved on its side in large letters. I bent down to examine it more closely. The broken stone was what I had seen earlier.

Now I understood why this place should hold such emotion for me. The name chiseled on the broken stone, the stone that had once fit on one of the pillars beside the entrance to the estate, was NEVILLE. I was standing at the gateway to the former estate of Sir James Marcus Neville, once Prime Minister of Khutule and father of James Martin Neville. It was in this very drive that Sir James Marcus had met his death at the hands of the ARC. I could feel what had happened here, could see it in my mind's eye, and I began to sob uncontrollably.

Jamul took me by the arms and physically moved me into the back seat of the van. He quickly jumped into the driver's seat and pulled away from the former Neville residence. He didn't speak, and I sat in the back and cried. By the time he pulled into the parking lot of the little wayside inn and café, I had no more tears.

Jamul left me sitting in the van and went inside. He returned minutes later with food and drink.

"Ms. Redmon, we must get you feeling better before we reach Sir James Martin's estate. I was hoping that you would not notice his father's home, but you did. The past is done. You cannot help James Martin's father now, but you can help him and his son. What occurs in the next few hours is critical. Do you wish to continue?"

Jamul's brief and forthright talk followed by the frank question served to clear my head. As he spoke, I ate and drank and listened. I excused myself to wash my face in the restroom and returned to the car with a new attitude. The Lord had not given me the spirit of fear. Whatever happened, however I was tempted to feel, I didn't have to be fearful. I recalled that He had provided for me the spirits of power, love and soundness of mind. The words of 2 Timothy 1:7 were clear. I was here because of love, and I would need the power and the sound mind over the next couple of days. There was no time now for anguish over past events I could not change.

"Thank you, Jamul, for your help. Yes, I am ready to continue our journey." I could see his somewhat grave smile in the rearview mirror.

In less than an hour, Jamul slowed and began to prepare me for what was ahead of us. "We are approximately five kilometers from the estate of James Martin. We do not know what we will find upon our arrival. The people who are sheltering Jack may be alone, or the estate may have become occupied by the African Re-Unification Coalition or some other group. We must, therefore, proceed with great caution. I know a back entrance from a sidetrack that is not often used. We can enter the property there some distance from the main compound. The track, not much more than a path, is largely sheltered from the great house by outbuildings and hedges. I think perhaps we would be wise to enter there and hide the van as quickly as we can to proceed on foot."

It occurred to me then that Jamul was much more involved in and aware of the particulars of this operation than I had realized. He obviously knew James Martin's home estate intimately. I didn't know exactly how or why he was involved, but he had more than shown he was committed to my cause. I was now sure I wasn't on my own. I had an ally who was much more than a tour guide and driver.

18

Finding Jack

Jamul found the back entrance to James Martin's farm, nearly hidden and overgrown by the savannah scrub. The roadway was old, maybe centuries old, and so worn that the roadbed was a foot below the surrounding land. Still, it appeared to be unused and would be hard to follow in the growing dusk. It was all but dark when we found a tall clump of grasses, small trees, and a dilapidated shack behind which we could hide the van. From there on to the main compound, about one half of a kilometer, we had to find our way on foot.

We had one small low-beam flashlight Jamul always kept in the vehicle for emergencies. Besides that, all the light we had were the moon and a cigarette lighter I had found on the floor of the back seat of the van. Jamul directed me to leave the small handgun I had not been forced to use during the riot in Limbarne hidden where I found it after he learned I was not an experienced gun user. I suspected he carried his hidden on his person.

We had to be careful and quiet as we made our way along the dirt track, which took time, and it was about half an hour before we began to come close to the cluster of buildings that made up the main estate compound. There were numerous barns and outbuildings, several small dwellings and the large, two-story, rambling great house. A high chain-link fence with barbed wire across the top surrounded the compound.

Following Jamul's lead, our immediate target was to reach one of the small dwellings behind the great house that was home to Obana and Gele Milward. I learned from Jamul that the old couple had been with the Neville family for decades, first at the estate of Sir James Marcus Neville and later here at his son, Sir James Martin Neville's, home. Obana had once been James Martin's nanny. She loved him obsessively and would protect his son, Jack, with the same fierceness that she had guarded his father years ago. Gele was as quiet and retiring, as his wife was sociable and mischievous. He possessed a strength and inner confidence that had carried them both past two lifetimes of triumphs and tragedies. The fact that they were both now well into their seventies did not diminish their presence and convictions.

Hearing about the couple who currently sheltered Jack gave me hope that he was well and within our reach. I had been warned to expect anything or anyone at the compound in James Martin's absence, but I still held out anticipation that we would find the place quiet and unspoiled. Slipping silently past the first buildings without encountering anything unusual brought us no small relief.

It was well past full dark now, and as quiet as only the deep savannah can be under its blanket of millions of stars. The moon was waning and only offered a weak light making intermittent use of the flashlight a necessity. Apart from the usual night sounds to which I had become accustomed on our walk in, there were no other sounds coming from the buildings. The great house was dark, and it lay like a great sleeping animal at the front of the compound. Dim lights glowed in two or three of the smaller dwellings and from one tall but faint area light, but the rest of the compound was dark and quiet.

I felt Jamul's hand on my shoulder and turned to look at him in the dim light. We could no longer afford to use the flashlight. We had come to the length of fence directly behind the largest of the small dwellings visible behind the great house. He motioned, and I took it to indicate that Obana and Gele Milward lived in the nearest cottage. The fence prevented further movement, and its height and the barbs at the top were a daunting obstacle. Apparently they did not deter Jamul, who slipped a small object from his pocket and with quick snips opened the smallest of passageways at the bottom of the fence. He slid soundlessly under and held up the jagged edges for me as I did the same. He replaced the fencing in such as way as to defy anyone to notice the breach.

As we neared the front stoop of the cottage, I could hear muffled sounds from within as if from a radio. We had decided that, since there was no obvious evidence the estate had been occupied by any outsiders, I should be the first to speak to the couple inside. As a woman, I might appear less threatening.

I stepped up and knocked lightly on the door. There was no response. After waiting for at least a minute, I knocked again, more loudly this time. Instantly, I heard the radio sounds cease. Footsteps shuffled inside, and after some time, the door opened an inch for an eye to peer out at me.

"Mr. Milward? Gele Milward? I am looking for Obana and Gele Milward. I am a friend, and I need to speak with Mr. or Mrs. Milward."

The door closed. I looked at Jamul, not sure what to do next. We could hardly storm the home of the elderly couple. What if they were not alone? What if hostile intruders who had learned about the presence of Jack were holding them? Or what if it were not the Milwards themselves who had greeted me but rather members of the ARC?

As I turned to step away from the door, crouching into a position to flee, the door opened just enough for a plump, stooped, white-haired black woman to walk through. She closed it behind her.

"I am Obana Milward." Her tone was strong, and her stance was challenging in spite of her obviously advanced age. She placed her hands on her hips and waited.

"Mrs. Milward." I lowered my voice. "Is it safe for us to speak freely?"

"It is safe," was all she said, without explanation.

I had to get right to the point regardless of the consequences, as time was of the essence. "I am Jannia Redmon. I am a friend of Sir James Martin Neville. I have come from America to escort his son back to the United States. We have received information that he is with you. This is my guide, Mr. Jamul Legassi. He is also acquainted with Sir Neville."

She met my eye contact with a level stare that did not shift, except to give Jamul a quick appraisal. She didn't speak for many moments, as seemed to be her way. I tried not to fidget, or look away or show the impatience I felt. She looked at me as if she could actually see into my soul. After enough of a wait to make me quite uncomfortable, she spoke.

"I believe you, Miss. You have good eyes. Your eyes are honest. Mr. Legassi, I do remember you as a visitor here from some time ago. Master Jack is with us. He is sleeping. My Gele is not well just now. What do you wish us to do?"

Jamul had decided that we should move Jack in the night, rather than by day. There was less chance of meeting a roadblock or encountering those hostile to us. We relayed our plan of moving Jack on to the small city of Mozuru where we would wait for the day to meet our plane, hoping and praying that his missionary guardian, Bertram Wallace, could join us.

There was a problem. Jack had sprained his ankle during the wild rush to help him escape from the mission compound when it was overtaken by government troops. Although Obana thought there was no break, walking was most difficult for him. We had planned to slip Jack out of the cottage and walk away from the compound down the dark path to where our vehicle was hidden. This news would necessitate Jamul moving the car as close to the cottage as possible.

Jamul started off in the darkness while Obana and I moved inside to ready Jack for the journey. We found Gele Milward sitting at the kitchen table, reading from a large Bible. When his wife introduced us, he greeted me politely and asked me a strange question.

"Miss, do you know the name of Sir Neville's new wife?"

The question took me aback. New wife? Had they learned something I didn't know? *Please, no!* Had James Martin married Branda VanderCross during my absence and somehow gotten word to the Milwards, his trusted servants?

My mind could not imagine that possibility and threw it aside as I answered. "Mr. Milward, I am not aware that Sir James Martin Neville has a new, a second, wife. Sir James Marcus had two wives, but I believe his son has had only one. She was Jack's mother, and her name was Elisia. She is not living."

"Bless you, child," the old man answered. "My Obana judges people by what she can see behind their eyes. I had to have more proof, more facts. You have spoken correctly. It seems that our Master James Martin has sent you."

I learned that Obana and Gele had put Jack to bed on a cot inside of a small pantry entered from a door in the kitchen where we were talking. In front of the door, they had pulled their small eating table, where Gele was now seated. They had cleverly hung a large, well-worn Khutulen flag behind the table to form a distracting backdrop and help hide the outline of the pantry door. I would never have expected the smaller room was there. It had no windows and was difficult to detect from outside of the home.

I helped Obana move the light table and chairs, and we pushed the hanging flag aside and entered the small pantry. It was lit by a long candle in a tin sconce hanging on the back of the only door. There was little light and only enough room to walk carefully around the cot upon which Jack lay sleeping. Jack was sprawled on his back with one arm raised above his head. He was covered with a quilt that had slipped off of his left leg, showing the bandage that Obana had wrapped around his ankle.

As I bent to get a closer look at the face of the child that had brought me to Africa, I almost exclaimed aloud. His face was that of James Martin almost twenty-five years earlier. The black hair cut below the ears, the determined set of his mouth. This boy seemed very familiar to me, though I was seeing him for the first time.

"He is so like his father," I whispered to Obana.

"That he is," she said with a sad smile. "And I am going to lose him too, just like I have lost his father."

As I turned to look at her tearing eyes, we were both startled by a loud sound coming from beyond the kitchen. I instinctively grabbed for Obana's soft hand as we recognized the sound when it came again. It was a knock on the front door. Not really a knock, but a pounding that became more insistent by the moment. Then we felt the door to the pantry closing and heard the soft scrape of the table being pulled back into place.

"Gele," Obana whispered loudly through the closed door, but there was no answer as we heard him shuffle out of the kitchen. Our breathing seemed to cease as we strained to hear what was going on at the front of the cottage.

The sounds of a loud voice reached us, but we couldn't make out the words or recognize the speaker. It was not Gele's voice and didn't sound like Jamul. Obana awkwardly started around the cot toward the pantry door when I reached out and took her arm firmly.

"No, Obana," I pleaded. "It may be dangerous out there!"

"I must go to my Gele" was all she answered as she listened intently to the direction of the voices and then slowly pushed against the pantry door. I moved to help her, and without much effort we were able to move the table enough for her ample form to fit through the opening. She placed her hand against my chest and put her finger to her lips in warning for me to stay put. The door silently closed behind her, and I could barely hear the table being moved into place on the other side.

I blew out the candle and listened.

The muffled voices continued for a while, indistinguishable, and then grew louder and clearer. Whoever was in the house with the Milwards was coming near the kitchen. The night was cool, but I found I was sweating in the small room. Jack stirred on the cot below me, but only briefly. I could see nothing in the blackness of the pantry but a thin line of light below the door.

"Mrs. Milward," a male voice spoke rather loudly and impatiently, "we have received word that you may have a certain young boy in your care for the last day or two. We have reason to believe he was brought here from Reverend Bertram Wallace's orphanage and school. While we are not absolutely sure about who this child is or even where he is, we need to question him. He may have important information about a man we must contact immediately."

It was Gele's soft old voice that responded. "Sir, you may look about our home as you please. My wife and I live alone. We do not receive many visitors these days. We have no children, and certainly not a young son. How old did you say the boy was?"

Gele Milward was choosing to misunderstand the information given by the intruder. It served to make the man more impatient.

"Mr. Milward, I am not speaking about your son. Do you have a boy in your care? If you are hiding him here, it would be best if you show me now. I can only say the word and my soldiers outside will not be kind to your home or you as they search it." His threat was menacing. I didn't need to be able to see his face to understand that he meant what he said and could command what he pleased.

Apparently the Milwards were undaunted. I next heard Obana's voice, firm and clear in its delivery.

"Mr. Rebel Officer, please understand that my husband is not a well man. He is well along in years, as am I. We have gone some fifty-five years without children in this house, and I suppose we are most too old to begin having children now. We are beyond putting much effort into the affairs of others. We try to keep mostly to ourselves. I would be most pleased to offer you a cup of tea and a look around our home." She finished this speech as firmly as she began with no hint that the visitor intimidated her in at all.

"Thank you, no tea." The visitor, who must be an ARC member by how Obana addressed him, responded abruptly. "But I will take a look through your rooms."

I could hear heavy footsteps as he tromped around the kitchen, opened the door to the small side porch, closed it again, and tromped into the hall toward the other parts of the house.

I had begun to pray fervently for the safety of the Milwards, and for Jamul, who was somewhere out in the darkness. He had left to get the van, unaware of the impending visit, and now who knows where he was or what may have happened to him? I prayed for Jack's safety, for the Milwards', and for mine. I prayed the intruder's eyes would be blinded to our hiding place and that he would be convinced the old couple was, and had been, alone.

Since the house was small, it didn't take the man long to see every room. He was soon back in the kitchen where the Milwards waited, most likely standing near the table opposite where I was hiding.

"Do you have a loft or attic? Is there a cellar here?"

"No, sir," Gele responded, "just the rooms here on the ground floor. We would have much trouble reaching an attic room anyway. You are most welcome to continue your search."

Then I heard heavy footsteps coming closer to the door behind which I was hiding. I held my breath but couldn't stop the thunderous drumming of my heart. And what if...what if Jack made a sound in his sleep?

"Such a nice flag," the searcher said, no doubt pointing to the Khutulen flag above the table that covered the door to my hiding place. I heard a thudding sound very close to where I stood. My mouth went dry with fear. He was tapping on the door through the flag. Was he trying to see if the flag covered something? I strained to hear whether the thuds sounded hollow.

"You must be quite loyal to your country?" There was more than a hint of sarcasm as the man spoke scornfully to the elderly couple. I remembered uncomfortably that the ARC was at dangerous odds with the government of Khutule. Loyalty to Khutule could be interpreted as trouble for the ARC. The rebel tapped some more.

"Yes, sir. I served in the military for my country when I was a young man." It was Gele again, and there was obvious pride in his voice. It was lost on this man.

"That must have been during the late colonial period. This is a new day for a new type of army." The intruder answered with disdain as if in dismissal of Khutule's past and Gele's with it.

Obana spoke, maybe to divert the man from his explorations. "Mr. Rebel Soldier, wherever this lost boy is and whoever he is supposed to be, I trust it will all come to a good ending. It worries me to see young people in some kind of trouble. You would have thought he was reared correctly by the reverend."

I realized she was choosing to act simple-minded about the seriousness of the situation facing her. It worked. The tapping on the door in front of me stopped.

"The other homes on this compound are dark. Who lives here on this farm?" It was the voice of the rebel officer again.

"The big house is unoccupied, sir. The owner is out of the country for a few months. One small house is home to a deaf and dumb man who keeps things clean about. A young man and his wife with their tiny infant live in the other. He does repair jobs around the farm; his wife sometimes bakes us a cake. She is a fine lady but a bit young to have a child, I think."

There was a long pause, and I strained to hear what would happen next. To me, Gele and Obana appeared believable, but I wasn't the judge. Finally I heard the man speak.

"You have satisfied me for the present that you do not have the child in your house. My men will search the barns and outbuildings. They have been ordered to harm nothing for the time being. I will place a guard outside just to be sure. I hope you have been forthcoming with me. Good evening."

It was a good five minutes before I heard Obana's voice, whispering to me through the door, "Miss, he is gone for now. Thank God for the thick wooden door. It is not safe for you to come out yet. Sit down, if you can, and I will come for you in a while."

I heard her talking to her husband, rather loudly, as if he were deaf himself. "Old Gele, my dear. We must go to bed now. These bones are tired, and the hour is late."

With that, I heard them rise from the table. I imagined the muffled sounds I was hearing were Obana turning off the lights, locking the kitchen door, and shuffling down the hall with Gele to their small bedroom beyond the kitchen.

All was quiet and dark for a long time, maybe a half hour, maybe an hour; it was hard to tell. I couldn't see anything, not even a light under the door. I was exhausted and uncomfortable, sitting cramped beside Jack's cot on the floor. I could hear his quiet breathing and prayed he would stay asleep until our dilemma was resolved. I knew that, with a guard outside and Jamul missing, I might be in the pantry for a long time. Although I was weary beyond words, to sleep now would have been foolish, so I contented myself with resting my eyes and continuing with my prayers.

I must have dozed after all because a rattle of the door handle startled me to awareness.

"Miss, you must be very quiet. I am opening the door a bit to give you some air. The guard is out by the gate in our yard. I think it best you stay hidden for now."

Just then, there was a light scratching on the screen of the side door to the kitchen. It was so quiet we almost missed it. It could easily have been a cat. It came again and lasted longer. We waited, and it happened for a third time.

"Obana!" I whispered.

"Shhh! Wait," she crooned, and I heard her shuffle quietly toward the door from which the sound came. Then I heard the lock move slowly back and felt the cool night air from underneath the flag curtain. It was agony to be able to hear but not see what was going on in the little kitchen. "Mr. Lagassi," I heard her whisper, "come inside quickly."

"I was on my way to move the car when I noticed lights entering the compound," he whispered. "I crept back to look around and saw the military vehicles. I stayed hidden as they searched the grounds. I'm sorry. I was outnumbered and afraid I would only make more trouble for you if I were seen. I would have tried to stop them, had they tried to take anyone away."

The voice was Jamul's.

"We had an official visit from an ARC officer," Obana explained. "A guard is posted outside.

"I saw him. He's leaning on the front gate. The others appeared to leave, at least for now. What did they want?"

Obana explained, concluding with, "There must have been someone from the mission, or perhaps a visitor, who suspected Sir Neville's son had been at the mission compound and was being sent here to his home. That someone must have been a friend to the rebels. Sir Neville is hated by the ARC, and the loathing runs very deep."

"And Ms. Redmon?"

"Ms. Redmon and Master Jack are still hidden."

"I'm fine, Jamul," I whispered. "What shall we do? Is there any way we can get Jack to safety without endangering the Milwards?"

There was silence. Then I heard Jamul's voice very close on the other side of the table from me.

"It will not be without risk, but we can try. The guard seems a bit casual in my opinion. I could distract him, and you and Jack might be able to slip away in the darkness out of this side door."

I didn't relish Jamul's plan because it would further jeopardize his life. Apparently Obana didn't either, for I heard her protest.

"Mr. Lagassi, any distraction from you might lead to your arrest or death. It would cast great suspicion on this house. We must find a way out of this that would not cause doubt in the mind of the guard. He must never know the three of you were present. It must seem as if only my old Gele and I have been here all the time. Jack's ankle is sprained. Ms. Redmon will need your help with him and finding their way in the darkness to your car. How far of a distance is it?"

When I told her, I heard her whisper, "Lord, help these friends just now. They need your strength and cunning, Lord, for what lies ahead."

Silence followed again for some moments, and we both knew Obana's active mind was working on the dilemma.

"I will take the guard some hot tea and apple cream tarts. He will not be able to resist, and it will look innocent enough. When I am outside, Mr. Jamul, you will take the Miss and Master Jack and flee through this door. You cannot see it from the front of the cottage due to the shape of the porch."

"No, Obana," I pleaded, "this puts you at risk. I cannot allow..."

The wrinkled and motherly old woman cut me off quickly. "There is no time for arguments. This deed, this distraction, will come from me." Her firm voice, heard only in a whisper, held a note of finality in it. To protest further would be to risk disrespect to an elder.

"First we must awaken Jack," she continued. "I will do that so as not to startle him. He has been forewarned that he may have to do things quickly without question. He is aware he may endure things unpleasant to him for the sake of his safety."

It was still dark in the cottage, the only light filtering in from the dim outside lights of the compound. Obana moved surprisingly quickly and soon had the table out of the way and the flag pulled aside. Feeling her way along, she knelt by Jack and turned a small flashlight toward his cot.

"Master Jack. This is your old Obana speaking. Wake up, sir. It is time to leave with some new friends."

Jack moaned softly and became quiet again. Obana spoke once more with the same authority I had heard previously.

"Master Jack, come awake. You must now go to your father with your new friends." She shook him gently several times, and he began to come around. When he would have spoken aloud about why it was so dark, Obana's "Shhhh, my son," swiftly silenced him.

"Obana, my leg hurts." Jack sat up on the cot.

"I know, my lovey. It will for a while."

"What new friends? Who are they? I don't wish to leave you. Where is Mr. Bert? I am not going with anyone except my father or Mr. Bert." He sounded tired, querulous, and a bit arrogant.

Obana met his challenge head-on.

"Master Jack, Mr. Wallace has problems of his own right now, and so does Sir Neville. It's time you behave like a man. I need you to be very strong and use good judgment. There is danger about, and you will need to be most cooperative and obedient to help us. Are you willing to do that?"

Jack caught her tone and the seriousness of her message. "Yes, ma'am. I can do that."

"I knew that you could," she responded with love in her voice. "After all, you are your father's son. I am very proud of both of you."

"I worry about Mr. Bert. Who else is here?"

"Jack, this is Ms. Redmon. The gentleman is Mr. Legassi. They are both friends of your father. Ms. Redmon is from America, and she has come to take you there to be with your father and your little sister. We hope that Mr. Wallace will be able to leave Khutule with you. We just do not know yet. I want you to go with these people. They will do their best to protect you. Think of your father waiting for you to come to him. That will give you strength."

"Yes, Obana. I am curious about meeting my sister. When do we leave?"

"You leave here tonight. I will miss you, but you are not safe here. Mr. Legassi and Ms. Redmon will lead you out to their vehicle. They will take you

131

somewhere to get ready to leave this country and go to America. You must obey everything they say at once. You can trust them as I do. They want to help you. You must not trust anyone else."

"Can you come with me, Obana?"

"I cannot, my child, but God will go with you. He will make you brave, if you let Him. I will miss you, but I will be here praying for you."

"I will be brave, Obana. Please tell Gele that I will miss him, too."

"The time has come for you to go. May the Heavenly Father go with you all."

I could hear the emotion in the old woman's voice, as she understood that this was very likely the last time she would see a member of the Neville family this side of Heaven. But she remained strong as she prepared Jack for departure. In the darkened kitchen, she managed to put his few belongings, what little had been sent from the mission, into a sturdy bag along with some biscuits for us all. As Jamul slipped out the kitchen door to make sure all was well, Obana prepared for the diversion of the guard.

A thermos of hot tea and a couple of apple cream tarts were placed in a small tin. Obana bade us good-bye with quick embraces and a whispered prayer. She then turned on the light to her front stoop and opened the door, carrying the refreshments with her on a small tray.

"Stop at once!" we heard the guard order. "What are you doing?" He sounded young and a bit unsure of what to do.

"Young man, it is only old Obana. I thought you might be cold and tired out here by yourself for so long. I just wanted to bring you something..."

I couldn't hear any more, for by this time, we were on our way. We had slipped undetected out of the kitchen door and off of the small porch into the side yard, out of sight of the guard. We were moving as quickly as we were able, given the darkness and the need to make no noise. It was possible the front guard was not the only one left at the compound to watch.

19

Narrow Escape

Our going was made more difficult by Jack's sprained ankle. He had to go the first several yards on his own, just holding my hand in the darkness, and I could feel him limping valiantly beside of me. Jamul was leading the way, but staying near, as we could not use a flashlight at all this close to the buildings.

We finally cleared the open yard of the compound and reached the high fence. Jamul again led the way under, then pulled Jack and me after him, replacing the fencing again to hide our exit. We moved into the tall grasses of the savannah. We were going to try to reach the van, almost a mile away, by cutting directly across the savannah. It might be safer. There was no path, but following Jamul's small compass we would cut through the grasses until we emerged on the dirt road, perhaps a quarter of a mile from the cottage. From there, we could follow the road to where we hid the van.

There was always the thought that the rebel visitors had discovered the van and were guarding it, too. If I had come to that realization, so certainly had Jamul, but nothing was said to Jack. When we reached the deep savannah and greater cover from grassy clumps around us, Jack gave a small moan and I felt his hand pull out of mine as he sank to the ground.

I knelt down beside of him.

"Jack," I whispered in his ear, "Are you in pain?"

"Yes, Ms. Redmon," he whispered back. "My ankle throbs terribly. I am trying to keep going. Really I am."

Jamul turned back to us and stooped to hear Jack's explanation for the delay. He rummaged in Jack's bag, finding a soft T-shirt. With his pocketknife, he cut the shirt into strips and bound them tightly around Jack's ankle, something Obana had forgotten to do.

"Now, young man, let's see if this helps. If it is still too painful, I will carry you."

"That will not be necessary, sir. I will be fine." He was trying hard to be brave, and we were able to move faster. Jack still limped but did not complain.

After about twenty minutes of picking our way through the grassy stretch, sometimes stumbling as we searched for good footing in the near total darkness, we came to the edge of the sunken dirt road. Jamul pulled us down into the grass covering and quietly cautioned us to be silent and watchful as he explored the road ahead. The going would be easier, but we would have little cover.

Jack and I waited and rested on the ground for some time until we saw Jamul's dark form appear in front of us.

Squatting again, he whispered, "It appears that the road is clear. I cannot be perfectly sure. Follow me, but stay close to the edge of the road. If anything occurs, move quickly into the grass, crawl as far as you can, and lie quietly." I felt his hand on my shoulder in reassurance. I had been following the Bible's command to pray without ceasing.

We moved onto the edge of the road. Clearly Jack was tired, but I knew he had to walk on his own as long as he was able. We made our way slowly along the road uneventfully for some time. I was beginning to feel as if we might make it to the van undetected after all when an unearthly sound arose from the savannah near us—a sound so utterly terrible and unnatural that it literally made my flesh crawl.

It was a guttural growl followed by a screeching bark, and it came from close by. The noise was soon answered by a similar cry from a little further away and then a chorus of howls. It sounded like demons from the very pit.

I was completely frozen where I stood. My brain spun with conflicting plans to grab Jack and run, sink down and give up, or simply begin to scream myself to drown out the awful sounds. I was so disoriented by the continued din that I covered my ears to blot it out. Suddenly, I felt two sets of arms go around me, holding me close and urgently whispering my name. I managed to calm myself enough to focus on what Jamul and Jack were frantically trying to tell me.

"It's only a pack of wild dogs. They are not after us." That was from Jamul, who shook me lightly as he spoke to ensure I was concentrating on his words.

Jack's reassurance followed. "It's okay, Ms. Redmon, really. They are only dogs. I hear them all the time at the mission. They travel in packs at night. They just sound horrible, but rarely attack humans."

My relief must have been tangible because they both hugged me simultaneously.

"I'm fine. I'm okay now. Please, let's go," I whispered back.

Jamul squeezed my hand and started off ahead of us again.

Taking Jack's hand, I move forward at a fast pace. I soon found that Jack couldn't keep up and slowed my steps. Surely we must be nearing where we hid the van. I felt Jack stumble and then fall, pulling me down on the dry, rough soil with him.

"Sorry, Ms. Redmon. I cannot go on. It hurts too much." The twelve-year-old had tears in his voice.

"I know, Jack. You've been wonderful. Jamul will be here to help you in a minute."

Indeed Jamul did appear a short time later, having scouted the roadway ahead. "Jack, you have helped us very much with your bravery. We are almost there. You must crawl onto my back and pretend that I am your fine steed."

I was amazed that Jamul could make a joke in our situation, but Jack obeyed immediately. He was tall and his legs dangled to Jamul's knees, but Jamul didn't seem to be bothered by the extra weight. We moved on much more quickly than before.

I sensed after some time that Jamul was slowing down, and soon he halted altogether. I thought it was to rest, but he slipped Jack down onto the roadbed and, putting his hand on my shoulder once more, pushed me down beside Jack.

"We are quite near where we hid the van. Wait here and be still while I check to see if anyone is near. If you hear anything, crawl into the undergrowth and remember what I said to do."

We were glad to have a brief respite and sprawled low in the dirt, ready to crawl away quickly if the need arose. I was so tired that I was tempted to close my eyes and let myself drift into sleep. That was much too dangerous, I knew, but still it was enticing.

At first I was relieved that Jamul didn't return quickly to lead us to the van. Then after a while I began to be concerned when there were no sounds indicating he was moving back toward us. The concern turned to overt alarm when at least an hour had elapsed. Just when I was on the brink of taking Jack and moving toward the van myself, we heard a soft crunch of shoes on sand marking Jamul's return. I found there was good reason to be uneasy.

Crouching on the roadbed close to us so we could hear what he said, he told us chilling news. While the van was still parked where we left it, hidden behind a large clump of grasses and a structure just off of the roadway, Jamul had seen the flickering lights of a large campfire and dark figures moving about it across a sizeable field about a quarter of a kilometer from the van.

Apparently a detail of men accompanying the ARC officer was left on the farm to observe from a distance. The camp was located where its occupants could oversee the comings and goings on the main road to the estate. Hopefully the rebel soldiers didn't know about this back road on which we were lying. But if they did, who knew what would await us as we returned to the main highway?

After our rest, Jack felt he could go further on his ankle. Jamul suggested that we might want to spread out so we would form smaller silhouettes in the event that someone chanced to notice. Perhaps we would be mistaken for animals or scrub trees. As we neared the van, Jack's ankle finally gave out, and Jamul again carried him on his back.

Jamul was afraid to start the van's engine so near to the soldiers' camp. The sound would carry and might be noticed. There was nothing to do but have Jack steer while Jamul and I pushed. Jamul insisted he could do it alone, but I was adamant. The site at which the dirt road joined the main highway was further from where the troops watched, and we might be able to pass for regular roadway traffic once we reached the highway. The going was slow and difficult. Naturally we couldn't use lights, and more than once Jack steered us into the tall grass on the side of the track.

Finally, when I felt I couldn't go another step, Jamul signaled for me to stop pushing, and he ran alongside to have Jack apply the brakes. We were less than a hundred meters from the highway. We waited, watched, and listened carefully for any sight or sound that would indicate the intersection was being watched. Five minutes or more must have elapsed before we were satisfied no watchers were waiting for us.

To make the van not to appear to have emerged from near the estate, we pushed it onto the highway and away from the soldiers' camp for several meters with no headlights. Jamul then got behind the wheel while Jack and I crouched on the floor of the back seat. Jamul started the engine and drove back in the direction from which we had originally come and away from the estate for some distance before finally turning on the lights. At a turnout about five kilometers down the highway, he reversed the van and began the return journey past the estate. It was not our route of choice, but this was the only viable highway to our destination, the small city of Mozuru, where Jack and I were to meet the plane out of Khutule in two days.

Jack and I stayed out of sight as Jamul maneuvered the van toward the estate's main gateway. As he neared the gate, he kept busy by giving us a running commentary on what he could see. The ARC soldiers were still in evidence at the entrance to James Martin's home, but he drove us past with no obvious moves on the rebels' part to flag us down. We were afraid to celebrate. This seemed too easy.

And then Jamul's voice took on an excited tone as he cautioned us to stay down and out of sight. A large transport vehicle had come up behind us with its lights on bright. It seemed inevitable that we would be pulled to the side of the road or maybe even forced off of it. Jack and I gripped hands and crouched lower to the floorboard.

I began to plan what I would say to the rebel militia...if we lived long enough to be questioned. It was hard to believe that this might be the end of my journey. At least this way, I wouldn't have to face James Martin and explain why I had not been able to free his son.

None of us talked. I'm not sure we even breathed. After several of the longest minutes of my life, we heard the large lorry drive around us. Jamul described what was happening as he watched the truck race away ahead of us down the road. The relief in his voice was audible when he told us it was safe to get up off of the floor.

I climbed back up to sit on the back seat next to Jack, breathing an audible prayer of thank you and brushing the dirt off my clothes and combing the grasses out of my hair with my fingers. When I turned to look at Jack, his eyes told me that his ordeal had far exceeded mine.

20

Reluctant Young Stranger

It was nearly two o'clock in the morning when we came to the outskirts of Mozuru. I was so tired I couldn't think straight and had fallen asleep several times already just to jerk awake whenever the van swerved. Jack slept without waking, his head against the corner of the seat and door. After driving around the sleeping city for some time, Jamul pulled in to a small hotel that still had a light on in its lobby. He registered us for two rooms as a family with one child, and we took only what we needed for the night from the vehicle and stumbled to our rooms.

Jamul and I settled Jack in Jamul's room, only pulling his shoes off and checking his ankle before covering him up. He cautioned me to lock my door securely and open it for no one. I suspect I would truly have slept through any intruder's visit.

I stood before the bathroom mirror and hardly recognized myself. I was dirty and smeared with sand and a brownish-red substance I hoped was soil. My hair was matted, and my eyes were dark against skin pale and puffy from exhaustion. I splashed water onto my face, took off my shoes, and collapsed onto the bed.

It was late afternoon when I awoke. My whole body ached from the activities of the last evening. A hot shower helped some, but not nearly enough. There were bruises and scratches on my arms and legs, and I had pulled a muscle in my back. I was also seriously hungry, but not being familiar with either the hotel or the city, I was not about to go out to forage on my own. A quiet knock on my door and the reassuring voice of Jamul from the hallway were welcome sounds.

"Good afternoon, Jannia." We were now long past the formality of *Ms. Redmon*. "I trust you are feeling rested. Jack is in our room eating just about everything the limited room service offers. I am guessing you are also in need of nourishment?"

"You have food? Close by?" We joined Jack at his private picnic laid out on a cart by his bedside. I noticed that he was clean, his newly wrapped ankle was raised onto pillows, and his appetite was unhindered. We didn't talk for some time, but communicated our satisfaction by the audible sounds of our munching. When we finally concluded our feast with a Khutulen version of chocolate cake, I felt I wouldn't need to eat again until Thanksgiving. And thanksgiving described our state of mind as we discussed our recent escapades at the Neville estate.

Jack asked a lot of questions about what had happened to Bertram Wallace at the mission and about the events at Obana and Gele's home. He also wanted to know about me, about who I was and why I had come for him instead of his father. I was beginning to see that he was advanced for his age of twelve.

Jamul addressed most of his questions directly and openly. Jack appeared to know Jamul from the past and to trust his forthright responses. Jamul didn't hide from him the seriousness of Bert Wallace's detention by the government officials nor did he minimize the threat posed by the ARC at the Neville estate. Jamul warned about the continued need for heightened caution since there seemed to be some reason why both the government and the ARC were on the alert.

The questions about me were asked with an uncharacteristic touch of petulance, much like a younger child would pout to show displeasure. I was willing to respond to his interrogation and decided to follow Jamul's lead and be direct. "I am a friend of your father and sister, Jack. I know your great-grandmother, GranJuel, also, though I don't think she would call me a friend."

"Why is that?" His eyes were the same color as his father's, and I just realized it. I struggled to keep my concentration as I answered him. It had been hard not to think about James Martin any more than necessary on this trip, but I had done rather well. Until that moment.

"I'm not sure, Jack. Perhaps she's afraid of losing Marta. They have been together for a long time. Maybe I make her think of her granddaughter Elisia, your mother, who died. There could be many reasons. She has not shared her thinking with me. I just think she sees me as an outsider in your family."

"How do you know my father?"

"I met him somewhat by accident when he was injured and needed help. Marta found me and led me to him. I couldn't help him that time, but later he did ask me to do something for him. We have been friends since then." There was no need now to explain how I had followed Banolo's taxi to the apartment and all of the details since that day.

"Why did you come for me? Why did he not come himself?"

Something in Jack's repeated peevishness about this subject bothered me.

I knew his guardian, Bert, had not left him in the dark about the danger his father would encounter if he came home to Khutule. Was Jack truly asking for his own information, or was he somehow testing me to find out what place I would play in his father's life? I didn't mind responding to anything that was asked in truth. I found I was less willing to play along with adolescent games at this point. I had to be sure of what Jack knew and did not know of his heritage.

"Jack, has Mr. Wallace ever talked to you about how important your father's family has been to this country's past? Do you know the story of how your great-grandfather came to the land that is now Khutule? Do you understand how important your grandfather Neville was in the political history of this place?"

Jack looked at me steadily with his clear blue eyes flashing. "Mr. Bert told me a lot about my family, but I was not allowed to talk about it with anyone but him, not even my friends."

"That's understandable. He was protecting you. Do you know what your father does now and why he is in America?"

"He went to play in a benefit concert. He is a famous pianist. I was never allowed to discuss him either, except in private with Mr. Bert."

"Do you know why? I mean, why you couldn't talk openly about your family or your father?"

There was a long silence while Jack alternately looked at me and looked down at his empty dessert plate. I rose and turned on the bedside radio to a station playing some version of African jazz. We needed background noise. I returned to my seat and simply waited while Jamul sat silent, watching us both. He seemed to sense this might be some sort of showdown that needed to happen between Jack and me.

"Mr. Bert said that people are trying to hurt or kill him." His answer was very quietly spoken.

"Who is? Do you know what people? And why?" I made him continue.

I could tell Jack didn't want to discuss this topic and especially not with me. But I couldn't let him avoid the subject. The way he faced the reality of his family situation might be critical to his survival and mine as well. It also might be crucial to his relationship with his father when they were reunited. Jack had to be realistic about his place in the Neville family and about why his father was unable to come in person to take him to the States.

"Talk to me about it, Jack," I prompted, my voice lowered and quiet as a model to him.

"Mr. Bert said the President of Khutule thinks my father wants to become

President, and the government is afraid of him because of that. He also told me that the ARC hates him because of what my grandfather did to them a long time ago. He said that my father even has enemies who followed him to America." Jack's voice was now as low as mine had been. "That's not really true, is it?"

"Don't you believe Mr. Bert?"

"I don't know."

I waited.

"Yes."

"Then you do understand why your father is not here now. You also understand why you couldn't live at home and you had a different last name while at the mission?"

"Yes." This time the response was a whisper barely audible above the music, but I had heard what I needed to hear. I was convinced Jack understood the situation clearly. No more games from him now. His father would have to fill in the emotional blanks with Jack. It was my job to help get him home.

"Then we are a team to get you to the States to be with your family for good. Are you in agreement with that?"

I took his nod for a *Yes*.

Jamul and I talked about moving to another hotel for the remaining three days Jack and I would spend in the country. We had picked this one simply because it was still open so late into last evening. We were about fifteen miles from the airport, and we would have to travel through the city to reach it. Perhaps we should move to a closer hotel to make things easier the day of our departure.

In the end we concluded that we would stick with what seemed to be working. We felt relatively safe and unobtrusive there. Hopefully no one dangerous to us knew we were in Mozuru. Let well enough alone.

The next morning Jamul ventured to a small café near the hotel for breakfast and brought back a takeout bag for Jack and me. After the incidents with the ARC at the highway checkpoint and the Neville estate and especially in light of the detainment of Bert Wallace at his mission compound, I was hesitant to appear in public with Jack any more than necessary. While it was reasonable to think that no one knew where we were, it was not out of the realm of possibility that we were still the targets of a specific hunt by one or the other of the groups interested in finding a way to harm James Martin.

When Jamul returned, he indicated that he needed to talk with me in private, and we went out onto the patio off of the first floor of the hotel. The sun was bright and warm for so early, causing us to seek shade underneath an umbrella at a poolside table. I knew he must have news of Bert Wallace. I was right.

"He has been released by the Office of Information officials who were holding him. He was not harmed. Fredric DeSoto just notified me by telephone. Wallace has left the compound, but no one knows where he is now. My guess is that he is on his way here and will find a way to meet you at the airport as scheduled. I hope that is wise. He may be under surveillance yet."

"Surely he would understand that and would not endanger himself or us unnecessarily?"

"I think he will be cautious, but he will want to be close to ensure that Jack is safely out of the country, as planned. All we can do is watch and wait. We must continue with the original plan for departure two days from now. You should have what you need by way of paperwork to be allowed to take Jack with you on the plane."

I hoped and prayed he was correct, but my heart ached for Jack and for Bertram Wallace, who had reared him. They might now be separated for a long time.

The next day passed slowly for the three of us. There was little to do. The television reception was poor and the choice of stations limited. Jamul managed to secure a checkers game for Jack and some magazines for me. We took turns challenging him to matches, which he generally won. By dinner I was reduced to playing hangman and tic-tac-toe with him on hotel stationery.

Jack was becoming more irritable and difficult by the hour, and it taxed me greatly not to lecture him on ingratitude. He continued to question me about his family in America, which was understandable, and I did my best to tell him what I knew. He also continued to ask about my relationship with them and especially with his father. It became clearer to me where this was leading, and he finally confirmed my fears when he blurted his suspicions.

"Are you my father's sweetheart? Are you going to marry him?" His tone indicated some displeasure at the thought.

Although I could understand how confusing all of the events in Jack's life had been up to now, including the extraordinary last several days, I had had enough of his rudeness.

"Jack, I am a friend, and I am here to help you and your father. That's all. If you have any more questions about your father's personal life or future plans, you will have to ask him. I am not privy to them. We will not discuss this further. Is that clear? It is important that we work together very closely for the next few hours. We must not let any personal concerns interfere with that. Our safety might depend on it. Do you understand what I am saying?"

"Yes." He would not make eye contact.

"Jack...is something else bothering you? If so, I will be happy to help. Do you have some problem you are finding it hard to talk about?"

"I'm tired. I would like to go to bed," was all he answered.

I had been in bed about two hours myself when I awakened with an uneasy feeling, and, without knowing why, got up and stood in front of the room's door to the hallway. After listening carefully for some minutes, I heard nothing unusual. I lay back down, and when an hour had passed and I still could not sleep, I knew the problem must be internal. I began to pray, thanking God for a long list of blessings that I failed to exhaust because I must have finally fallen asleep.

My next awareness was of an early morning light coming in the hotel room window. After feeling relief that morning had come, my next thought was that hopefully this would be my last morning in Khutule.

21

Flight for Freedom

Jack and I had reservations to leave from the small Mozuru airport at 11:30 a.m., which meant we needed to be at the airport by 9:00 to clear security and any other red tape barriers that might arise. Jamul suggested we give ourselves even more lead-time for the unexpected. Before rising, I spent more time than usual praying for the safety of all involved in today's efforts to help Jack and me make our exit from the country. I would be sad to leave Jamul, who had become a good friend, as well as protector, guide, and invaluable traveling companion over the past weeks. I was concerned for his continued safety in Khutule, and for that of Bertram Wallace, who might make an appearance sometime during the morning.

Jack was subdued and hollow-eyed as we ate a hasty breakfast, tucked some packaged snacks in our hand luggage in the event that we might need them later, and made our preparations to depart for the airport. Jamul was all business as he checked us out of the hotel and maneuvered the relatively light traffic across the city to the entrance to the unremarkable Mozuru International Airport. The three of us spoke little during the drive.

Bert Wallace had informed me that this particular airport was chosen for our departure point because of its small size and usual quiet atmosphere, uncommon in an international airport. While most airports since September 11 have been carefully guarded, this was one of the more relaxed and open. We were slightly concerned, then, as we drove near the single, one-story departure building and saw two government vehicles idling at the curb with uniformed soldiers at the wheel.

Jamul felt that this one sign was not enough to alter our plans, and we pulled up to the curb behind a waiting taxi. Jamul prepared to help us out of the van and lead us to the check in area. He had no more opened the door to step out first when someone unfastened the front passenger side door and sat down beside him. Jamul turned to face the newcomer and discovered Bertram Wallace in such a disguise as to be hardly recognizable. He was rumpled and unkempt in a dirty white suit, had several days' growth of stubbly beard, and carried a cane. He seemed to have aged ten years.

"Wallace, I hardly recognized you!" Jamul's usually calm, controlled voice was raised in obvious excitement. "My man, what are you doing?"

"Drive off, Jamul, slowly as if you do not expect to be pursued, but drive off right now. Do as I say, man, and I will explain as we go."

Wallace's tone meant business, and Jamul complied instantly. As Jack hurled questions impatiently at Bert Wallace from his seat in the back, Jamul drove out of the loading area of the airport and headed back toward the city. When we drove past an abandoned industrial complex, Bert indicated that Jamul should drive behind one of the ramshackle buildings out of sight of the highway.

As soon as the van was stopped, Jack threw open his door and ran around to the side where Bert was sitting. As Bert opened his door, the youth fell into his arms, overcome by sobs.

"You're okay. I was so scared! Mr. Bert, I'm so sorry."

We could hear him repeating such phrases again and again through his sobs as Bert Wallace, who had stepped out of the van and shut the door, soothed him quietly. After a brief conversation, which Jamul and I could not overhear, Jack rejoined me in the back seat. Bert Wallace returned to his place in the front next to Jamul, wiping at his eyes with his handkerchief as he came.

Once inside the van, Bert Wallace began. "I was hoping you would be early. I knew that, with Jamul driving, you most likely would be. We need the extra time to talk about an alternate plan for leaving the country."

"What do you mean, we need an alternate plan? Has something happened?" Patience was not a virtue of mine. "Is there a problem?"

Wallace turned to look directly at me.

"We have reason to believe that someone at the mission compound may have leaked information, inadvertently or otherwise, about the presence of the son of a famous person being protected on mission grounds. We think it was reported that the child's family represents a threat to the present government. Apparently...and fortunately...the information quickly became garbled as it was transmitted, and thus was of less use to its recipients, but it was still enough for government representatives to visit me at the compound and make certain threats. Unfortunately, the information also appears to have spread quickly within government and rebel factions. Both groups would have reason to benefit from this information. It is not yet certain that those interested in the news have guessed the true identity of the child. We have to assume the worst. One good point is that Jack does not bear the Neville name, but rather one that I gave him years ago, Murphey. It was my mother's maiden name, and that is the name his credentials currently bear."

I was stunned at what Bert Wallace was saying. While I always knew the distinct possibility of danger existed, I must have refused to accept the reality of it. Now it was before me. The events of the past days took on a new and more ominous meaning. The hope of getting Jack out of Khutule without incident sseemed to be fading quickly.

I struggled to keep my face calm and my voice steady as I asked, "What do we do now? Will we try to keep our plane reservations or try some other means of leaving the country? Or will we be able to leave at all?"

Jamul was the first to answer me. "The fact that Mr. Wallace was released at all could be a positive sign. Bertram, do you believe you have been followed here to Mozuru?"

"While I can't be certain, I do not believe I was. I traveled by my own car and made no move to avoid detection, at least not until I reached this city. I gave anyone ample time and opportunity to follow me, and I observed carefully all along the journey. I saw no evidence at all. Once in the city, I took great pains to ensure I lost any followers. As you can see, I also have attempted to alter my outward appearance, although I still must use my name and usual passport."

Jamul thought for a moment before responding. "There may simply not have been enough information passed along for the government officials to hold you any longer or to risk harming you, especially once their trip to your compound revealed nothing. It would not be popular with the religious community to have such a respected missionary injured or his home destroyed. It may also mean, however, that the strategy being played out was to follow you at a distance, hoping you would lead your watchers to Jack. At the least, they may be watching the airports and borders carefully for any sign of someone fleeing with a child under questionable circumstances. We have to be realistic about all possibilities."

That speech by Jamul chilled me thoroughly, although again, I labored hard not to show it. It was now Bert's turn.

"With the assistance of Mr. DeSoto, I have worked out a plan that involves some risk, but it does give us a way to explore whether it is safe for you and Jack to board the plane this morning. Fredric is inside of the airport as we speak and has informed me by cell phone that all appears to be quiet, with business as usual.

"Now listen carefully. We will return to the airport now. Jamul will put me out some distance from the main doors, and I will go in alone to observe the status of the security in the building. I should be able to tell in short order whether security appears elevated or there is evidence of unusual tension among the staff. I will signal to Jamul, who will be at curbside with his hood up, examining his engine.

"If all appears to be normal, you and Jack will enter the terminal and proceed as usual. If all is not well, Jamul will drive you both away immediately, and we will meet back at this spot to plan another means of exit as soon as I can join you."

I was not entirely in favor of this plan. I decided to voice my concern. "What if you should go into the airport and are detained? We may have opportunity to escape, but what about you?"

Jack chose that moment to voice his own worries. "Mr. Bert, I'm afraid. I do not want you to go to prison for me. Please be careful, Mr. Bert." He was pleading and close to tears again.

"Jack, I have taught you that God's strength is made perfect in our weakness. We are not without Divine assistance here. There will be two of us, Mr. DeSoto and I, looking for trouble in the airport. We must keep in mind that it is also possible there is no one here searching for you and Ms. Redmon. There simply may not have been enough information passed along to warrant further attention. Do you understand me?"

"Yes, sir."

"It is absolutely essential that you act as if all is normal. Is that clear? Can you do that?" Wallace was firm but kind.

"I can, sir."

"I knew that you could. Now, let us return immediately to the airport.

We followed the plan laid out by Bert Wallace. We put him off some way from the main terminal, and then pulled over as if we were moving luggage around in our van. We stalled long enough to give Wallace sufficient time to reach the terminal and then we approached the main entrance. Parking just shy of it, Jamul raised the hood of the van and began tinkering underneath, as if we had a bad radiator or some other problem. Jack and I remained in the vehicle, watching carefully for any signs from Bert Wallace or Fredric DeSoto from within the terminal. When none came, we began to gather our hand luggage in the event we received the all-clear signal to come inside.

We must have sat about ten or fifteen minutes with no glimpse of those inside the building when suddenly I noticed Fredric DeSoto standing on the sidewalk opposite our vehicle. He began striding up and down as if looking for someone, taking care not to pay any attention to us. He made a great show of looking at his watch as if his expected party were late. After about two or three minutes of this, I saw him speak to Jamul without looking at him when no one else was nearby. Immediately he strode off down the sidewalk, and Jamul closed the hood of our van.

I heard him say, "It's time, Ms. Redmon. Master Jack, are you ready?"

We quickly gathered our belongings, which had been pared down to carry-on luggage only, and stepped out of the van. I turned to Jamul with my hand outstretched. He formally shook my hand and then Jack's.

"Jamul, I don't know how..." I began.

"I know, Ms. Redmon...Jannia. And there is no time now. We must say our good-byes later. You and Jack must proceed directly to the security check. Just go quickly. Jannia, be ready for anything."

His words were odd to me, but I knew there was no time to analyze anything. I pasted a smile on my face and nudged Jack forward; taking him by the wrist in what I hoped didn't look like a death grip. We did not look back.

In spite of our fears, check in through security went smoothly. Our persons, passports, and tickets were inspected without incident, as well as the papers giving me clearance to travel as Jack's escort. I began to feel a sense of relief when we were directed toward a departure gate.

As we walked down the short concourse toward where our plane was waiting, I made sure that my confident smile remained in place, but a quick look at Jack indicated he was as pale as a ghost. As we followed the signs indicating the direction to our gate, it dawned on me that there was an odd absence of other passengers moving up and down the concourse. Given that it was nearing midday and that the airport had been relatively busy when we entered, the concourse had an eerie, deserted feel.

I slowed our pace as we neared two doors on our right, one that led to restrooms and one marked observation deck. I could see that a left turn in the opposite side of the hall led to our departure gate. The sensation that all was not well became overpowering, and I stopped in the middle of the hallway. Jack looked at me with increasing awareness that something was wrong. I felt him take hold of my hand in a clammy grasp. At that moment, the door to the observation deck opened slightly, and a movement inside caught my eye. It was Bertram Wallace, and he motioned to me frantically.

Without further thought or hesitation, I pulled Jack toward the doorway to the observation deck and pushed him through it. Just as I nearly fell through the door on his heels, I heard quick footsteps coming from the direction of our departure gate. The door clicked quietly shut behind me, and I could only pray that whoever was on the other side had not seen the door's movement.

"Follow me," was all Wallace said, and he began to run along a narrow metal walkway attached to the outside of the building. I could see that we were above the tarmac at least one story. We passed the stairs leading up to the observation tower and came to another set of stairs leading down, which was blocked by a chest-high locked gate. Wallace stopped at the stairs only long enough to whisper, "We must go down there."

Wallace grabbed my hand luggage and dropped it over the side, then turned and did the same with Jack's bag. He then indicated that we were to climb over the locked gate. In any other circumstances, I would have declined and told him it was too dangerous. To drop to the steps below would be to risk spraining or breaking an ankle, and Jack was already running on a badly injured one. These were not, however, any other circumstances, and Bert's face told me to do as he said with no questions.

I grabbed the top of the gate with my hands and used his hand as a step as I threw my leg over, tearing my skirt and dropping without dignity to the steps below. I cut my hand, but that and my torn skirt were my only casualties. Jack was next, and Bert had to work harder to hoist him up high enough to get over the gate, but with me to break his landing, he made it without too much pain.

There we stood, Jack and I on one side of the gate and Bert on the other. We looked at each other for a moment and then he spoke to me with great emotion evident on his face.

"Jannia, get Jack down the steps and onto the side of the tarmac. Stay hidden by the walkway above as long as you can, and run toward the right. You will see a small white plane parked about 20 meters down the tarmac. Make sure you get on that plane. Do not turn back for anything. Gather your bags quickly and go now."

"But you...?"

"I'm coming, but don't wait for me. Keep going...no matter what!"

I grabbed Jack's hand, and we clattered down the metal stairway. We snatched our bags from the ground and took off at a serious run toward the right as Bert had ordered. Above us, we could see the windows of the departure gates; we tucked as close to the building as we could and still have room to run. Only once did I turn around, and that was to see Bert Wallace, as short as he was, make a most remarkable flying vault over the locked gate to land in a crouch on the step. Just before I turned back, I glimpsed movement on the walkway in the direction from which we had just come.

"My foot hurts too much to go any further!" Jack said beside me.

I sensed that he was slowing. I jerked his duffle from him and spoke firmly through clenched teeth as we ran. "You will go on. You will not stop. Forget your foot. Think about your father. You will go on!"

And he did. Stumbling often but staying upright, he somehow kept up with me.

Just when I was beginning to get dangerously winded myself, I looked up to see the small white plane that Bert had described ahead of and opposite us on the tarmac. The door was open, and the steps were down. I told myself these were the steps to Heaven and herded Jack ahead of me in their direction.

When we reached the plane, I realized that the engine was running, and I saw a face appear in the doorway while a hand reached down to help Jack on board. The same hand again appeared to assist me when I heard a sound from behind that caused me to spin around to confirm what I feared. It was certainly a gunshot, no...two shots in rapid succession. I could see figures running along the tarmac, and in front of them the rotund figure of Bert Wallace was going faster than I would ever have thought possible. I hesitated in my movement up the steps and turned toward him before a voice above me reached my ears over the sound of the plane's motors.

"Give me your hand. Do not look back. You must come aboard now." The crisp authority in the voice shook me out of my indecision, and I threw our bags into the doorway and allowed myself to be pulled inside. The plane began to move, its engines revving in eagerness to fly. The door remained open as it began the taxi down the runway, slowly at first, and then picking up speed as soon as the body of Bert Wallace was dragged on board.

Bert lay inert in the small entranceway as the door closed. A man I didn't know pushed me into a back seat next to Jack and fastened my seat belt. I strained against the straps to see what was happening to Bert as we gathered speed.

At Jack's tug on my arm, I looked out of the small window to see a group of soldiers crouching on the tarmac, and I felt the distinct thud of what I was sure were more bullets against the side of the airplane. I grasped Jack's head in my hands and pushed it down as low toward the floor as we could reach as we felt the small plane leave the runway. We were frozen in place, and it was not until I heard a voice say, "Ms. Redmon, it's okay. You are safe now," that I opened my eyes and relaxed my grip on Jack.

The first thing I saw was the body of Bert strapped into a seat in front of me, his head hanging to one side. I reached for him, trying to see if he had been injured when the same unknown man, now bending over Bert, spoke in the most comforting voice I had ever heard.

"I believe he will be fine. His vital signs are good. He may have passed out from over-exertion, but he was not shot."

It was then I heard Jack sobbing softly beside me.

There are times to be strong, and there are times to keep on being strong, even when you think you can't go on. After that, when the reserves are gone, there is a time to crash. This was a fine example of the latter. I pulled Jack's head onto my shoulder, rested my own head on top of his, and crashed with him.

I didn't ask where we were going or who these people were. At that point I really didn't much care. Jack and I were out of Khutule. His guardian, Bert Wallace, we prayed would soon recover. That's all there was. I thanked God just before Jack and I fell asleep.

When I awoke, I could feel the plane descending and could hear some communications from the cockpit to someone on the ground. Jack was still asleep, and Bert was either asleep or still unconscious. I hoped that was all. I couldn't tell what time it was or how long I had slept, but I knew that I was sore in multiple places from the activity of the morning. I could see scratches on my arms and the large tear in my skirt as a result of my climb over the gate. But I was alive, and I wanted to go home.

22

Warm Farewell, Uneasy Welcome

Jack stirred beside me as the plane dropped its landing gear with a thud. There was still no evidence of activity from Bert, but by watching him carefully I could tell he was breathing. That was enough for now.

Jack sat upright and glared at me defensively. The old Jack was returning. "Where are we going? What's going to happen to us now?"

"I really don't know, Jack, but I think we're fine. We will have to wait until we've landed to find out more. Is your seatbelt fastened? Good. How are you feeling?"

"Is Mr. Bert dead?"

"No, he's not dead. I can see him breathing. There, I think we've landed. Just sit still until we get further instructions."

As the plane taxied down a dimly lit runway, I could see lights in a long, low metal building near where the plane came to rest at last. We sat and waited but not for long as the exit door soon opened, and four persons from the ground entered the plane. I could tell two of them were medical personnel by the way they went to work immediately on Bert, taking his vital signs and setting up an IV bag. Two of them greeted Jack and me with warmth and welcome, assisting us as we prepared to leave the plane. As they helped us down the steps, I could see the others continuing to work with Bert, who showed signs of movement.

We were ushered into a sitting and office area of the corrugated tin building that seemed to serve multiple purposes as terminal, maintenance area, and conference room. The lights were bright, and the furniture was functional, giving the whole environment a no-nonsense, practical, and secure atmosphere. After the distress of the past hours, this was a safe-haven.

Before we could even get our bearings and begin asking questions, we were made comfortable and served sandwiches and soft drinks. Two of our hosts joined us and introduced themselves as Stephen and Jacklyn Simpson, the Director of the Sub-Saharan African Mission of South Africa and his wife. It seemed we had been flown onto their mission compound near Messina,

South Africa, by their mission plane at the request of their friend, Mr. Bertram Wallace, who was even now resting quietly in their infirmary.

Steve and Jackie had served in South Africa for twenty-five years, and they were looking forward to having Bert join them as part of their staff now that he had left Khutule. I discovered they were fully aware of the circumstances of my trip to Africa and why I had come for Jack. Even before Bert's detention by the government at his Khutule compound, the Simpsons had offered their mission plane as a standby means of escape, should we need it. When word arrived of Bert's confinement and the probability that we would all be allowed to leave Khutule peacefully became questionable, word reached the Simpsons to send their Cessna 421 to the Mozuru airport just in case. Such trips into Khutule were not unusual as members of the Sub-Saharan African Mission family frequently traveled by plane among the several African countries in the region on medical or other mission business.

The couple explained that in the past few months, relations between the Sub-Saharan African Mission and the Khutulen government had become strained, but not yet to the breaking point. The use of their plane to effect our escape would, in all probability, bring an end to such flights in the foreseeable future. This prospect didn't appear to be surprising or disturbing to the Simpsons as they praised God for the safety of Jack and me and for the delivery of Bert Wallace, for whom they had prayed diligently.

After meeting other members of the mission's staff and being shown to comfortable guests' quarters in the compound, I requested that we be able to see Bert, if he was able. I knew it would help Jack, and I wanted to see for myself that he was all right. We were taken to him immediately. Jack was thrilled to see him sitting up in a hospital bed in the infirmary eating a light meal complete with yellow jello. Some things don't change regardless of the continent.

"Jannia, Jack, come closer. Don't be shy! I'm back, and as you can see, in my usual good form. I'm hungry."

I took his outstretched hand and kissed him on the cheek. "Bert, you gave us a fright, for sure. And also saved our lives, I might add. How you managed to get word to this mission about all that was going on and the need for the use of their plane right under the nose of the government of Khutule I don't understand."

"God enabled it, Jannia, and my cell phone and email were the vehicles. I'm just thankful my mission friends were willing and able to stand by. I will admit, their assistance came in handy." His eyes twinkled, letting me know he was a master of understatement.

During our exchange, Jack had been silent. He approached the bedside slowly and, after standing there for a long time with his head down, spoke quietly. "Mr. Bert, may I speak with you, sir?" He looked at me. "In private?"

"Of course you may, Jack." I turned to go. "I will wait for you in the hallway." I closed the door behind me.

When Jack emerged about ten minutes later, his eyes were red, but he held his head high. He appeared somehow different, almost as if he had undergone some fast-forward maturity. We didn't talk but walked back to the guesthouse and into our rooms to sleep for the next twelve hours.

The next morning, we met with the Simpsons about plans for our departure. We would travel immediately by car, Jack, Bert and I, to the U.S. Embassy in Pretoria. We would work through the embassy there to obtain permission for Jack and me to remain in South Africa for the short time needed to make travel arrangements back to the U.S. Bert, mostly recovered now from his exhaustion, was also a U.S. citizen. He would seek asylum with the South African government to remain at the mission station in Messina as a refugee from Khutule. There was little doubt he would be allowed to do so.

After four uneventful but successful days in Pretoria, Jack and I were again at the airport, this time anticipating a long and complicated series of flights finally landing in Boone's Summit, North Carolina. There were few words remaining to say to the Simpsons of the Sub-Saharan African Mission that I had not already said. They quickly turned all praise upward rather than inward, as they bid us Godspeed.

Bert embraced Jack for a long time, whispering quietly to him until it was time for us to go. Jack was brave but barely held in his emerging adolescent emotions. When Bert turned to bid me good-bye as I gathered my few belongings for the walk to security, I had one remaining question for him.

"Jamul? What about Jamul? Will he be safe in Khutule?"

"He is no longer in Khutule, Jannia. He is also in South Africa. He is even now on his way to Pretoria to the embassy. He wants to join his half-brother, Banolo Benadie, in the U.S. Perhaps you know him?" Bert Wallace again had a decided twinkle in his eye.

"It is, indeed, a small world, Mr. Wallace. I have had the pleasure of a ride in Banolo's taxi. I will look forward to thanking Mr. Jamul Legassi one day in America then."

Jack and I had flown for so long and our internal time clocks were so confused that we hardly had the energy to interact. I was long past chirpy cheerful conversation, and he was too done in to maintain his almost-teenage image. We communicated in as few words as possible out of near exhaustion, but strangely our circumstances seemed to draw us together. Finding comfort in each other's presence as we flew, we slept, ate, and slept again, staggering through several layovers in various cites we never saw.

Sometime late into the night over the ocean on one of the final legs of our journey, I felt a clammy hand touch mine. I was sitting with my eyes closed, but I was not asleep, and I turned to look at Jack in the dim light of the airplane's cabin.

"Ms. Jannia, I have something I need to tell you. I am afraid you will be very disappointed in me, but I have to make it right with you before we get...home."

"Yes, Jack?" I waited without pressing him. It was obvious he was struggling with what he wanted to reveal.

"I am the reason we had so much trouble getting out of Khutule. It was my fault Mr. Bert was visited by the government officials. It was because of me we were almost shot at the airport where Mr. Bert...almost died trying to help us."

I could tell by his eyes he was completely serious. I knew I had to hear him out, regardless of how hard it was for him. "Why do you think you are responsible?"

"Because I bragged to someone at Mr. Bert's mission compound about my father. It was one of the African students. He was older than I and better at sports. I was jealous of him because his father is famous in the Khutule military. He is one of the fellows who boards at the school because it has such a good reputation for the education we receive. He is not one of the orphans."

"Jack, what did you say to him?" I had to be careful and not sound judgmental. A lot rested on this conversation.

"I never told him my father's name; I just said he was someone very talented and famous. I hinted that he might even become President of Khutule one day. I mentioned that my family was important in the history of Khutule. It was a stupid thing to do, and I had been forbidden to talk about my real family at all. The boy must have reported what I said to his father or someone connected with the government. I never meant for it to cause anyone harm. I was tired of him being better at everything. I guess I wanted to appear more important. I was terribly wrong."

"That's what you wanted to talk with Bert Wallace about in the infirmary. You told him?"

"Yes. I was unable to stand it any longer without talking to him. I asked him to forgive me. I know there is nothing I can change, but I am sorry. I think I will always be sorry."

155

"He forgave you, didn't he? He forgave you. Mr. Bert loves you very much. He's been a father to you for most of your life. Nothing you do can change how he feels. You must remember that. You may be the closest thing to a son he will ever have. Do not ever forget that."

"What about you?" His voice was not adolescent now. It was childlike and pleading. "Will you forgive me? I am very sorry, Ms. Jannia."

"Jack, what you did was foolish and childish. It could have gotten us into a lot more trouble than it did. God is good, and we are now on our way home. I didn't come half way around the world to get you to be angry with you the rest of my life. Of course I forgive you.

"Look at me, Jack. I said I forgive you, and furthermore, you have behaved very maturely to make this right. I'm also glad to find out what's been bothering you. Frankly, I was beginning to think you were just a whiny kid. Now I know you had a lot on your mind." This brought a hint of a smile. "Now try to get some rest. We'll be in New York in the morning."

I pointed out the Statue of Liberty as we prepared to touch down in New York City. Our stop there was brief. We barely had time to change planes, which involved a ride on an airport trolley, before it was time to begin the final flight to Boone's Summit. I watched Jack out of the corner of my eye as he grappled with the unfamiliar scenery around him. He hadn't traveled out of Khutule until now, and Khutule was light years behind New York City, even from the airport.

Jack gripped the armrest of the seat until his knuckles showed white. I knew it wasn't from fear of flying because I had seen no signs of that. I suspected it was the overwhelming new surroundings, coupled with anticipation of meeting his father and sister in the next couple of hours. Bert Wallace had managed to arrange some clandestine visits between James Martin and Jack over the years, so they weren't strangers. But they had been afforded little time to bond as parent to child.

James Martin. The thought caused a physical reaction in my stomach. Within two hours I would also see James Martin. I had consciously set any thought of him aside whenever possible. When mention of him could not be avoided, I steeled myself not to react and distracted my attention as quickly as possible. In light of such a self-imposed indifference, my current reaction surprised and frightened me. I had to be sure our meeting was professional and efficient. My job was completed, and I needed to excuse myself as quickly as possible. I could do that.

When the pilot announced we were preparing to land, told us the weather conditions, and wished us a pleasant stay in the Boone's Summit area,

I turned to Jack and found him watching me closely.

"Are you nervous?"

He nodded in the affirmative and smiled. He didn't even try to cover, and I could see him swallowing with effort.

"Hey, this couldn't be as hard as Khutule. We're fugitives, remember? Runaways. Desperados. Why, we're famous on two continents. We might find our wanted posters on the Internet."

My feeble attempt at levity left Jack looking at me as if I were speaking Latin. I had to remember how sheltered he had been. We felt the landing gear drop.

"Welcome home, Jack."

I made a great show of gathering all of our belongings, which by now were few, from the overhead storage area. I was stalling to let other passengers get a head start. This would give us a little more time to prepare ourselves. Actually, this was mostly for me. I was shaking, and I suspected it was due to more than jet lag.

When I couldn't delay longer, I pushed Jack ahead of me to the exit ramp. He had spoken with his father from South Africa, so James Martin knew we were safe. I wanted Jack to be the first to see him and Marta. Jack was silent as we negotiated the airport passageways to the terminal, and I refrained from filling the void with useless chatter. When we reached the waiting area filled with passengers being greeted on all sides by friends and family, it seemed we were surrounded by everyone else's loved ones. I pushed Jack forward through the happy greeters.

When I felt Jack stop beside me, I looked to where he was facing. James Martin was standing at the edge of the crowd with Marta and Banolo beside of him. Even GranJuel was there, looking as out of place as Queen Elizabeth in the busy waiting room. They saw us, and I saw Marta clap her hands and begin pulling her father forward. Jack took my elbow in his hand, almost as he would an old lady, and began to steer me forward in a paternal way. I knew he simply needed to hold onto something, and this was more acceptable than holding my hand in public, so I allowed myself to be herded.

The two Neville men, so much alike in the way they looked and carried themselves despite their age difference, stopped in front of each other. I saw Jack make the first move by offering his right hand to James Martin for a handshake.

"Hello, Dad."

James Martin hesitated, then offered his own hand to Jack. They shook formally, as if sealing a business deal.

I was astounded, and I know my mouth was open. James Martin was surely not going to greet his son, whom he could so easily have lost, in such a stiff and formal manner. Just as I was about to say something, anything, to break the formality, James Martin took matters into his own hands.

"Son," I heard him say in a voice that broke, "thank God you're safe."

When James Martin enfolded Jack in his long arms and lifted the boy off of the ground, I was gratified to see that Jack had his arms around his father in a tight hold also. I know anyone listening would have heard me let out an audible breath of relief.

Jack was passed from James Martin to Marta, who hugged him quickly and then stepped back, shy, looking up at him with wide blue eyes. I caught a glimpse of GranJuel dabbing at her eyes with a monogrammed handkerchief as Jack kissed her paper-thin cheek.

James Martin turned to me. I had been standing with our belongings, watching the family reunion with great joy.

"Jannia, welcome home. We will talk later at length, but I can tell you now I will have no adequate words ever to express my gratitude for what you have done." He enfolded me also in a brief embrace, one that was proper and chaste and one from which I never wanted to disengage.

Before I could answer, something behind the family group caught my eye, and I looked again to see Branda VanderCross standing in all of her blond beauty a few feet away. Any words I had for James Martin left me, and I stepped away from him awkwardly, nearly stumbling over my bag as I did so.

Of course they were together. Nothing had changed. This was normal and to be expected. I mustn't visibly react now by showing any emotion other than what was natural and appropriate. I had no right to think any action on my part deserved anything special. I had done what I felt was right. That must be enough.

I used self-talk to make it through the next minutes. *Breathe. Breathe. That's right; keep on doing that. Smile, pick up your bags, smile, and speak pleasantly to GranJuel. Give Marta a hug and a wink. Smile some more and speak cordially to Ms. VanderCross. Greet Banolo warmly in honor of his cousin, Jamul. This drama will end soon, and I can go home. All I have to do is pretend to be just fine and keep on smiling.*

"I am sure you are quite exhausted," I heard James Martin address me. "We have much to discuss, but this afternoon is not the time as I can see you are asleep on your feet. I have asked Banolo to see you home safely. You will hear from me as soon as you have had time to rest." I felt his hands on my shoulders. "Jannia, you have been a gift of God to my family. Thank you, and

158

bless you. Please go now and rest."

I remember trying hard to walk toward the exit door to the street. I know that I turned in the direction of the door because I saw that it led to fresh air and took me away from the little group of Neville people, but my legs were lead-filled, and I couldn't pick up my feet.

Then it felt like my feet were water-filled balloons that wouldn't hold me up when I took a step.

The last thing I remember is wondering why I was going down toward the floor instead of forward in the direction of the door.

23

Quiet Resolve

The events of the next few days I relate from snatches of memory mixed with what I heard from those who cared for me. Weakness in others or myself has never been acceptable to me. I consider the airport episode a supreme show of weakness, and it has been no small source of shame and self-assessment as I reflect on this time.

Apparently, I collapsed from exhaustion, dehydration, anxiety and other accumulated stressors interacting with each other and gathering strength during my activities related to getting into and out of Africa. I neither saw it coming nor realized its symptoms when they arrived.

One minute I was trying heroically to get home, and the next I was unconscious and staying that way for two days.

For three nights and three days I rested in the hospital, physically depleted, insensible to stimuli around me, nourished artificially by IVs and resting a rest induced by little shots to my hips.

I understand my pastor was there, my editor Jake Bean, my friend Al Lanier, James Martin, and the children. I have been told that even GranJuel made a crusade to sit by my bed for several hours.

Sometime late in the second day, I began to come to my senses...at least enough to know that I hadn't made it safely home as planned.

Medical tests were negative, and a brief visit from a psychiatrist assured me I had not suffered a nervous breakdown but rather had simply stretched my resources too thin for too long. He assured me there should be no lasting consequences. The doctor encouraged me to talk about my experiences in Africa, which he thought had influenced my fragile behavior. I carefully omitted mentioning what I thought of as the poignant capstone, the effect of seeing James Martin still in the company of his lady friend. I knew the symptoms of an adolescent crush without having it confirmed by medical credentials.

When I began eating on my own (why is that such a universal sign of recovery?) and could stay awake for more than an hour at a time, there was talk of my being discharged. All I wanted was to go home...alone. No one would even consider that escape for me. It appears that the extended Neville-Everston family won custody of me, and I was bundled into a limousine for the trip to GranJuel's apartment in the elegantly crumbling old building where I first met Marta and James Martin.

This all happened with such firmness and efficiency I felt I had no choice but to comply and cooperate. I tried to protest that I didn't want to cause anyone trouble and explained that I needed to be left to recuperate on my own. When no one listened, I just didn't have the energy to do other than murmur "Thank you" and submit to the loving care I was to receive.

I was grateful for the attention to my needs and efforts to make me comfortable. But it became apparent that I might soon smother from so much consideration. The more those around me tried to help me, the more agitated I became. To try to explain would sound unthankful.

Jack brought me books, GranJuel fed me sweets, Banolo tried to cheer me with stories of his youth in Khutule, and James Martin must have thanked me a thousand times for bringing his son home to him. Even Branda VanderCross, who usually moved quietly in the background, was solicitous and offered to shop for any little necessities I lacked. Only Marta didn't overwhelm me but sat quietly beside me with her head on my shoulder and her hand in mine.

The family gave me a beautiful private guest room in which, unfortunately, I was unable to do more than toss and stare and have flashbacks of being pursued by faceless men in jeeps with guns mounted on the back. Being alone didn't work any better than being coddled to death.

After a day and a half in GranJuel's grand apartment, I was, again, in a state of near exhaustion. It was late evening; Jack and Marta had already said their good nights. As bedtime neared, I found myself lying on a delicately brocaded couch, covered with a blanket, shaking, feeling confused and vulnerable and dreading the long night ahead. My emotions were out of control; I was verging on a panic attack and oblivious about how to prevent it.

James Martin and Banolo came into the living room where I was lying, and to my horror, I found myself crying and incoherently warning James Martin about some imagined attack on his life. I was appalled by my behavior but unable to stop my near hysterical actions. Clearly I was in trouble.

Instead of reacting in disgust or making light of my imaginary fears, James Martin practically sent Banolo for water and my sleeping prescription while he gathered me up in his arms and carried me, blanket and all, down the hall into Marta's darkened bedroom, where he put me into bed beside the sleeping child.

When Marta stirred to see that I was lying near her, I heard her father say quietly that Ms. Jannia was very, very tired and needed her help to sleep. I remember taking the medicine that Banolo brought and lying back on the soft pillow to feel the child put her arms around me and curl her tiny body next to mine. I knew that safe and restful sleep would finally come.

I think that I stayed for four or five days with Sir Neville's family before it was clear that I was back to my old self again. I remember it now as a quiet and healing time during which I was able to grow strong without worrying about practical matters related to my care. Always a family member or the housekeeper anticipated any needs before I had to ask. I tried to keep my mind free of anything that might cause pain or worry, which meant I automatically disallowed any reflective or contemplative thoughts. I just drifted until I felt sound enough to return home.

Banolo drove me home in his taxi. We talked of my time with Jamul in Khutule and of how we both hoped and prayed he could soon come to America. I was much more comfortable with Banolo now and felt I had another friend as he delivered my luggage and me to my apartment. As much as I had benefited from being with Marta and Jack and their family during my much-needed rest, I found great comfort in knowing that I was alone at last.

The next morning was Sunday, and I slept through church time. This was not my usual practice, but I knew I still needed the rest. I had always thought jet lag and the hazards of travel were matters of imagination versus will power. I was wrong.

When I finally got up to face the day, it was almost noon, and I went about doing the everyday things one does to begin to feel normal again after having been away from home for so long. I fixed a sandwich and read my mail and unpacked my few belongings that had survived the trip.

By late Sunday afternoon, I was feeling restless and confined, a sure sign that I was better. I needed some physical activity to further clear my mind. After dressing in a simple summer dress, I left the apartment for a leisurely walk around my neighborhood. Walking had always been useful processing time for me, and today I desperately needed to sort out the events of the last few months and consider what impact, if any, those events might have on my future.

In truth, I wanted a long, uninterrupted stretch of time to rethink my whole life's purpose and priorities. I needed to do a mental survey of everything important to me so that I could rearrange my time and activities to concentrate on those things, rather than squandering my personal resources on the irrelevancies of life.

These thoughts whirled in my brain as I walked. There was an intense desire to re-establish order to my world, which I felt was presently characterized by disorder, disarray and confusion. I wanted to reorganize my life into the efficient and well-defined categories that seemed to exist before I met Sir Neville and the entourage that accompanied him. My life needed to feel safe, structured, well thought out and controlled again.

The more I reflected, the more I began to suspect the comfort of my former existence might not return. It surprised me to realize that my purposes and priorities may have shifted during the events of recent days. Six months ago I thought singularly, evaluating everything in the light of how it would affect my time, my personal convenience, and me. In Africa I had grown accustomed to thinking about how to make Jack comfortable, how to keep him alive and how to get him out of Africa. While frightening, it had not been an altogether unpleasant change. I might, in fact, need new habits that involved thinking about someone other than myself.

And then there was Marta. Her beautiful, thin, pale, blue-lined face disturbed my privacy as much as Jack's emerging adolescent one. I now had emotional attachments, whether I wanted them or not.

I had made a commitment to become the children's guardian in the event something happened to James Martin. I wasn't sure whether I'd be expected to keep that commitment now that they were finally all together. There was also GranJuel to consider. She might be old, but she was still a strong, opinionated force in the children's lives and hopefully would be for some time to come.

Surprisingly, it now mattered to me whether I would have a place in the children's lives. Instead of savoring my possible freedom from commitment, I wanted assurance that I was still their back-up plan. I needed to know that I could have a continuing relationship with Marta and Jack, even if it included GranJuel. And it was the children's father who would make these decisions.

Their father. Sir James Martin Neville. He was the critical part of this equation and the part that I had pushed out of my mind for too long. It was now time to look squarely and honestly at my relationship with him or, more accurately, at the absence of a relationship with him. The subject was painful, and I had steered clear of it during my recovery. Maybe I could face the hurt better sitting down.

Serendipitously, there was a small, quiet park near where I was now standing with ferns, oak trees, and cool stone benches. I chose one that gave me privacy from the street where I could continue my encounter with reality.

I had not asked to meet James Martin in the first place, nor had I sought out his company. Not specifically. While I'd pursued the taxi with Marta in it, finding her father had been a byproduct. I also had not asked to continue a relationship with him. He was the one who had asked me to get involved with his family. True, I could have declined, but that would have meant turning my back on Marta. While I had volunteered, insisted I take James Martin's place on the trip to Africa to bring Jack to the States, what choice did I have? Either I went against his will or he would go, risking his death and, quite likely Jack's also.

I was a grown woman. Despite my unrequited infatuation for James Martin, I had remained involved primarily for his children. The children were, at present, safe. Wasn't that enough? Why then was I feeling so betrayed by James Martin?

I had made my choices freely; he hadn't promised me anything in return. There was no basis for my hurt feelings. I had engaged in adolescent dreams about a handsome, talented, and mysterious stranger in need who asked for my help. My own mind added the ending in which his gratitude and indebtedness toward me resulted in an outcome of happily-ever-after. When put to myself this bluntly, my feelings sounded clearly pre-pubescent, especially to me, the one who had always liked biographies about real life rather than made up novels. It was pitifully clear. I had been caught up in the mystery and romance of the whole unlikely situation and allowed myself to become more deeply drawn in as it unfolded.

Granted, I could have bowed out at any point, but the gravity of the circumstances and my conviction that I was doing the right thing kept me involved. All of that was acceptable, but my expectations imposed upon Sir James Martin Neville were not.

The fact that James Martin had found someone who interested him more than me was of no consequence. If he owed me any level of gratitude for help with his children, a simple "Thank you" would cover that. The most I might expect was a lasting friendship with the children. But happily-ever-after was not part of what he owed me.

I could deal with that. I had been happy with my work and my friends before James Martin. I had endless possibilities of the rest of my life to consider, and Heaven literally only knew what that might bring. I was okay. I would be okay. I was certainly no worse off than when I followed that taxi so many weeks ago. Indeed, I had a much clearer view of the precious and short nature of life and of my relationship with its Author.

I heard vesper bells chime from the little church I attended located a couple of blocks over. I could still make it for evening service if I left the park now. The idea sounded good.

24

Back to Business

The following day was Monday. Unlike most Mondays, there was joyful expectation, anticipation, and even relief in the prospect of getting back to my job, sitting at my desk among familiar things and continuing my career in journalism. Sweet normalcy.

I met with my editor, Jake Bean, for about an hour, catching him up on the events of the past several weeks and thanking him profusely for his part in supporting and helping to finance my African adventure. He listened intently to my saga, brushed aside my thank you, and expressed gratitude for my safety. He concluded our time, as I knew he would, with a cryptic comment about hoping I had lots of good information for our column on extreme vacations. Our column? That column was his pride, his one place to practice journalism as he once had before his editorial years.

We would share responsibility for this column. I was to take the lead and the byline for this three-part series on Extreme Vacation Possibilities in the South African Country of Khutule. I returned to my desk knowing, without false pride, that I was good at my present job, but that I also had enough ideas now stored up to write a dozen novels, should I desire to go in that direction. I didn't have to chase taxis any more to find good story ideas. This Monday was an excellent one, as Mondays go.

The deadline for the first installment on the Khutule vacation series, which was looking like it might lead to other African vacation ideas, was Friday. There was much to be done quickly as my notes were mostly in my head due to downsizing my belongings so continuously during our flight from Khutule.

As I wrote, the sights and sounds all came back almost as clearly as I viewed them. All too quickly it was early afternoon when I surfaced enough to notice my colleague, Al Lanier, standing in front of my desk.

"It's good to have you back. We missed you."

"Thank you, Al." His words were simple and direct, but I knew he meant them, and I was reminded again of his friendship and support. Indeed, many of my co-workers had shown me this kindness since my return, even those who knew little of the reasons for my absence.

"Are you stopping for lunch today? You've been working mighty hard for the last couple of days. Would you like to take a break and join me?"

Yes, I found that I would like to and readily agreed to accompany him to our local favorite deli. I needed to come up for some air after getting a good start on the first installment of the travel column and making some plans for a series format for the African travel feature.

We talked first about the generalities involved with catching up on our friendship. Then he wanted to know about my travel excursions in Khutule. If he knew about my real reason for being there, he steered clear of any mention of it, asking extensively about my safaris, extreme water sports, and other adventures. He was vintage Al, attentive, interested and kind. I found that I had missed his company and was genuinely enjoying our time together. He was safe ground...steady and predictable. Those characteristics were appealing in my present circumstances.

And then, as we were lingering over coffee after our lunch, the conversation took an unexpected turn.

"Jannia, I thought you might be interested in a recent follow-up interview I had with a gentleman you met at the Please and Thank You Benefit Concert a couple of months back. You remember meeting Sir James Martin Neville, the Khutulen pianist who did such a magnificent job when he and the other African artists performed here?"

So Al didn't know of my recent involvement with James Martin and his family. Could he be fishing to see how I would react? That hardly seemed to be Al Lanier's style.

He genuinely seemed unaware of my true reason for going to Africa.

"I remember. When was the interview?"

"We met for dinner one evening this week. He had quite a story to tell, actually. He's in the process of seeking political asylum in the U.S. due to death threats against him in his country and here. It appears his request may be granted too, as the threats are verifiable. Apparently his family was quite prominent in his country at one time, and some leaders in Khutule fear that he might pose a political menace to the existing government if he returns. In fact, he has a son who has just joined him from there. I think he has two children, but he was rather close-mouthed about his family. He made for quite an interesting interview."

"What are his plans now that he's here to stay?"

As I asked, I caught a mental vision of myself as a moth flying into a flame. I was a slow learner in the ways of practicing self-preservation.

"Continue his musical career, certainly, if he is granted asylum and an extended visa to work here. In the meantime, he has acquired an American agent and is making plans toward signing a recording contract, including a promotional tour. It's a great survival story. The U.S. is fortunate to inherit him. The loss is Khutule's. He must have been quite a commodity in his country."

"What a wonderful opportunity to begin afresh with his talent intact and his family together." I meant what I was saying. That part was easy.

"Well, I did learn that his wife was deceased, apparently as a result of complicated childbirth. He did have quite a lovely lady with him during the interview. They made a striking couple. She stuck pretty close to him...cordial enough...but didn't have much to say."

"Who was she?" I couldn't help myself, really.

"He introduced her as Ms. Branda VanderCross. Never really explained whether they were engaged or whatever, but there was some sort of connection that was hard to explain. She seemed so focused on him all the time. Lucky guy. I'm a sucker for a good romance."

His words, thankfully, provided me with the perfect cover for the disturbing emotions at work within me. "Why Al, I didn't know you were such a romantic. You keep that side of yourself all hidden behind your competent journalistic persona."

I hoped that my teasing tone concealed any real feelings I might expose in the face of hearing more about James Martin and his beautiful friend, Branda. And I hoped to turn the conversation in another direction.

It must have worked and maybe too well. I looked up from rummaging in my purse for my lipstick to find Al Lanier's eyes on me.

"I really am glad you're home and safe. I want you to know that I worried about you, what with foreign travel like it is now. Journalists are especially vulnerable to terrorists, it seems. And Africa is not the most secure of travel destinations these days."

"Thank you, Al. I appreciate your concern. I'm happy to be home. I must admit, I had my moments over there." The understatement was lost on Al, and I intended to keep it that way.

"Jannia, I hope that we'll have some time to spend together...getting to know each other better. I enjoy your company."

This I had not expected. It was clear from the gentle tone of Al's voice and the soft look in his eyes that he was not talking about furthering our professional relationship. I was at once caught off guard but flattered. I liked

Al. His friendship had meant a lot to me since I first came to Boone's Summit. But the possibilities of an involvement with Al Lanier that exceeded friendship and moved into the dating arena? I wasn't sure...

On the one hand, what he was suggesting might not be that big a deal. He certainly had not asked me to marry him. Maybe I should simply be pleased that he was interested and see what he had in mind. No question that he was a wonderful man. Spending more time with him could be a pleasant distraction from my recent...disappointment. If James Martin had decided where he wanted to place his affections, I needed to respect him in that decision and continue to move forward in my own life.

On the other hand, would I be disingenuous to use Al as a way to forget about my unrequited feelings for James Martin? Was I interested enough in Al for his own sake or would he be merely a salve for my ego? I had no interest in toying with the affections of a real friend.

While I was thinking these thoughts, oblivious of the time it was taking to respond to Al's last statement, I didn't realize I was sitting and staring at him with my mouth open and my Heavenly Blush lip gloss stick open in my hand. I came to when I heard Al laugh.

"Jannia, it's okay. You don't have to commit to a binding relationship today. Why don't we just take it easy and see what happens? This isn't a matter of life and death, and certainly not a reason for you to get that little frown line in your forehead. Look, why don't you come with me to the kickoff of the Boone's Heritage Annual Art Exhibition this Saturday evening at the City Museum? We both love fine art. It's the biggest show of the year in this part of the state. We already enjoy each other's company. What's not to like about this opportunity? What do you think?"

"I think...it's a wonderful idea," I answered. Bless Al for his perception and his maturity. Keep it light. I needed that, and he knew it. Good friends are valuable commodities.

Work had been good, even therapeutic, since my return. I found comfort in the familiar—the wordsmithing, the research, the routine of deadlines. I had missed it and was glad to be back. These thoughts reassured me as I slipped back into task mode following lunch with Al Lanier. His friendship, even his personal interest, was reassuring. Besides my spiritual hope, which was growing more certain and precious to me daily, it was good to know that there was something to contemplate and look forward to on a personal level, as well.

I was beginning to feel quite settled and even happy for the first time in several days as I punched in the code to check my cell phone messages before tackling the afternoon's writing agenda. I had left it behind during my lunch with Al.

The unexpected voice of James Martin Neville acted as a projector to flash his face before me and with it came a quick pain.

"Hello, Jannia," I heard his deep, quiet voice say. "This is James Martin (as if I could forget to recognize the sound of that voice ever). I would like to meet with you some time in the next couple of days, if your schedule permits. I have some papers connected to our agreement with the children that I would like for you to review and sign, if they are acceptable. I am sorry to have missed you. I will try again later."

He was certainly always the gentleman. I was ashamed of how much I instantly looked forward to that next call and to the possibility of seeing him again. This battle of forgetting was going to be uphill all the way.

His reason for calling raised questions for me. Why would he still need the arrangement giving me legal guardianship of his children if something should happen to him now that he was seeking political asylum and would likely be remaining in the States? And especially why, now that he might soon have another wife, the flawless Ms. VanderCross, to fill that role?

Turning my attention back to my writing after this disturbing phone message took main strength. And a silent but desperate prayer.

25

An Exhibit to Remember

I still had not heard from James Martin again before the weekend, and the weekend meant my *date,* or my *see what happens,* or whatever we were calling it with Al Lanier. The art show we were attending was the major highlight of the annual cultural arts events in Boone's Summit and the surrounding counties. It was always an affair not to miss, which showcased the latest works by carefully selected local artists as well as sponsored a spotlight feature of some nationally known figure in the art world.

This year the spotlight was on wildlife watercolorist George Maxwell, who had captured the fauna of the Southern wilderness areas in a breathtaking collection drawn from his travels across thirteen states. The opening reception would be Saturday evening, and, wth or without Al Lanier, I wouldn't have missed it.

Boone's Summit was not New York, but we did know how to be ritzy enough to put on a first-class exhibition opening reception. To attend the event, most of the men wore their black ties while the women displayed their sequined finest. Even I found a little silver whisper of a dress that made me feel like I was thirty-two pretending to be seventeen. Pretending a bit did lift my spirits, and so did Al's boyish smile when I opened my apartment door to join him for the evening.

The opening event was scheduled for a fashionable eight o'clock, but most of us couldn't wait, so by seven-thirty the parking lot of the vintage, awe-inspiring City Museum was already plenty busy. Al took my arm as he escorted me up the long flight of marble entrance steps. Usually reticent to be led along, I was grateful for the extra help, as I had also selected nearly nonexistent and too-high silver evening sandals in which I tipped along as if they were my first pair of heels.

An interesting cross-section of the city's well-known citizens, including members of the arts community, politicians, educators, the clergy, and the social set, was attending. Mixed in were others Al and I couldn't recognize but knew they were as interested as we were in tasting the artistic delicacies of the evening.

We moved from small cluster to small cluster of our acquaintances, greeting and meeting as we entered the museum's lobby, waiting for the official opening of the exhibition gallery for the evening. We had just turned from speaking to Jake Bean and his wife when I realized that we were face to face with James Martin Neville and Branda VanderCross.

By now, I had gotten quite adept at removing any sign of give-away emotion from my face and replacing it with an all-purpose smile. I was formulating a greeting as glittery as the dress I wore when James Martin took the lead.

"Ms. Redmon, you look lovely this evening," he said, taking my hand and actually giving the back of it the briefest of kisses.

I didn't know people did that anymore.

"Mr. Lanier," he continued, "I enjoyed our conversation the other evening. Your article was quite well-written, and that is not something you will often hear the subject of an interview say."

The two men shook hands a bit warily, in my opinion, but the impression was subtle and may have been my imagination.

"Good evening, Ms. VanderCross. How nice to see you again. Thank you for being so kind to me during my...recent illness." My smile was genuine, really it was.

Some small talk followed during which I had vague feelings that James Martin was overly serious and a bit distant while Branda VanderCross was watchful and preoccupied. The scenario that played through my haze of hurt was that they were eager to be away from me and from all of the other patrons in favor of being alone and in love. Acting on this assumption, I took my first opportunity to excuse myself and turn away to greet someone else with great vivacity, someone who was most likely surprised because I hardly knew her.

Al followed cooperatively, and we were caught up again in the whirl of the evening. It was soon time for the reception to commence in earnest beginning with effusive appreciation expressed by the Museum director for those who supported the exhibition and those who were in attendance. The director was a master at making such ceremonies glowing, witty, and brief. He followed these remarks with fascinating introductions of the participating artists and their works.

The doors to the exhibition gallery proper were then ceremoniously opened, and we collectively moved inside to taste both the artistic and edible treats in waiting for our consumption. The evening was off to an enticing start. I smiled and stumbled along with it, lecturing myself as I went.

In spite of the fact that this was a date of sorts, Al had explained that he needed some minutes to gather additional background and comments from the major contributors and sponsors of the evening. I was happy to use my time wisely by visiting the refreshment table, and then finding a nice, quiet, potted plant with which to screen myself. Fortunately, the plant was positioned near an intriguing collage by my favorite local artist, which I could pretend to scrutinize. Unfortunately, my examination of the creation did not last as long as Al's mission, leaving me feeling a bit closed in and restless.

I needed fresh air and solitude, both of which I found as soon as I slipped out of the exhibit rooms, through the lobby, and onto the vast front portico of the City Museum. The building was a magnificent structure built in the middle of the architectural excesses of the nineteen twenties. It was a wonder of cement, massive columns, wide steps, marble floors and chandeliers. What it lacked in practicality, it made up for in ostentatious arrogance.

In preparation for the exhibition, the museum staff had softened the appearance of the façade by tastefully but abundantly staggering potted evergreens up the front entrance steps and clustering them decorously across the front. For this dazzling evening, they were festooned with tiny white Christmas lights, making it Christmas in June.

It was in the darkness behind a large column amidst a clump of the greenery that I found my privacy. The cool of the smooth cement bench placed close against the old building gave me a place of respite to catch my breath and my composure. The gallery was situated in the middle of the downtown section of Boone's Summit, and the height of its porch offered a brilliant view of the inner city and its gracefully aged buildings, all of which were lost on me hidden safely where I could struggle with my emotions.

For reassurance, I was literally engaged in repeating some of my favorite verses to myself about God's planning for us, such as, *"A man's [or a woman's] heart plans his way, but the Lord directs his steps,"* from Proverbs 16:9, when my attention was caught by the sound of late arrivals and a car door slamming some distance below me.

As curiosity is my constant companion, I stood and walked behind the huge fluted column nearest me to see who might be arriving so late in the evening. When I did so, I observed a black limousine at the bottom of the long set of steps below where I stood. A striking, dark-skinned couple emerged from the car and began walking up the steps of the museum.

They were young, late twenties maybe, and most stylishly dressed in what I could only describe as neo-African couturier fashion. From the bottom of the steps I had taken them to be merely late arriving art patrons, but as they drew nearer to where I was hidden from their view, I began to have a strange feeling that they were not in attendance for the same reasons as most of the others inside of the building.

What gave me that impression? What caused the alarms to sound inside me? I'm really not sure. Something in their movements or something I pre-imagined in my highly charged state? Or was it the Lord figuratively tapping my arm in warning? I prefer the latter explanation, but there was soon no longer any doubt that they had no good intentions for the evening.

The entrance to the museum was otherwise deserted except for the beautiful couple and me. They had no idea I was standing there in the darkness hidden behind layers of concrete column and greenery. They paused at the top of the steps nearby, and I moved silently further back into the darkness. I heard them conversing with each other but couldn't quite make out the words. This forced me to be a little less cautious and move slightly closer to where they stood.

My heart skipped when I recognized that their exchange was not in English at all but in what sounded like an African dialect. I didn't understand the language, and I couldn't be sure, but the intonations sounded like something I had heard recently...in Khutule.

I had especially noticed the unique cadences of the dialect, so much so that I had asked Jamul about it. Now it appeared that I might have native speakers standing within a few feet of me halfway around the world in western North Carolina. Was this an innocent coincidence? Late-arriving friends of James Martin and Banolo from their home country? Maybe.

I was mentally processing my theories when the man reached inside his stylishly cut long black coat and pulled out an object that he briefly displayed in the palm of his hand. The shadows made it hard for me to see clearly, but I thought I saw a flash of metal. He gripped the object, and the reflection off of a thin blade was clearly visible just for a moment as he folded the blade away and offered the object to the woman. She placed it into her small evening bag, which glittered in the lights from high above the entranceway, and they moved toward the massive doors to the museum. The man's arm was around her waist, and he gave her a brief embrace before disappearing inside of the building.

This brief scenario convinced me with a thorough and horrifying assurance that my initial instincts had been correct. These two visitors meant immediate harm to someone, and I was sure that person was Sir James Martin Neville. What should I do? What could I do? There was no specific plan, but inaction was out of the question.

With one of those, *Oh God, help me right now please!* prayers hurled upward, I grasped the handle to a big entrance door and pulled it open. The couple was less than ten feet ahead of me moving across the lobby toward the exhibition gallery.

I had another flash of memory about the biblical David avoiding capture by the Philistines by acting crazy. I could do that!

"Hey ya'll, wait up!" I clattered on my high heels as loudly as I could, nearly tripping as I moved into the lobby and making my voice as faux Southern and smoozy as possible.

"Are ya'll late too? Whoo-eeh, I had so much trouble finding a place to park! Ya'll were smart just to park your big old limo right smack in the way at the bottom of the steps." This I followed with a high-pitched nervous giggle that even grated on my ears while I continued to wobble and clank my three-inch heels against the marble floors.

All of this commotion seemed to have a useful effect, as it caused the couple to turn toward me with surprised and less than friendly expressions on their faces. Now that I clearly had an audience, the real show was on. I stopped and pretended to straighten my dress and hair as they watched me intently. I had won the high school drama award my senior year, and I was putting it all to good use.

"What a mess I am. Really, I had to run almost two blocks. I'm scared to be out on these streets by myself at night, aren't ya'll? But then, one of you is a man, and men don't seem to have that much trouble."

I laughed the awful laugh again, and all the while I was hurrying across the lobby toward them as they turned and proceeded on their way toward the gallery doors. That was not good.

"'Scuse me, sorry to hold you up, but do either one of ya'll know where the little girls' room is? I'd just love to repair all this damage before I go inside. You see I'm dating this real good-looking man, and he asked me to meet him here at this shindig tonight. *(Shindig?)* By the way, what kind of get-together is this, anyway?"

By now I was even with them but not too close.

"Do I look all right? I'm so late I just hate to take any more time. Is my hair okay?"

The man brought his hand up as if reaching toward the inside of his tuxedo. Just when I fully expected to be shot dead while standing there in the lobby badly overacting, the woman smiled broadly and answered me in the most syrupy Southern accent I have ever heard.

"Honey, you look divine. That's some lucky man you have. Now don't you keep him waiting, you heah?"

I was stunned. Could I have been mistaken? Was she really just a Southern woman who also spoke an African dialect coming to an art exhibit with a well-dressed man who was simply handing her a...a what? Who was I kidding? He had handed her a retractable stiletto. I had watched him demonstrate it, dark or not dark, on the porch of the building in which we were standing. This girl was a great actress, much better than I, but she didn't know I knew what she was doing.

"Why thank you now," I crooned as I sailed past them both, swept open the gallery doors and moved into the room several steps ahead of them.

Now what? What was next?

I could scream "Fire!" and clear the room, losing all chance to stop the couple for good. I could run frantically up to warn James Martin and maybe embarrass myself and a lot of other people unnecessarily, again losing further prevention opportunities. Or I could act smart.

Oh, Lord, please help me to act smart. I'm scared to death here.

I moved as fast as I dared off to the side of the room, where the refreshment tables waited invitingly. I could pretend to have punch and cookies while I scoped the room to place the people I needed to locate—James Martin, Al, and hopefully members of the Museum security team. I had noticed that security was armed, and while I had not seen any weapons but the stiletto on the African couple, I had not forgotten the menacing way he reached toward the inner pocket of his tux when I first called to them in the lobby.

At that moment, the gallery doors opened and the couple slipped elegantly and unobtrusively inside. I leaned over, pretending to inspect the caviar presentation, while watching them circulate around the perimeter of the room, pretending to appreciate the paintings displayed on the walls.

I was not fooled by their feigned attraction to the exhibit, because they were moving far too quickly for any genuine interest in the pieces of art. Their movements in the general direction of James Martin and Branda VanderCross were beginning to confirm what I suspected earlier about their intentions.

My concentration on the drama unfolding in front of me was rudely broken by a movement at my side and the unmistakable sounds of the local gossip columnist for my employing newspaper.

"Why, Jannia Redmon, don't you look the sight of lovely tonight! I heard you would be in attendance on the arm of our esteemed Albert Lanier. And here you are all by your lonesome. It must be hard dating a man who's also on duty, so to speak."

"Markie McCrae, it's nice to see you too. Actually I'm here with Al, although I must say I don't feel like I'm playing second fiddle to his job. I knew he'd be working."

All of this was spoken without turning to face her or losing sight of the couple still conversing and gesturing appropriately, as if immersed in each other and in the art they were viewing. All the while they were drawing closer to James Martin.

"Markie, you must excuse me as I am working on a project at the moment also."

Maybe I could explain later, but at the moment I had no time for distractions. The couple, acting so obviously oblivious to anyone else around them, had stopped their forward motion about twenty feet away from James Martin. I also began to move rapidly in his direction, waving two cups of punch in front of me as if I were taking one of them to a friend.

I noticed that Branda VanderCross had also seen the couple and was eyeing them with a slight frown as I saw her reach for James Martin's arm. He was talking to another patron and seemed to be unmindful of anything out of the ordinary.

When I was about the same distance as the African couple from James Martin, I saw the two exchange a significant look, a signal. I was sure that some action was imminent. I had to stop the impending attack myself, and I had to do it without risking James Martin's life or causing a general panic.

What to do?

There was no time to evacuate the room or get help from security. I knew the plan was to get as close to James Martin as possible, use the retractable blade quickly and cleanly, and move away before anyone realized what had happened. In the confusion, they would be gone, and he would be hurt or probably worse. It was now or never, and my earlier dumb Southern act would just have to suffice.

I was now about five feet in front of James Martin, and the couple was moving up quickly to his side. This was it.

"How dare you bring that woman here with you when you told me you belonged to me?" I spoke stridently and loudly enough to be heard by all standing around us. Moving between the couple and James Martin, I threw the contents of both of the cups of punch directly into the faces of James Martin and Branda VanderCross. They could not have looked more stunned. Then I turned to face the African couple directly behind me, engaging them in my desperate drama.

"Can you believe this?" I made eye contact with the woman as if she were a close confidant. "Isn't that just like a man to tell one woman he loves her and then play her for a fool with another woman?"

I was moving right into her personal space, and she was looking at me as if I were crazy and moving back before my advance. My diversion was working. It was then that I noticed she had an exhibition program wrapped in one hand and was clutching it tightly with the other. I knew what was hidden in that program.

At that moment our eyes met again. She knew that I knew, and in an instant she was playing my own game by moving against me and pushing me toward James Martin. I was not her prey, so I was not afraid of her knife, but she was going to use my body as a shield to move toward him. She was going to use my tactics to divert attention from what she was about to do.

"Somebody get this crazy woman off of me," she spoke loudly, as she shoved me harder the last few feet toward James Martin, still moving with me. "She's trying to hurt me! I think this woman is insane!"

It must have been quite a scene. By now two of the security guards were closing in on us, and the African woman had pushed me back against James Martin but was making it appear as if I were the aggressor. I had clearly underestimated this lady. All she had to do now was reach past me, still using me as cover, and stab James Martin. She was thin but strong, and her eyes were cold and determined.

I felt more than saw her arm pull back enough to gain momentum and sensed she was about to use her weapon. What if I couldn't save him even if I shrieked that she had a knife...even if I used myself as a shield? There was no more time. I managed to angle my body slightly toward her and slightly more in front of where I thought the knife might go. I prayed that was enough.

Apparently I had also underestimated Branda VanderCross. Just before I sensed the hot sting in my side, I felt her iron grip pull me away from the African woman and down toward the floor. As I was sliding down, I saw Branda's beautiful blond figure, weapon drawn, reach out an elegantly clad foot and trip the other woman who had turned to flee.

Someone somewhere shot off firecrackers. Surely I must be at the county fair. People screamed as the roller coaster we were riding came over the crest of the hill, and then I was lying on the nice soft grass and watching the carousel go around and around. I felt good...really good because I could see James Martin alive and reaching toward me before the lights of the fair went black.

26

Close Call

The first person I saw when I opened my eyes again was Al Lanier. He was holding my hand, and I was content. After all, we were on a date, of sorts. Except that I was wearing a bloody white sheet instead of my sparkly silver dress, and his face was the same color white as my sheet.

"Al, what's happening? This isn't the art exhibition!" Apparently my mastery at understatement of the obvious added some color to his cheeks because he laughed disproportionately loudly to my remark. I failed to see what was funny.

Another face appeared above me. "Ms. Redmon, I'm Dr. Burns. You're in the emergency room at Mountain Memorial Hospital. Please try to lie quietly while we make you comfortable."

"You see," I told Al, "I was right! This is not the art...this is where? Am I under arrest?"

Now the doctor laughed.

"No, but you have been injured, Ms. Redmon. You'll be fine, but you need a few stitches. I've given you a little something for the pain and now we'll take you to the operating room."

I tried very hard to focus, but my eyes were not under my control. If I closed them for a minute, I could think more clearly and know how to ask Al what was going on. He was my good friend, and I knew he would tell me. He would help me escape out of a window if I needed him to. Why was it hard to breathe? I thought we had been at the county fair all night. I was having fun. Why were we here?

My next journey into consciousness came two days later in a hospital room after having spent twenty-four hours in intensive care. It was not my injury, which was significant but would heal, that had slowed my recovery but a severe reaction to the pain medicine given in the emergency room. It was rare but frightening enough for the hospital to keep me on close watch.

As I became aware of my surroundings I felt weak and fragile but overjoyed to have my faculties about me again.

When I moved my head to look around, I met the eyes of GranJuel Everston watching me closely as she sat by my bedside, ramrod straight, every hair in place, and her hands folded in her lap as if in church. I wondered whether she had been there for minutes or hours.

"Good morning...afternoon...?" I found that I had lost all sense of time, and it was hard to talk. My throat hurt.

"It is evening, Ms. Redmon, and I am pleased to see that you are awake. Are you in any pain?" This communication was spoken most articulately and precisely, as GranJuel did everything.

"Thank you, Mrs. Everston. I'm not in any pain." I began to notice the IV to which I was attached and feel the pull of bandaging on my side.

"Please tell me what..."

The lady interrupted my question. "No, Jannia. We will not speak of unpleasantness now. We will discuss all events of the past few days at another time. Suffice it to say that much gratitude is due you and many apologies as well. Now, if you will please lie quietly, I shall inform the nursing staff that you are awake."

She arose gracefully for a woman of her age and glided elegantly from the room.

Eventually, I would learn that the bandage on my side closed twelve stitches mending a deep cut carved into me by the African woman's switchblade. There would have been a lot more, I am told, or worse, had not Ms. VanderCross pulled me away from the blade in time. As it turned out, my body had deflected the sharp edge from its intended victim, and James Martin was unharmed. Branda had tripped and detained the attacker, and while the companion had finally used his gun in a desperate attempt to flee, the security guards had stopped his escape permanently. His life was the only one lost.

As the investigation unfolded, it came to light that the two assailants were indeed in America on a mission from Khutule related to James Martin's past. While they were not really a couple in marriage, they were joined by a deep hatred of anyone who bore the Neville name. Sadly, the lovely woman was the granddaughter of the former head of the African Re-Unification Coalition—the same man who had killed James Martin's mother and aunt and had been hung by his father, the former Prime Minister. The woman's companion was her cousin and the son of the ARC member who had killed James Martin's father.

The African Re-Unification Movement had done great harm to the Neville family, but they had paid a high price for it. Upon learning that her beloved cousin had been killed in the gallery, the lady's bravado collapsed as she relayed a troublesome plot of revenge and murder against the proclaimed enemies of her relatives.

Equally astonishing was the role that Branda VanderCross played in the scenario that occurred at the art gallery. In fact, to my great amazement, she had really been play-acting in quite a drama for the past several months.

Branda, I learned, was actually an FBI agent who had been given the assignment of helping protect Sir James Martin Neville, a recent celebrity emigrant from Africa and more recently an applicant for political asylum from Khutule. While not at liberty to discuss her professional role with anyone due to security reasons, not even the members of his household, she had successfully posed as his lady friend until the events at the exhibition caused her to reveal her true identity.

Apparently James Martin's narrow escapes while in the U.S. had been brought to the attention of our government by those sponsoring his tour. In response to the convincing nature of his story and to political pressures from his supporters, the FBI had agreed to provide protection to him while in the States as long as he required it. His subsequent political asylum interview with the Immigration and Naturalization Service and the accompanying evidence documents and testimonies convinced the INS that there were sufficient grounds to grant him temporary asylum pending further investigation. The decision on whether to grant asylum would almost surely be made in his favor, especially now.

It seems that the U.S. government didn't wish to answer to the wrath of the international music community in the event that harm came to such a global treasure as Sir James Martin Neville on its watch. This last piece of information had come to me during a visit from James Martin himself. The twinkle in his eye indicated that he fully enjoyed being considered an international treasure, even though he was clearly and thoroughly in touch with the fickle nature of fame.

His amusement increased, at my expense, as he quoted back to me the words of the diversion I had used to turn the attention of his attackers away from their mission: *"How dare you bring that woman here with you when you pretended to belong to me?"* Jannia, I would never have suspected you could be so jealous." His laughing eyes told me he had no idea of the truth of the matter—he really didn't know how I felt about him.

I found it difficult to be in such close proximity to James Martin without reaching out to touch him. I needed to be reassured he was all right. I couldn't allow myself even that small luxury as I lay in the narrow hospital bed listening to his talk and laughter, smelling the roses he had placed in a vase on the table beside of me.

Then I heard his tone change.

"Jannia, there are some things I need to say to you." He fastened his eyes on mine, and it was all I could do not to turn my face away from them. I was afraid of what he was going to say. Somehow, it didn't feel as if he were about to declare his eternal love and offer me a place on the back of his winged stallion as we galloped away to his stronghold in the clouds. No, this was not going to be that kind of speech. I knew by the way his eyes failed to twinkle any more.

Oh, how I hoped I could be strong just this once more. In spite of all of my resolutions, my heart had already decided the way I wanted this to go. I could admit that to myself now. But I knew the verse in Proverbs 16 about the Lord making the final decision. Suppose He had not directed James Martin's steps in my direction? Or mine in his? What would I do?

"Jannia?"

"Yes, I'm sorry. I'm ready. What did you want to tell me?" My game face was now in place.

"I must ask your forgiveness for involving you in the circumstances of my life that have brought you to this place." His gesture indicated the hospital room in which I lay. "You were a stranger to me, but you showed me compassion. You showed caring and self-sacrifice to my children at a time when I admit I was feeling rather desperate."

I must have looked surprised at this admission because his next words were spoken with a self-conscious smile.

"Yes, I do remember the *I am a Man of Faith* speech I delivered to you that day we met in the cemetery. It was not untrue, the part about my faith I mean. But I have also come to understand that desperation is not a becoming characteristic in a Christian. We have more hope than that. I am afraid that my anxiety, my lack of faith, has caused me to endanger your life on more than one occasion. For that I am filled with sorrow and regret. It also makes me ashamed that I have not been more forthcoming with all of the details about my life."

I wasn't sure what he was referring to, but I know I was thinking about his alleged relationship with Branda VanderCross. Suppose now it wasn't so alleged. What if he had grown genuinely fond of her during the time they were constantly thrown together? Maybe they were even now planning a...?

"I ask your forgiveness, Jannia. Will you grant me that favor?" This time he placed a firm, warm grip over my cold hand as it lay on the top of the hospital blanket.

181

"If there were anything to forgive, I would do so. There isn't. You've forgotten that I found you and Marta on my own accord. Don't you remember how I chased Banolo's taxi after seeing them at McDonald's simply to satisfy my curiosity about why she was there in his taxi? I used you, remember? I wanted a story line for a novel. I should be asking your forgiveness. And besides, were it not for you, I might never have seen what beautiful vacation spots Khutule has to offer."

I could do this. I could meet his eyes and make light of his attention. I was doing it and succeeding.

"Now I know you are out of your head, my dear Jannia."

His laugh brought levity back to the moment and made me able to catch the breath I felt like I had been holding since he came into my room.

"I must thank you for each of us—Marta, Jack, GranJuel, and for myself. We are together because of you. We have never been a family...not really...until now. There are no words of appreciation for that. I would like to release you from your promise to take my children in the event of my death. That also was unfair of me to ask, even under the circumstances, although it gave me great comfort. You had your own life, which you nearly sacrificed for ours. It is time we let you go back to living your life. We hope that you will continue to share some small part of that life with us. My children, I am afraid, have become quite attached to you."

A nurse who had entered on a mission to administer my pain medication interrupted us...medication that would do double duty. It was not so much the pain in my side from the knife that hurt so much, but the pain in the middle of my chest threatened to do me in.

As James Martin told me good-bye and turned to leave, I was utterly aware that he had been caring and grateful and kind, but he had not been personal. He had done his duty by me as I would expect from such a gentleman, but the obligation appeared to end there.

I was glad for the sting of the needle, followed gradually by the sensation of being removed from present reality. I knew, as I began to slide toward sleep, that it was a brief and artificial reprieve from my feelings, but a reprieve nonetheless.

27

Marta's Request

A ll in all, I was in the hospital only four days, but that was enough to make me feel weak and frail. I was glad for Al Lanier's comforting arm to lean on as I walked the short way from my wheelchair to his car waiting at the hospital exit.

Al and I were friends. We had somehow come to understand, almost without words, that friendship was suitable to both of us. We realized before it was too late that we didn't want to sacrifice the friendship we already had for the possibility of something more permanent, which we might never have.

On the drive from the hospital to my apartment, I told Al I had been thinking of making a move. Three years at one job was a long time for me. Up until now, I had been at ease in Boone's Summit. I liked my job at the paper, and I loved working for Jake Bean. Getting back to work in a couple more days would be a blessing after being so inactive.

I realized, though, that I had begun to feel the first stirrings of restlessness, as if there were something more...somewhere for me to do. It was hard to describe, but I tried as Al drove me home through the most glorious day of early summer.

"I can't say I feel the way you do, Jannia. I've lived in Boone's Summit all my life. I can't see doing otherwise. True, there are still some things left undone that I want to do—some challenges." He looked at me and smiled. "Like finding a nice wifely type, settling down, and winning a Pulitzer Prize for excellence in reporting on a story really worth telling...maybe someday." Al sounded like he was joking, but I think he was serious.

"I want you to grant me one request, Jannia, just one. I'd like for you to wait at least three months before making any move to find a new job in a new place. Give it time. You've come through some major life-challenging events. Don't make any decisions too quickly, no matter how much you're tempted to run for your life."

Run for my life? I looked at him quickly to see if he had any idea how close to the truth he spoke. It was as if he knew how lost and sad I was feeling without further need to help protect James Martin's little family...and James Martin.

"Al, you've been a good friend. I'd like to agree to your request. I really would. All I can say is that I'll think about it seriously. I will do that much."

The normalcy of Monday was welcome. I dressed for work slowly. My side still hurt when I moved. The sunshine outside was welcome, and so was the drive to work on my own. Even the walk from the parking lot felt good because my destination was not another hospital room but my usual desk in my small office on the third floor at the newspaper building.

From my office window I could see the green city park alive with summer color, thanks to the Women's Club members who tended it carefully each week. I stood at the window for a long time enjoying the calm and the beauty. Some of the trauma was beginning to fade and, with it, the sadness. Being despondent was hard on a day like this. For that I was thankful.

Over the next few weeks, my pre-James Martin routine began to return at a comforting pace. Work was good, I was busy and there was no time to think. I played a game to see just how much more I could get done each day than the one before. So far I was way ahead.

One month from the day I left the hospital, there was a note on my desk when I arrived at work requesting that I check in with Jake Bean. I always looked forward to our visits.

"Jake, you look great. How was your week at the lake? Was the fishing good? How's Mareen?"

"Mareen's good, the lake's good, and I'd rather be fishing now. Retirement's beginning to have a certain magnetism. It's good to see you feeling better, Jannia. Thanks for coming by. Have a seat."

"Is this a business call, Jake?" I was beginning to feel a bit uneasy. "Is there a problem?"

"With the job? No, my dear, your columns are superior. Your writing's better than ever. The vacation pieces make even me want to travel to Africa, and I barely leave the state."

"Did you get a chance to read the draft of the new piece on tandem HALO jumping? I'm hoping it'll appeal to a totally different set of readers. I'm planning an interview with...what?"

His look was serious. "Actually, this is a personal visit, Jannia. Professionally, you're at the top of your game. No problems and some of the best writing I've witnessed. Personally? Honey, you know you're like my daughter. I'm afraid I've held off on this conversation longer than I should have."

"What's wrong, Jake? What do you need to say to me?"

"You're in a frenzy, Jannia. I've never seen anyone work as hard, or as compulsively, as you are now. Granted it's a quiet frenzy, and you're very productive. But there's no way you can survive this pace. I'm worried. Tell me what's wrong?"

Jake was not a man who spared words...or feelings...when he knew he had a job to do and knew he was right. I was busted. Good thing, too, because my working game was beginning to wear me thin. I had revved my brain to such a level that I was having trouble stopping long enough to sleep. Sleep seemed a waste of time. Sitting still and doing nothing was out of the question. I had honed multi-tasking to an art form.

"Jannia, this is not a conversation I would have with just any of my employees. I'm confident you will understand what I mean. In the spirit of the verse in 1 Peter, are you casting your worries where they belong, or are you trying too hard to take care of what's bothering you by yourself? I recognize the telltale signs of do-it-yourself faith. Take my word...it doesn't work."

He was willing to sit and wait when he saw that I had trouble responding. Jake didn't make me uncomfortable; he just waited. We both knew he was right about my recent actions. We also both knew this was not the time or place to go into an extended discussion. It was enough that he had seen my predicament and moved to intervene.

"Thank you, Mr. Bean, sir. As usual, you are most perceptive. I consider myself admonished. May I be excused?"

"You may. Let me know if I can help."

It was time for the morning break, long recognized as a tradition in the newsroom. It was a corporate coping skill to add some refinement to our otherwise rather unsophisticated existence. Usually there were sufficient pastries available in the coffee shop on the ground floor of our building to keep us satisfied without going further abroad. Today I needed fresh air more than a pastry.

To be in the middle of the city, the little park across the street was an unexpected touch of country comes to town. There was even a concrete banked stream that appeared from nowhere and returned to nowhere but provided a suggestion of serenity within its urban ecosystem.

I sat on a bench beside the water and marveled at Jake's insight. My game of replacing the empty place inside me with frenzied work-related activity was ill conceived. I was clearly not my own answer to my needs. I knew Who was, and I spent the next minutes wisely in conversation with my Heavenly Father.

Two days later the phone on my desk rang while I was putting the final touches on coverage of the summer celebrity wedding that had graced the mountain just above Boone's Summit.

"Jannia? Is that you?"

"Jack, how wonderful! How are you?"

"Good, I'm good, thank you." He sounded so...adult. "Look, if you're not too busy, I have somebody...Marta wants to talk to you. I will put her on the line."

This was followed by silence.

"Marta, are you there? Talk to me, honey. Is everything okay?"

"Jannia, I thought you forgot about us. Jack said you didn't, but..."

"Darling, I'm sorry! Of course I didn't forget you. I've been working very hard, but I think about you all the time. Are you all right, Marta? Is something the matter?"

"I miss you, Jannia. Can you come see us?"

"Of course I can, Marta. I'll come today, tonight if it's okay. Can you put your brother back on, please? Let me talk to Jack now, darling."

"Jannia, I want to see you too." He didn't sound so adult now. "Daddy said we shouldn't bother you. He said..."

"Jack, where is your father?"

"He's away. I think he has gone to Chicago. He's hoping to begin his work again soon."

"Is GranJuel there with you?"

"She is here. Marta became upset. GranJuel told me to call."

"Jack, tell GranJuel I'd like to come there right after work. See if that's all right with her. I'll hold on."

I could hear him talking with his great-grandmother close by the phone. I could hear my own heartbeat louder. *She had told him to call me?*

"Ms. Redmon?" It was GranJuel herself on the phone. "Ms. Redmon, I would very much appreciate a visit from you this evening. My Marta is quite disturbed because she has not seen you of late. Jack has also requested that you come. Would you be so kind as to grace us with your presence, if it is convenient for you?"

"I'll be there as quickly as I can after work...maybe about five-thirty. Please tell the children."

"Yes, I will. Thank you." The click I heard as she hung up was as precise as her response.

The children missed me! The children wanted me. They called for me. That was all I could think of as I rushed through the final copy of my story, filed it, straightened my desk, and left the office at five for the first time in a month.

Today I would have welcomed the sight of Banolo's battered taxi as I walked to my car. It would have been a relief to sit back and let him deliver me to the Everston-Neville apartment instead of having to battle the early evening traffic on my own. He would not be waiting for me, I knew.

Since James Martin was in Chicago, Banolo would be there too. He seldom left James Martin's side since the night his friend barely escaped death. James Martin's celebrity status and the persisting grudge against him held by the Khutulen government dictated his continued need for a bodyguard. After the incident in the gallery in which she had helped to save his life, James Martin had insisted that the services of Ms. VanderCross were no longer needed. He argued that the immediate danger from the ARC was over, at least for now, and that his own handpicked protector, Banolo, would be sufficient protection for the time being.

I learned all of this during a brief and unexpected visit from Branda during my recovery time in the hospital. She came late in the evening, long past usual visiting hours. Later I would wonder if she came when I was sure to be alone. She told me she would be leaving and wished me a quick recovery. Naturally I thanked her profusely for saving James Martin's life. To that, she looked at me strangely for a while before responding.

"It was a life worth saving, without a doubt. He's an amazing man. And I credit you with saving it, almost single-handedly."

When I tried to dissent, she merely shrugged and changed the subject. She told me she was leaving for her next mission...she wouldn't tell me where.

"You're a fortunate woman, Jannia. I'll miss getting to know you better. I wish you happiness. Good-bye."

Before I could think of a suitable response to her curious farewell, she was gone.

When she left, I lay awake for hours, deep into the night, trying to figure out what she meant. What could she, as beautiful and self-assured as she was, possibly have learned from me? We hardly knew each other, had only spoken a few times. On most occasions, when I knew she'd be present, I had avoided her. Jealousy had been a hard emotion for me. I found it still was. She was leaving Boone's Summit, but was she leaving her contact with James Martin?

Never mind. With determination, I forced my thoughts back to the present and my immediate destination. I would concentrate on fighting rush-hour traffic and not being followed with the anticipation of being with James Martin's children.

When I pulled up to the curb across from the apartment building, I was struck by the same feeling I had the first time I saw the place. The evident deterioration on the outside, I now knew, belied the elegance and comfort within. It was a strange place, but a good one in which James Martin's little family could be relatively safe for now.

As I opened my door to step onto the sidewalk, I looked up to see two sets of eyes watching me from the top step outside of the first floor apartment that had once belonged to their deceased grandparents. This was the place where I had met Marta. This is where it started. I looked up again and the same delicate, paper-thin face, aged and proud, looked at me from the window of the second floor apartment. It was GranJuel, just like on that first day.

Marta leapt into my arms, nearly knocking me off of my feet. The tiny child was growing long legs and arms that wrapped around me as I held her little body close. Uncharacteristic chatter tumbled out as if she wanted to tell me all of her news in one long, unbroken sentence.

Jack stood quietly at the top of the steps and watched.

When I reached him, I put my hand softly along the side of his face. "Jack, I've missed you so much."

He hesitated for only an instant before he, too, threw his arms around my waist over Marta's, wrapping the three of us together in a tight hold.

GranJuel's greeting, when we finally made our way to the second floor foyer of her apartment, was more restrained. She did offer her fragile hand, but her grasp offered little warmth.

"Please come in, Ms. Redmon. I have planned a light supper for you and the children, as they often eat informally when their father is not in residence. I regret to inform you that Sir Neville is not presently at home. He is out of town on business, I am afraid." Her bright eyes watched me closely for disappointment, I was sure, or any other telltale sign of emotion.

"I understand. I'm here to see the children. It was kind of you to invite me." Surely I was disappointed, but she wouldn't know it.

The children and I had our supper on the private balcony. While it was still warm during the day, the evenings were beginning to offer the first twinges of fall, and I had to send Marta in for her sweater. We talked and laughed and ate the formal little sandwiches and fancy cakes one would have at high tea, but we drank lemonade instead.

Marta soon inched onto my lap, and Jack moved his patio chair as close to mine as he could and still maintain his adolescent image. They competed with each other to tell me something new that had taken place. I could see that Marta was much less shy, and the constant worry lines that had been present between Jack's eyes had softened, allowing him to look much more like the growing boy he still was.

I knew not to overstay GranJuel's welcome, but pulling myself away from my own personal fan club was harder than I had expected. It took cross-my-heart promises to both of the children and considerable exercise of self-discipline on my part before I could tell them good-bye.

GranJuel joined them at the doorway as they told me goodnight. When I had given each one a hug, she asked them to prepare for bedtime, and they reluctantly obeyed, leaving me alone with their great-grandmother.

"Mrs. Everston, I would like permission to take the children for an outing on the Saturday after next. Do you think I could pick them up in the morning so that we could spend the day together? There are some special things around the city I would like to show them. Do you think their father would approve?"

She looked at me steadily without smiling. GranJuel was an inscrutable personality, and I felt like I still didn't measure up in her eyes.

Finally she answered. "We are expecting Sir Neville home on Thursday evening. While I will certainly discuss your request with him, I am afraid he already has plans for the family on that weekend. I'm sure, however, he will be in touch. Good night, Ms. Redmon."

I understood that I had been excused, and I found I was incredibly tired all of a sudden. The door closed quietly behind me before I even had time to reach the nearby elevator.

28

The Invitation

T he drive home was lonely and empty. I missed the children more after being with them than after weeks without seeing them. It was clear that keeping up our relationship was going to take patience and fortitude to navigate around GranJuel, as well as strength to hide how much I also missed seeing their father. I loved the children. Would I be strong enough to manage seeing them under such circumstances? Would it be worth it? Could staying away be the best alternative, if not the most pleasant?

My personal doubts and arguments continued during the next few days as I waited to hear whether I would be allowed to see Marta and Jack on Saturday. Thursday came, and still I had no word. This was the day James Martin was to return home. Surely I would find a call waiting on my answer machine at my apartment. For the second time in a month, I left work on time, but no message reached my cell phone or greeted me when I reached home.

By eight o'clock I was considering calling James Martin's apartment to pursue a response for myself. I hadn't told the children what my plans were ahead of time, as I didn't want to raise their hopes and risk disappointing them. But by calling, I would also risk having to speak directly with James Martin, and on that basis, I waited.

At nine I had worried myself through a medium sized box of chocolates, thus risking a migraine. I had finally given up and was just stepping into the shower when I heard the phone. It rang four times before I had the courage to pick up the receiver. It was James Martin.

"Good evening, Jannia. I'm sorry I missed your visit. The children were ecstatic. Thank you for coming to see them. Did they overwhelm you? I told them you had been quite busy catching up since you were in hospital. How are you?"

"Well, thank you. They explained you were away. We had a wonderful visit. I've...missed them. They caught me up on all their news. Jack seems to be coming along nicely. He's such a gentleman. How have you been?"

I might have been auditioning for a movie role. I was warm yet subdued, not too eager yet sincere, genuine yet a bit removed. The fact was, I had trouble making words form correctly and was so near to panic that I was having difficulty breathing. I closed my eyes as he responded to my question, trying not to sound like I was hyperventilating.

"Jannia, GranJuel informed me that you wanted to spend some extended time with the children on Saturday. She may have also informed you about our plans to go out of town for a long weekend."

There was a long pause, as if he didn't quite know how to let me down easily. I knew how to help him.

"Yes, of course Saturday wouldn't be suitable then. I completely understand. Perhaps next week, or whenever it's convenient. I just wanted to take them to the zoo and downtown to the new children's café. It has a menu of entrees selected by a panel of children. I can't wait to see what interesting dishes might be available. Actually, I'm very fond of peanut butter."

Keep it light. Keep it casual. I knew the call would end soon, and I could go on with the rest of my life. James Martin's response stunned me.

"As a matter of fact, I was going to ask if you would like to join us. GranJuel will be along, and of course Banolo. Marta and Jack would be most pleased."

He sounded hopeful, but I noticed that he failed to add, *And I would especially love for you to come along so that we can spend some time together also. I've missed you, Jannia. I'm not sure I can go on without...*

But I hadn't answered him yet.

"I'm sorry, James Martin. Yes, I heard your invitation. Actually, it sounds like a wonderful idea, but I have some stories to finish up that I...excuse me?"

It was not like James Martin to interrupt. I listened, and then asked him to repeat. "Jake Bean told you what?"

"He told me you were working far too hard. He's quite worried about your health, Jannia. He says you're working yourself into a *spell*, whatever that is."

That made me laugh. "A spell is an old Southern expression that means...what am I saying? Thank you for your concern, but I'm feeling fine, really. It's just that I've been very busy lately on some new projects. Maybe Jake worries too much."

"Will you come with us, Jannia? Please?"

"I...I'm not sure...I have some things...I will need to get back with you. Could I let you know tomorrow, say by two o'clock?"

"That will be fine. We will speak then, if I may call you at work? The children would love for you to come, if you can. Good evening, Jannia."

James Martin's phone call left me feeling more vulnerable than ever. If I agreed to be a guest on the family outing, I would get to spend the time I wanted with Marta and Jack. That was a point for the pro side. But it might also mean that GranJuel would subject me to further lukewarm-to-cool treatment. While that prospect didn't appeal to me, I could withstand it for the sake of being with the children.

On the other hand, I would have to be in close proximity to James Martin. That would be especially painful, knowing I was likely invited only because the children wanted me along. Some situations aren't worth the cost. This might be one of them.

In fact, I would soon have to decide whether pursuing a close relationship with the children was worth the ongoing emotional trauma of being near their father. Maybe moving away was the best plan after all. Still, I had promised Al Lanier I would not make a hasty decision.

I looked at the clock. Nine-thirty p.m. I had less than twenty-four hours to decide what to do about the trip. This decision would take some momentous prayer.

I slept little that night and had made no decision when my alarm sounded. I couldn't see my way clear to decline the invitation, but neither did I feel the freedom to accept. The struggle continued as I dressed for work between my strong need for self-preservation and my intense desire to play some part in Jack and Marta's lives.

The little-used back staircase leading from the street to my office provided a respite from the usual morning social interactions. I simply was not in the mood for office chitchat with my emotions already at risk. And I didn't want to explain to my boss once more why my eyes had blue bags under them. It worked, and I slipped into my little workspace early and unnoticed.

My plan was to work as hard as I could until the phone rang, when I would be forced to make a decision. I prayed that, by then, I would know what to do. It was fortunate there was no efficiency expert looking over my shoulder as I read and reread the same sentences in my copy over and over, trying to focus on proofreading them. Everything I did took three times longer than usual.

I tried to concentrate so hard that I got a headache. I'd skipped breakfast altogether, which I knew was a mistake. Break time took me slipping down the back stairs again in search of caffeine and sugar. Fortified with chocolate doughnuts, cola, and a fast walk around the park, I returned to my desk, determined to think about the work before me and not about when the phone would ring and I would talk to James Martin.

With renewed energy, I reached for my unfinished papers and found instead, in the middle of my desk, a homemade envelope of red construction paper. It was addressed to me in a child's handwriting with a hand-drawn stamp in the wrong corner.

It took me only a second to open the envelope and find a yellow card decorated with crayon flowers, a sun, and a rainbow. A magic marker map showed a road winding up a hill from a funny little town labeled *Boones Summet*. The road zigzagged to a mountain-like structure with the words *Where I'm goin* scrawled beside of a black **X** mark. I opened the card and found a note that read: *Pleas come, Jania. Its O.K. I love you. Marta.* This was followed by, *P.S. Jack dos to.*

The decision just got easier. I wiped the tears off my face but smeared them across the map. The phone rang, and I told James Martin I would join his family for the weekend.

As part of the more relaxed security measures James Martin had requested for himself and his family, there were times when he allowed Banolo to arrange for their travel by limousine with a trusted driver other than Banolo himself. This trip was to be one of those times. James Martin's family was leaving on Thursday morning, and since I was working until Friday afternoon, I told him I would drive up to join them that evening. He insisted that Banolo, who was joining the family a day late, would come for me instead. I tried to convince him otherwise, but in the end nothing would do but for me to ride up in Banolo's taxi.

Friday came quickly and, at the risk of looking over-eager, I was on the curb in front of the office when Banolo pulled up. He loaded my small suitcase and seated me in the back. His greeting, as always courteous, was also quiet and subdued. After asking a couple polite questions, I could see that he was preoccupied with the late-afternoon traffic. I sat silently, enjoying not having to drive while he moved quickly in and out of traffic, crisscrossing around the town in a strange pattern. I didn't have to ask what he was doing. The need for caution was still present.

I realized Banolo was finally satisfied that all was well when he took an exit ramp off of the interstate onto a north-bound state road I knew led out of town toward the more remote areas of the mountains. We drove on in silence for about an hour until he pulled into a convenience store at a small rural crossroads.

Still without speaking, he left me in the taxi and went inside. It was growing dark, and I rolled down the window to feel the cooling air. The night sounds had begun, and the lights came on in a couple of houses across the way. I hadn't felt so peaceful in years.

Banolo was not gone for long, and when he returned he was carrying a small brown paper bag. "Ms. Jannia," he started as he reached in the bag and pulled out an icy cola and a candy bar, "these are for you. Thank you for coming."

"My favorites. Thank you, Banolo. How did you know?"

"I observe, Ms. Jannia. I cannot afford to miss details."

"Is it much farther?"

"Not so far as you have already come, Missy, not nearly so far." And then he smiled.

He spoke the truth as the rest of the trip took less than half an hour, but we made good use of that time.

"Do you know, Missy, that you gave me quite a scare when I learned you had followed me to where James Martin's family lived that first Saturday? I am a good bodyguard and a better taxi driver. You gave a shock to my confidence, I must say. You let me lead you to the very people I was trying to protect."

"Banolo, you never knew I was following you? No any of those times? Not the last time?"

"I never knew."

I laughed. "I'm sorry. I certainly meant no harm to anyone. I was just curious."

"Curious and a bit determined as well. Yes, Ms. Jannia, and a lot of folks are happy that you were. We are almost there."

29

Granjuel's Confession

The road had climbed significantly and had gotten more deserted. It was now almost fully dark, and I could sense dark green all around us as we wound through an area of dense forest. Banolo called ahead on his cell phone, which was having trouble getting a signal, to announce our impending arrival.

I felt him slow the taxi and turn off onto a narrow paved driveway. It started to rain, and the lights of the taxi shone on the wet pavement. I was having trouble breathing from anticipation. I sat forward and held onto the seat in front of me until my hands hurt.

We came around the last curve in the drive, and the taxi's lights illuminated a large and sprawling stone building banked against the side of the mountain as if it had been built in stages across decades. It had, and the sign beside the front door read *Boundary Inn, Circa 1929*. The historic old ivy-covered inn was beautiful and inviting in the taxi's lights. More beautiful was the sight of the small group of people standing in front of the Boundary; one was jumping up and down and clapping her hands.

"She's here, she's here, I knew she'd come, tra la!"

I could hear Marta's little song before Banolo ever got my door open. By then she was inside the taxi and in my lap, smothering me with kisses. We laughed and hugged, and I handed her off to Banolo as I stepped out to greet the others. Jack stuck out his right hand as if to shake but changed his mind and put his arms around me instead.

When I turned around, James Martin was watching me with a most serious look. My first thought was, *What have I done?* I quickly decided I didn't care, and I stood still and watched him back just as seriously. We stood like that for several moments until he spoke.

"Thank you. I wasn't sure you would come."

I resisted the urge to ask, *Are you happy to see me?* I answered instead, "I told you I would."

At that point, the innkeepers, Rory and Keating Magenis, appeared to usher us inside. GranJuel, it seems, was resting and would join us for a late supper. Marta took my hand, eager to show me the room we would share. We were the only guests, and it became clear that GranJuel knew the couple well and had been a frequent visitor over the years.

The inn was decorated in the manner of an old hunting lodge, but one that had modern conveniences and intimate sitting areas, making it warm and welcoming. The Magenises were an engaging middle-aged couple that had lived their adult lives at the inn. Once a private home, the inn had been in the Magenis family for almost four generations. It was vast and rambling, and the tour we were given before supper included intriguing vignettes and artifacts of local history.

We dined at eight on a light but comforting supper served at a big round table in the inn's huge kitchen. Banolo had eaten earlier and already gone to his room. GranJuel joined us, apparently rested and refreshed. She was in an agreeable mood and unusually talkative.

James Martin was amiable but subdued. He conversed with GranJuel, and I only joined in when asked a direct question. The children were quiet, as they often were during meals, and I could see that they were fading fast. Just before we lost them for good, I excused myself and accompanied them upstairs.

Jack gave me an exhausted smile before he disappeared down the hall into his father's room. Marta was asleep on her feet as I washed her face and pulled on her nightgown. There was a single bed she claimed tucked in the corner of our big room. The last thing I heard from Marta as I pulled the quilt over her little body was, "I love you, Jannia."

"I love you too, darling. Tomorrow we'll have some real fun. Don't forget to say your prayers..." but I could see it was too late for that.

The trip, the excitement, and the sleepy children had all affected me, as well, and I readied myself for an early bedtime. A twinge of extravagance enveloped me as I stretched out between the 400-count cotton sheets and caught the fragrance of lavender sachet.

While I was sure that sleep would come quickly, I was mistaken. I found I was too wound up to relax and too tired to think clearly. Those edges between rest and reality were strange places filled with snatches of prayers, dreams, and simulated conversations. To soothe myself, I tried to pray. I got as far as being thankful for the worthiness of God and the gift of His Son. My gratitude was drowned out by my pleas for time to spend with James Martin.

When my prayers stopped, I'm not sure, but they were followed by a vivid dream in which James Martin and I were walking together down a mountain road in the rain. I jerked awake when as I heard myself say, *I wish you could love me.* I listened to the quiet footsteps and hushed voices of GranJuel and James Martin in the hall as they went to their rooms. The last I heard for several hours was the rain in the trees outside our window.

During the night there was a storm, unusual for the time of year. The thunder was loud, and the lightening was close. I felt a jolt as Marta propelled her tiny body onto my bed and scrambled beneath the covers as close to me as she could get.

"Jannia, are you awake?" she whispered, and so I whispered in return.

"Yes, are you frightened?"

"No, but I thought you might be." There was a pause. "Yes, I don't like thunder. Do you like storms?"

"Not really, Marta. They scare me sometimes. But I know a Bible verse that helps when I get frightened. Do you want to hear it?"

"Is it, 'Jesus wept'?"

I laughed, also in a whisper. "No, this one's from Psalm 56:3. *'Whenever I am afraid, I will trust in you.'* It's talking about trusting God to help us when we're scared. Let's do that now, okay? Let's trust God and let Him worry about the storm."

"Good idea." Some moments passed. "Jannia?"

"Yes?"

"Do you love my daddy?"

Oh, out of the mouths of babes...

"Well, I care about him very much, just like I care about you and Jack. Why do you ask me that, darling?"

"I think Jack and I need a mommy. May I sleep here for a while?"

"Of course you may. Good night, Marta."...

The morning was splendid. The touches of early autumn were evident in everything I could see from my window that looked out through the near trees and across a narrow valley to the next ridge of mountains, and the next, and the next. The layers of green and blue were just beginning to take on traces of color, and the early morning sunrays held a slant that crossed the line from summer to fall. I stood for several minutes, too tangled in conflicting feelings to make a move to start the day.

My gratitude at the beauty of the morning and my joy at being in such a place with James Martin and his family clashed with my frustration that this could well be a fleeting experience that would soon leave me empty and alone.

Such double-mindedness was not productive; I knew better. Realism was acceptable, but not to the point that it would ruin what I had right now...this time with the children...and their father. This was the day my Heavenly

Father had given me. I would rejoice and be happy in it.

Breakfast was cheerful and lively. The children were rested and eager to be at some adventure, and GranJuel was cordial toward me in a way that she had not previously been. James Martin's mood matched that of his children; he seemed more relaxed and at ease than I had seen him.

I tried to sit back and observe the fun without being intrusive, but the children drew me into their conversations and plans for the morning. They wanted to hike to a place the Magenises had described about a mile's easy climb behind the inn. Called Angel Drop Falls, it had a rock formation shaped amazingly like an angel with spreading wings overhanging a small waterfall.

"Jannia wants to see the angel too, right, Jannia?"

"Wellll, Marta, let's see, I do have some letters to write and some books..."

"Please, Jannia, please, please, pleeze, puleeze!" Her drama was admirable.

"Jannia, we would like for you to come with us, right Dad?" This time Jack was at work. "It's not a bad climb, really. That is what Mr. Magenis said."

I felt a cool, soft hand on my arm. It was GranJuel; I think it was the first time she touched me willingly. I searched her eyes for a hint of her motive.

"Ms. Redmon...Jannia," she said softly, "I promise you it's worth the climb. I really do not see how you can decline such invitations as these. Could I ask that you give me a few private moments while the children and James Martin are readying themselves? I promise I won't keep you, but I really must speak to you alone before you all go off to enjoy the climb."

I looked at James Martin, who had been quiet for some time. He nodded and rose, taking the children with him as he left the breakfast room.

When the room was empty except for the two of us, GranJuel reached for her water glass and took a sip before placing it precisely in its place and blotting her lips. She visibly squared her frail shoulders and looked directly into my eyes. It was as if she prepared for some sort of ordeal. As I had no idea what she had in mind, I simply waited.

"Jannia, I owe you a profound apology for my inappropriate and mean-spirited behavior over the last months. There is no excuse, and I ask your forgiveness."

Speechless, I believe, would be a good description of my reaction. What prompted this address from the iron lady? "Mrs. Everston, of course I accept any apology you offer. If I have offended you in some way...?"

"Please call me GranJuel. No, there has been no offense. As I stated, I have no excuse. I do have an explanation, as inadequate as it is, if you care to hear it?"

I nodded my interest, and she continued.

"My husband died of an illness many years ago, so I have grown accustomed to his absence. At least I had my daughter and her husband, who were Elisia's parents, living near me. There simply weren't many members to our family. I was an only child as was my daughter and her daughter after her. I missed my granddaughter, Elisia, terribly when she went to Africa to marry James Martin. I never thought it was a good idea because I knew she was delicate of nature.

"When Elisia was sent home from Africa after the birth of Marta, I knew immediately I was going to lose her too, and I soon did. She died three weeks after arriving back home with the baby. Little Marta was less than six weeks old at the time, and Elisia's parents were devastated. Naturally they took the child. Caring for Marta gave them great comfort, and me as well, for they were all in the apartment below me.

"Marta was four years old and staying with me for the weekend when my daughter and her husband died in the crash of a small plane along with some friends. Because their deaths were accidental, they were even more shocking than those of my husband and my granddaughter. Their absence left me virtually alone except for Marta."

I would have made a move toward her at that moment, reached for her hand or something, but I was restrained by a slight lifting of her chin that told me she wanted no pity, only understanding. I waited for her to continue.

"At first I was overwhelmed. I did not inform James Martin of the deaths of his in-laws for months. I was resentful toward him for not coming to Marta when her mother died, and I was certainly not going to allow him to take her from me years later. I considered her to be mine, and she had been with me for almost a year when I finally wrote to inform him that I was the child's sole caretaker."

"What prompted you to change your mind about telling him?"

"Jannia, this will seem strange, coming from one who has shown you no Christian love during the months I have known you. Nevertheless, I have always attended a small Episcopal church in our neighborhood. A new and quite young pastor joined our congregation when Marta was about five. I considered him a novice as a shepherd until he began visiting me for tea and conversation on a weekly basis. Over time, his fine leadership helped me to realize my bitterness and selfishness might rob Marta of the parent...the father...she needed.

"I can see the surprise in your eyes. Yes, I have been a believer for many years. I regret you could not tell. In any event, my pastor convinced me I should inform James Martin that his daughter was now with me. That was two years ago. It took him a year and a half to make arrangements to come to America. He moved into my apartment while he was here so as not to disrupt Marta any more than necessary. I had no idea James Martin's personal and political risks would be such as they have been. I was unaware of Jack's living arrangements. The circumstances have proven most challenging at my age."

I felt I knew where she was leading next. "And my intrusion upon the situation provoked even further complications, I'm guessing?"

"You are most correct. At first you posed a physical threat to James Martin and Marta, because I was suspicious that anyone might be trying to harm them. I knew that he was under repeated physical attacks. Later, when I saw you meant no physical harm, you posed another type of danger. I imagined you were pursuing him for his...and my...money. Of course, ultimately, I feared I would lose Marta to James Martin's new wife. I presumed you planned to become his wife by whatever means necessary. Your unselfish and ladylike behaviors have since proven me wrong, I am pleased to admit.

"But I have kept you far too long from the hike, and the children will be anxious. Before you go, I need to be sure that I have your forgiveness."

The confession had cost her. Her aging face clearly showed it.

"I forgive you, GranJuel. Thank you for your explanation. And as for any unsavory designs on James Martin, I assure you there is nothing to fear. I am grateful to him for allowing me to spend time with his children, whom I have come to love. Other than that, I don't think you have anything to fear."

Speaking without showing the emotions I felt cost me dearly also, but I did it by taking my cue from her and lifting my chin confidently as I spoke.

She studied me closely for some time before she answered. "I am not as fearful as I once was, Ms. Redmon, about many things." After another pause, she continued, "Run along now. I want to visit with the innkeeper's wife as we are old and dear friends."

30

Family Outing

The air outside of the inn was snappish, as I joined the hiking party on the patio at the back of the inn. This was definitely what is called *sweater weather*, and I had to send Marta back for hers before we started our climb. We must have appeared quite a picture to anyone watching us start up the trail. James Martin and Jack led the way with their stout walking sticks picked up along the tree line while they were waiting for me. Marta was next, dancing like a woods elf in her bright green sweater and brown pants. I came last, walking slowly and content just to watch the other three take on this climb as if it were Everest itself.

Mrs. Magenis had slipped me a shoulder bag filled with provisions for the trail in the form of a plastic flask of lemonade, paper cups, homemade brownies and ginger cookies, perfect fare for the end of our trail. I could hear James Martin telling Jack about his own treks in the northeastern highlands of Khutule when he was Jack's age. I could also hear Marta humming what sounded like a homemade climbing tune as she tripped up the trail ahead of me. Life was very good at that moment, and I determined I would not waste the goodness worrying about whether it would all end for me when the weekend was over.

With the children along, the climb up the winding path to the falls area took almost an hour. The trail crossed a large open field behind the inn and then disappeared into the evergreens beyond. As we were the only travelers, the field and the woods were quiet, and our track was narrow but clear.

Remarkable rock formations along the way slowed us as their shapes enticed the children to imagine their origins. Jack was certain they were the remains of a pioneer fort from the days when the Blue Ridge Mountains were the end of the map going west. To Marta the pointed rocks were the very tips of troll houses built sturdily underground to protect their owners from curious humans.

James Martin seemed relaxed and comfortable with his son and daughter, interacting with them easily and providing answers to their countless questions. He spoke little to me, but I noticed he watched me often. I wasn't uncomfortable, but I was curious about what he was thinking.

I refused to consider this weekend as an audition for a place in James Martin's life or the children's, for that matter. I was firm with myself on those points. Besides, there was little I could do or not do to change his opinion of me. What he thought or felt was most likely already decided. I simply wondered whether he was missing Branda and wishing she were here in my place.

Near the end of the trail, there was a large, flat rock into which someone sometime had chiseled wide steps leading ten feet downward into a narrow gorge through which a small river flowed. We followed a trail beside the river, listening to loud rushing noises that grew louder as we walked. Rounding a bend, we found the source of the sounds. A falls high above us dropped its lacy water curtain to land with a spray in a pool at our feet. Looking up, we could see, jutting out from the side of a stone cliff, a rock structure that looked surprisingly like an angel with widespread wings watching over the falling water.

We stood there looking up at the exquisite display of God's creativity in nature. A tiny hand slipped into mine, and I heard a whisper from beside me.

"Jannia, she's beautiful! She's just like the guardian angel GranJuel says looks after me."

I stooped to look into the blue eyes of the child who had expressed so well what I knew we were all thinking. "Marta, she surely is. Our Heavenly Father does send His angels to guard over us to help keep us from stumbling. That's what He tells us. Aren't we thankful? And isn't that a wonderful thing to think about just now?"

"Yes, it makes me think about how real God is," Jack said. "Except for, Marta, I don't think angels are girls."

I was thrilled that he also got the truth suggested by the rock formation above us, despite his display of superior knowledge over his sister.

I looked at their father and found him looking back at me. I believed he was remembering the work of the angels in protecting us during Jack's escape from Khutule. My thoughts were confirmed when he put an arm around each of his children and prayed aloud.

"Heavenly Father, how grateful I am that you have reunited my family. How blessed I am to have these children. Thank you for taking care of Jack and Jannia in Khutule and for bringing them home safely. In Your Son's name, Amen."

He held them both close for a moment, and I moved to sit on a smooth rock beside the little river. Hungry hikers need sustenance for their journeys, and I opened the bag sent by the innkeeper's wife....

The children were tired after their hike. After a late lunch with GranJuel, we settled them down to play board games in the inn's library with Banolo. What a quaint idea. Not having come from a board-game-playing family, I hadn't tackled Monopoly in years. GranJuel served as banker. Most of us plodded our tokens around the properties conservatively. Not so for Jack. He proved to be the investment shark that soon owned most of the real estate east of the Mississippi.

Scrabble followed Monopoly as Marta and I teamed up against James Martin and Jack and Banolo challenged GranJuel to a singles match. She took no prisoners, defeating him and astonishing us with an unbelievable production of the word *kaleidoscopic*. After a brief lecture on what the word meant, GranJuel sent us all to our respective rooms for a rest before a late dinner.

Marta was asleep almost immediately, but not I. I forced myself to lie still without tossing and fidgeting, as I re-ran the amazing events of the last two days: the trip up with Banolo in his taxi; the revealing talk with GranJuel at breakfast that seemed to have cleared the air between us; the poignant, quiet moment at the falls when James Martin had prayed in gratitude for his children; and the pleasure of seeing this family play together in relative safety after the trauma of recent months. Each of these would be a treasured memory...regardless of the outcome of the weekend.

Something about James Martin during our time at the inn had left me a bit concerned. It was hard to pinpoint just what. He had been pleasant, cordial, and polite to a fault. He was always dignified, but now there was a certain reserve, an unusual quietness about him that seemed uncharacteristic. It was difficult to explain...almost as if he were a watcher more than a participator in our activities. His mood was subtle, and the children didn't seem to notice anything. GranJuel made no comment either, but I noticed.

On the occasions when I found James Martin watching me, I tried to take no notice of it. Speculation can be a dangerous pastime. Still I couldn't help wondering what was on his mind. Maybe it had nothing to do with me and everything to do with Branda VanderCross, who was absent from this family outing. He might be missing her and replacing my face with hers whenever he looked at me. Or he might be thinking of a kind way to let me know that, following this trip, he and the children would be fine, and I could go back to my life as they went on with theirs.

I was actually glad for this couple of hours to myself to reflect...and prepare. For that's what I felt I needed to do...realistically prepare for the end of this little respite and the return to the business of getting on with my life. I knew I would only feel safe if I were proactive. Waiting to be dismissed, even lovingly so, would be reactive and make me feel vulnerable. I had to have a plan.

The plan would require that I make a decision soon about whether to stay in Boone's Summit to be near the children, if that remained an option, or to move on to my next job...I was not sure where. Staying would inevitably mean also seeing the children's father on occasion. At the moment, that didn't seem to be the best plan for either of us. There was no need to tell the children yet, if I was going, but it wouldn't wait for long.

Dinner was planned for eight o'clock. I decided to dress for a special occasion; at least it was for me. I had packed an ankle-length black dress with my favorite sparkles around a neckline that was low enough to be flattering but not too low. A fringed shawl would keep me warm if I needed it.

After watching me, Marta decided she would wear her blue *swirley skirt*, as she called it. Putting it on obviously made her feel grown special, judging by the way she moved. She declared us to be the *beautiful people*, and just before we went down to join the others, she whispered in my ear.

"Jannia, I'm not to tell you, but I know a secret." Her blue eyes danced as they begged me to plead for her information.

"Marta, be my best friend and tell me your secret."

"No, ma'am. Nothing doing." This was her best game.

"Please don't torture me, Marta. Please, please, pleeze, pulease, one thousand times please."

"Lucy lips sink the ships! These lips of mine are sealed." She pretended to lock her lips and throw away the key, all the while laughing merrily at me through her eyes.

"I'll give you a bribe. How about a million gummy bears?"

"Wellllll...no thanks, ma'am. You must wait and see. Now let's go, I'm hungry," and off she swirled.

31

Unexpected Offer

ranJuel and the gentlemen, James Martin and Jack, were waiting for us in the sitting room as we descended the grand old staircase like two very fine ladies. They applauded and whistled softly as we made our entrance, causing Marta to give a smart curtsey and nearly fall down the final three steps.

"You both look lovely," said GranJuel as she took Marta's hand. "And now, if Jack and Marta will kindly come with me, we will be dining in the theatre room. We will be watching a special movie selected just for us, if you will excuse us please."

To my surprise, she led the children out of the room. Just before they disappeared through the doorway, Marta turned to me and twisted the key to her lips once more, as if holding on to her secret.

I stood uncomfortably in the presence of James Martin, who was also dressed for the evening wearing a dark sports jacket and tie. I think he was the most handsome man I had ever seen at that moment, and the thought made me sad, so I pretended to search for something in my evening purse. I was at a complete loss over what to do next. Would we follow the children for the dinner theatre? This was all so awkward.

When I looked up after finding nothing in my evening bag at all, James Martin was offering me his arm.

"It appears as if we have been abandoned. Perhaps we will have to fend for ourselves. Fortunately, I believe Banolo is waiting for us in the library. He has a surprise for you, if you will come this way?"

I took his arm, and he led me across to the library on the back of the house. It was a long chestnut-paneled room filled with the smell of old leather and shelves housing hundreds of books. At one end was a fireplace in which a small fire had been lit. It was early in the season for such a luxury, but on this night, it seemed appropriate. There were bay windows on either side of the fireplace, and in front of one was a small table covered with lace, candles, and a dinner service for two.

My heart began to hammer in the face of the shimmering, romantic setting before me. This man was so thoughtful, so proper, so much the gentleman. What a kind way to thank me for my assistance to his family and to let me know how much he and his children think of me because of it. What a fitting way to show his appreciation before easing me gently out of further obligation to them...or them to me. We would all be free to move on.

I was feeling a little faint and recognized the early signs of a panic attack. It was growing increasingly harder to breathe. What was I going to do? I loved this man. Surely he knew it. How could I sit here with him and eat a meal and make sparkling conversation and pretend that all was well...and wish him well...and say good-bye casually and cordially? I just couldn't, that was all.

I would smile and turn and walk out. I would call for a taxi on my cell phone from my room and leave at once. Or maybe Banolo could be persuaded to take me home. (Where was he, anyway? James Martin said he would be here.) I would return to Boone's Summit and give my notice at the office on Monday morning. In two weeks, maybe three, I could be gone. I was not without means; I had savings. I would be fine until I found another job in Maine or South Dakota or Idaho or Romania. It would work. I had nothing now to lose.

I turned to present my pasted-on smile and begin my exit when the door to the adjoining room opened and Banolo entered, smiling broadly, with a linen napkin draped across his arm.

Banolo of the slightly battered white taxi and the unswerving loyalty to his childhood friend was now going to play server for the evening. Before I could move, he held out a chair, inviting me to sit at the lace-draped table. His eyes shone mischievously. Banolo was having fun!

How could anything be fun? Certainly nothing seemed fun to me at this moment, and I found I really couldn't endure this any longer. I would be gracious. I would say the right things, make up something, not upset anyone, but I must be excused now before I embarrassed myself by sobbing into my iced tea.

My thoughts were spinning, and my mind was a whirl of confusion. I felt the first twinges of a headache. There. I could use that. *I'm so sorry but my head...*

As directly as if in a letter straight from on High, the words from 1 Corinthians 14:33 came to me: *"For God is not the author of confusion but of peace..."* It was written for me.

"Ms. Redmon...Jannia, if you please."

I smiled back at Banolo and sat down. James Martin sat opposite, and

Banolo quietly and carefully served us the loveliest, the most appetizing meal. The two and sometimes three of us talked freely and easily as Banolo anticipated our every need. When he brought the final course of espresso and dark chocolate truffles, he bid us a good evening and slipped away.

We sat in comfortable silence, listening to the sounds of the fire and a classical guitar from the speakers tucked among the books. We could see scattered lights across the darkened mountains from the bay window. This would end, but it was the perfect moment. I would be fine. I was not without fortitude or hope. It would be sad, but I would survive. The room and my heart were now peaceful.

"Jannia."

We had been quiet for so long that his voice startled me.

It was time.

"Yes, Sir Neville?" Keep it light, playful. It will be easier for him, for us both.

"Thank you for a wonderful weekend. I appreciate...we all appreciate your coming."

How well I had anticipated the script. "I wouldn't have missed it. Thank you for the invitation."

"There is, you must be aware, really no way to tell you how grateful I am for what you have done for me and my family. I do not tire of telling you that. When I think of how close..."

"God is very good. He's the One to thank. Of that, we can be sure." And I was.

"I do thank Him, continuously, for His blessings to my family. And for you also. I thank Him for the gift of you. Perhaps you have guessed how I feel about you, Jannia."

I responded with stunned silence. Of course I had not heard him properly. He must have missed his cue. These words weren't in my anticipated script.

"I am offering you my love without any assurance that you want it or will return it. I am well aware of my position. I love you unconditionally and without apology. Whether you feel the same or not, please know how much you have come to mean to me over the last few months."

I was looking directly into his gray blue eyes now and not believing the words I was hearing.

"Since you first found me injured on the day you followed Banolo to Marta, I have watched you closely. I have come to know and love both who you are and what you stand for. You tried to help us from the beginning and you continued to try, in the face of significant physical danger, until you got Jack home. Then I almost lost you as you helped to save my life. Jannia, no one would do what you have done for me."

I found my voice. "James Martin, please don't confuse gratitude for love. There is a difference. I understand your affection based on what we have been through together. It means so much to me, as do you and Jack and Marta. Knowing the three of you has changed who I am forever. Thank you for that, but your gratitude is enough."

He looked at me for a long time. The look was searching and serious. "Do you not understand what I am saying or are you rejecting me gently? I really can't tell. Jannia, what I'm expressing is not inflated gratitude. It is not misplaced guilt for putting your life in jeopardy. It isn't affection born of relief."

He stood and walked to the fireplace, his back to me. I couldn't move, could barely breathe. When he turned back to face me, there was still one question between us. I had to ask.

"Forgive me, James Martin, but what about...Branda VanderCross? I was sure...I thought that..."

"I know what you thought. You were mistaken." His response was swift and firm. "It was Branda who helped me understand what you might be thinking. For that, I'm grateful. Please understand, Jannia, you have been quite difficult to read over the past several weeks. Branda was assigned to protect me. It was her job, and we also became friends. Her work is over now, and I doubt we will see her again."

I believed him and I was out of arguments. James Martin, however, wasn't finished.

"I love you, Jannia Redmon. Of that I am quite sure. I haven't told you before now for many reasons, which we can discuss at length sometime in the future, if you're interested. If my declaration comes as a shock to you, I'm sorry. Perhaps I should approach this some other way. I apologize if my manner lacks sophistication...I fear I'm a bit rusty. I do, however, love you and want you to be my wife. Will you have me? Will you become my wife and Marta and Jack's mother? Not because they need a mother. Of course they do. But because you love their father. If you need more time, you may certainly have it, but I may not survive in the meantime if you keep me waiting."

Perhaps he saw something in my expression that gave him hope because his rambling discourse became more confident.

"I know that I am a temperamental musician, and a foreigner besides, and I know that GranJuel can be difficult and Marta flighty and Jack stubborn. We collectively can be overwhelming and a considerable amount of trouble, as you have experienced. Having recognized all obstacles, please tell me that you will have the lot of us for your own."

"Banolo," I said.

"I beg your pardon?"

"Banolo. You forgot to add Banolo. Doesn't he come as a part of your package also? And his taxi? You must remember, without his taxi I wouldn't..."

"...have found us," he finished. "That is true. We do owe him a debt of gratitude as well, do we not? Yes, he does come with the package. Will you have us all? Will you have me?"

He was simultaneously serious and vulnerable, Jack in grown-up size. The question in his voice asked me to confirm that what he thought...what he suspected... might be true.

He was right. This man standing in front of me was asking me to spend my life with him and his family. There was so much about him I didn't yet know. There was so much more about me he would have to learn. We had barely touched. He had never even kissed me. But I was sure what we were being offered was not ordinary and was not from this world. We were not coming together by chance.

"I accept your kind offer of marriage, Sir Neville. As it happens, I have loved you as well for quite some time, despite my best efforts to the contrary."

I watched him bow his head for just a moment and then take a step toward me. I stood to meet him and held out my hand.

"This was Marta's secret?" I asked.

"It was." James Martin took my hand. "Let's go and tell the children."

Epilogue

Waiting Taxi

We were not married immediately. We decided it would take some months to sort through the details of what our marriage would mean to each other and to the lives of our loved ones. Those were worthy months, though the waiting was hard. We wanted to grow our love stronger and unite our spirits more closely together in the love of our Father before we became a family. The children seemed to understand.

In fact, we waited a year and were finally married on the anniversary of our engagement. A small group came together for the long-anticipated occasion in the library of the Boundary Inn, the same room in which our commitment as a couple had begun, on the most lovely of all fall afternoons.

Pastor Terry would perform the ceremony. The Magenises, of course, were there as were my parents. Jack and Marta stood with us, bearing our rings. Banolo held the arm of GranJuel, in whose eyes I now saw genuine acceptance. Jake Bean, my editor, and his wife had arrived with Art Lanier. To my great pleasure, there was one more special guest.

At the last minute we learned that Banolo's cousin, Jamul Legassi, would join us. After many months of waiting, he had just arrived in the States for good. It was a sweet reunion. We missed Bertram Wallace, but we knew he was thriving in his new work in South Africa.

I looked around the circle of friends and loved ones present to help us celebrate our wedding with deep gratitude and a full heart.

Pastor Terry began the service with the traditional words, "Dearly Beloved." The phrase was well chosen, for it suitably described my feelings for those around me.

I was filled with joy and gratitude. Truly God had given me the desire of my heart. Still I couldn't help feeling that someone, something was missing from our little gathering.

As Pastor continued with the service that would seal my union with James Martin, I looked past my husband-to-be standing beside me toward the tall panes through which the late afternoon sun streamed into the room.

I could see the rich and brilliant foliage just beyond the windows...and something more. The picture was now complete. I glanced at Banolo's smiling face before looking again to catch the faintest glimpse of a slightly battered, but proud white taxi waiting outside in the autumn sun.

About the Author

With a BA from Wheaton College in Literature, an M.Ed. in Speech Pathology and Audiology and a Ph.D. in Special Education, JENNY JOHNSON has been writing nonfiction for many years in her role as a university professor. She has coauthored book chapters, journal articles, and conference proceedings related to her professional field.

Jenny prefers writing fiction and has pursued that objective seriously for the last few years. Her poetry and short stories have won local awards. *The Taxi* is her first novel. She is currently at work on two inspirational romance novels, *Copper's Run* and *By the Light of Your Face,* and a children's book with her daughter, *The Misadventures of Eulajalylah Picklethwight.*

"My goals as a writer are simple," Jenny says. "I want to write quality Christian romantic fiction that is worth reading, tells a good story, promotes values consistent with my beliefs as a Christ follower, and leaves readers feeling positive about their investment of time and money."

Jenny wants to provide similar clean and elevating entertainment today that Grace Livingston Hill did in the first half of the twentieth century. "If my novels can provoke thought about authentic Christianity through the actions of my characters, so much the better," Jenny says.

She and her family live in North Carolina.

To email the author: **jennywjohnson@gmail.com**

http://jennywjohnson.blogspot.com/
www.oaktara.com